RUTHLESS

By Sarah Tarkoff

Sinless
Fearless
Ruthless

RUTHLESS

EYE OF THE BEHOLDER

BOOK 3

sarah tarkoff

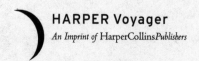

HARPER Voyager
An Imprint of HarperCollinsPublishers

HarperCollins books may be purchased for educational, business, or sales promotional use. For information, please email the Special Markets Department at SPsales@harpercollins.com.

Harper Voyager and design are trademarks of HarperCollins Publishers LLC.

FIRST EDITION

Designed by Paula Russell Szafranski

Library of Congress Cataloging-in-Publication Data has been applied for.

ISBN 978-0-06-245642-7

20 21 22 23 24   LSC   10 9 8 7 6 5 4 3 2 1

For Eva

I'm dreading what comes next.

Recounting all the steps that brought me to this point, the stories you didn't know, that was easy. Because while I made plenty of mistakes along the way, becoming a prophet wasn't a mistake in and of itself. It was what I chose to do next that keeps me up at night.

I've gone over and over the chapters that follow, agonizing over each word. I've convinced myself that if somehow I find the right ones, in the right order, you'll see things the way I saw them. Now that the dust has settled, maybe you'll understand me. Or at least, maybe you'll hate me just a little bit less.

I'm sorry I failed you. I believed I could help, and I hope that in some ways I managed to. I hope that despite everything I made worse, I made some things better, too. I hope that in time, you'll forgive me.

Dear readers, it turns out, it is your forgiveness I wanted all along.

With all the love of whoever and whatever you still believe in,
Grace Luther
c/o Arlington Federal Prison

BOOK
ONE

1

Welcome home, Prophet Grace."

Home. My feet had touched the ground for mere minutes; this little Outcast outpost in northeast Brazil couldn't be *home.* But Tutelo, Virginia, had stopped being home the moment I gave that speech in South Africa. It couldn't be, not with a father who was so disappointed in me, where death lurked, waiting to pounce if I came within the prophets' reach. No, I was a girl in search of a new home. And for now, this one would have to do.

After escaping from the stadium in South Africa, Dawn, Zack, and I had managed to traverse the turbulent Atlantic Ocean to find a perch on the coast near an Outcast metropolis called Redenção, named for the Portuguese word for "redemption." Even from afar, it was a massive, glittering marvel, the ocean lapping right up to its feet.

As I took in the sparkling sight, I was skeptical; how had I never heard that this massive city existed? But as Dawn reminded me, any achievement by Outcasts was seen by the mainstream world as a thorn in the eye of Great Spirit, a sign that following the prophets wasn't the only way to achieve success and prosperity. So Redenção had remained no more than a whisper . . . until now, as it shouted its majesty loud and clear from the shore.

Hundreds of Outcast citizens of the city had assembled by the docks to pay their respects, to welcome me. Their furious adoration overwhelmed us, the smells of their bodies permeating the air. *It's okay*, I wanted to tell them. *It's all a big con. None of this is real.* But without access to the pills that would cure them of their guilt, I couldn't tell them the truth. Couldn't do anything but smile and nod and perform my part. After spending months playing double agent in Prophet Joshua's army, I hadn't thought there could be any role more difficult. Apparently, I'd been wrong.

As the crowd grew more excited, pressing closer to me, I was startled by a faint buzzing from high above us—a drone, whizzing above the city. Before anyone else could react, the captain of our ship whipped out a gun and took it down in one shot, sending it careening into the ocean in a blaze of flaming metal. "The prophets will use those to track your movements," the captain warned us. "Stay out of sight, or the missiles will come next."

Fear lodged itself in my throat. Everywhere we went, we'd be targets, endangering whomever we came close to. And seeing the fervor in that captain's eyes, I worried what might have transpired if that metal spy had been a human one—would this devotee have been just as willing to kill in my name?

The longer we stayed out in the open, we knew, the greater

our risk of being spotted again. So the mayor of Redenção shuffled us away from the fray, leaving the crew of our boat behind. "We cannot hide you in the city," he said ominously. "The prophets will find you. But I will take you to someone who can help."

He introduced us to a small, well-dressed man with skin that shone like amber and a fast-talking charm that made you quickly forget his Outcast appearance. His malformed face twisted into a warm smile. "I am Eduardo Sousa," he introduced himself. "Your new best friend."

And indeed, Sousa immediately began living up to that promise. As his hunched frame limped ahead of us, hurrying to open the town car door, he barraged me with compliments, keen to befriend the so-called prophet. While he was eager to protect us from the dangers we'd told him were closing in, it was clear he wasn't ready to stop there. He hoped that some of my prophet's aura would rub off on him, that my imaginary specialness would somehow make *him* special. I wished I felt special, felt like anything other than a fraud.

As Sousa helped us traverse the roads around Redenção, I realized those worshippers at the shore were just the tip of the iceberg. I was stunned to see my own face plastered on walls all throughout the area—fliers, graffiti, banners hanging from windows. I was everywhere. "How did they all know she was coming?" Dawn asked, nervous.

"They didn't," Sousa said simply.

"This isn't some kind of show they're putting on for me?" I asked, confounded.

Sousa shook his head. "You are Grace, prophet of the Outcasts. And this is a city of Outcasts."

As we passed banner after banner, Zack's eyes glazed over in disbelief. "I guess they like you."

It suddenly hit me. I was a worldwide phenomenon. A role that came with obligations and consequences so huge I couldn't yet comprehend them. And there was no turning back.

As we drove, the sight of my own face emblazoned everywhere gave me a strange thrill. I'd never run for student council, never done anything that required leadership skills or real responsibility. My father had always taught me that the way to make Great Spirit proud was to be of service, to be humble. Making myself a prophet . . . that wasn't exactly humble.

My stomach churned with regret. I was just an eighteen-year-old kid with no idea what I was doing. Why had I put myself in this position? How had I convinced all these people that I had any kind of wisdom? Sooner or later, I knew they'd realize I was a fraud.

"I need to find a way to tell people the truth," I whispered to Dawn when Sousa stopped to refuel the car. "You know, that I'm not really a prophet."

She handily refuted, "No one's really a prophet."

"Then shouldn't I be saying that? That all the prophets are lying, not just me?"

"And risk billions dying because they question the truth?" Dawn challenged.

"Being Prophet Grace has its own risks," I pointed out. "Pretending I'm godly feels wrong, and against everything we've been fighting for."

Dawn shook her head, firm. "It's a lie that will save lives. Letting the world believe in some new prophet is safer than taking all their prophets away at once. You know how people are . . . they need something to believe in. Who knows, maybe you'll even be able to inspire some good in them."

I nearly laughed in her face. "So what, you're an idealist now?"

Her cynical tone gave away the truth behind her words. "When you're desperate, idealism's all you've got left." I accepted that wisdom—right now, I, too, was clinging to idealism's desperate hope.

I shifted in my seat, anxiously scanning the horizon for more of those flying cameras. "My mother said Prophet Joshua had allies left. Do we have any idea who they might be, who might be after us?"

"Any of the hundreds of other prophets you didn't sic a murderous crowd on?" Zack muttered sarcastically. Dawn had already warned me that the Brazilian Prophet Daniel would be hunting for us if he got even a whiff that we were in town—and if that drone had spotted us in Redenção, he'd already be on our scent.

"If we don't know who's allied with the prophets, how will

we ever find anywhere truly safe?" I asked, the fear seeping into my bones.

"Sousa's working on it," Dawn said, trying to reassure me.

I glanced at Sousa outside the car, hoping he wouldn't catch my gaze. "And are we sure we can trust *him*? My mother sent us to him, after all." I was wary of trusting anyone who might be working for Esther.

Dawn nodded; clearly she'd thought of that, too. "Esther sent us to this city, knowing Outcasts would protect you. I don't think anyone here knows the truth. Sousa may not be a part of the resistance, but unfortunately we're out of members of the resistance, or the means to make more." For safety, we'd gone radio silent since leaving South Africa, which meant we'd lost access to our supply of uppers—fine for the three of us, who'd acclimated to our own heresy. But it meant that for the moment we had to keep mum about the truth to anyone outside our circle of confidence, for fear that doubting what they'd been told was gospel might kill them. "But luckily we have you. People will do anything for Prophet Grace."

That was the real reason she didn't want me to recant. She needed my influence to protect us. "Where is Sousa taking us?" I asked.

"Inland, as far from the prophets as we can get."

Zack moved closer to me, voice light, trying to cheer me up. "Hey, we get to go on an adventure. Things could be worse, right?"

As he smiled, a bit of a thrill went through me. Despite what we'd been through, and despite what might lie ahead, I was secretly excited to share this journey with him. I looked at

Zack, thinking of all the roles he'd held in my life. Macy's cute, aloof older brother. Then my enemy, a seeming assassin. And now . . . I wasn't sure what he was to me, what we were to each other. But I knew I wanted to be close to him. I squeezed Zack's hand as Sousa returned, and our car hurtled toward its destination: the Amazon rainforest.

3

We traversed the bleak, dusty slums surrounding Redenção, teeming with poor Outcasts going about their daily lives. Seeing my name emblazoned in graffiti on these tin roofs, it finally sunk in, the sheer number of strangers my words had reached.

When the run-down structures finally gave way to the scrabbly brush of open country, I noticed Zack was asleep beside me. My adrenaline was wearing off, and after many sleepless nights on the boat, it felt nice to drift away from the world into an anxious, fitful slumber.

It wasn't until the first few rays of morning light streamed into the car that I stirred and looked around at the muddy brown roads. Though we seemed to be out in the middle of nowhere, this certainly didn't look like the rainforest. "Are we close?" I asked Dawn.

"Are we there yet?" Zack ribbed me.

"I'll take that as a no," I grumbled, and Dawn pulled out a

map. As she traced our path with her finger, I remembered just how huge Brazil was—we had another day's drive ahead of us still. As morning slipped into afternoon, rain started pelting our windshield, and I took that as a good sign that we were getting closer. Indeed, before my eyes I could see the trees growing taller, as the roads became bumpier.

Dawn and Sousa traded off driving, one sleeping as the other piloted, stopping only for fuel and bathroom breaks. "We can't risk coming into contact with too many people," she explained.

"Do you think anyone's following us?" I whispered, once I could see that Sousa was asleep in the passenger seat. "Maybe one of those cameras spotted us and we didn't see it."

"I'll feel better when we get off the road," she whispered back.

"You said all our safe houses were burned. Where are we going, if it isn't somewhere the resistance hides people?"

"Sousa has a place out in the country, remote enough that we should be able to avoid scrutiny." Despite Dawn's assurances that we could trust this charming stranger, I still had my doubts.

My worry for the three of us quickly blossomed into concern for all my other friends. I'd hoped that by now we would've heard something out of Turkey, but I knew they had no real way to contact us. I thought of Jude and Layla and Mohammed and Irene, everyone whose survival had hung in the balance since Joshua's army had surrounded their stronghold. The standoff must have resolved itself one way or another by now. My stomach churned with worry as I imagined where Jude could be right now . . . or not be.

Even now, with Jude's life in danger and our relationship

far in the rearview, I still felt a warmth in my chest when I thought of him. Like we were tied together by some thread, across oceans, which would always connect our hearts. As massive as the forces that threatened us might be, Jude's fate would always loom even larger in my mind. I'd once been prepared to leave the rest of the world behind for his sake, and some part of me still felt that way, still felt like the needs of the people I loved were so much more important than the well-being of a globe full of strangers. My stomach tightened with a sick thought: If we gave those strangers freedom, but I lost Jude, would all this still be worth it?

As the sky grew dark outside, I found myself nodding off again. Zack wordlessly pulled me closer to him, letting my head fall into his lap, as he stroked my hair. A silent acknowledgment that there was something between us, though neither of us had the courage yet to voice exactly what it was. Feeling safe in his arms, I fell into an easy, comfortable sleep once again. I had no idea what might be coming next, but I had a feeling I'd want to be well rested once we got there.

Well into our second day of driving, we finally arrived at a ramshackle outpost with a battered terra-cotta roof. Sousa parked the car and gestured for us to get out. "Here?" I asked. This little structure didn't look very secure, nor did it seem particularly stable. I doubted this shack would hold up to a rough shake, much less Prophet Daniel's artillery.

"No, there." He gestured to an overgrown path behind the building, and a lurch went through my stomach.

Don't trust him, the voice in my head whispered. That darn voice, the malicious nanotech that had made me fear those I was supposed to trust. While with mental focus I'd managed to mute it most of the time, we still hadn't found a way to fully get rid of it. Though we'd stolen the secret code that was supposed to be able to destroy all the bugs in our brains and restore the world to the way it used to be, the machine required to activate it was back in South Africa.

Ironically, the voice's resurgence now was enough to give me the confidence that I *could* trust Sousa—as long as the prophets didn't want me to trust him, that was as good a sign as any that I *should* trust him, right? I hopped out of the car, lugging as much baggage as I could carry through the thick mud at our feet. Seeing me struggling, Zack hurried to grab a bag and lighten my load. "Prophets shouldn't be carrying their own luggage," he teased.

I grinned, hauling what I could. "What can I say, I'm a woman of the people." As the four of us arrived at the end of the path, we found a small dock with an old rowboat, large enough to ferry all our supplies, but half rotted out. Sousa found a rag to plug a hole in its hull as we loaded it up.

Zack eyed our transportation. "You'd have to be a woman of the people, to ride in that."

Within a few minutes, we were rowing off. "Welcome to the Amazon Highway," Sousa said proudly. I looked at the wet "road" ahead of us—hoping desperately that it would lead somewhere safe.

Our boat wasn't on a river exactly, so much as the whole forest had become a lake, a slick, expansive pool that stretched as far as the eye could see, with dense pockets of trees piercing its surface. "It's rainy season," Sousa explained, as he navigated us through the maze. "Those trees are twice as tall as they look. In the winter you can walk here, but in the summer, it floods like this." That reminded me that we were in the Southern Hemisphere—it was summer here. I leaned over the edge of the boat, trying to see down to the bottom, but Sousa pulled me back. "Careful."

"What's down there?" I asked.

"Anacondas. Piranha. Eels. Caiman, like big alligators . . ."

"Got it!" I said, hoping he'd stop naming terrifying things. I stayed as close to the center of the boat as I could, squinting my eyes against the blazing sun. The air was thick with the sounds of cooing birds, calling monkeys, and the mosquitoes buzzing around our necks.

"I grew up there," Sousa said, and it took me a minute to notice the little house in the distance, resting on a mound of dirt between the trees. I tried to imagine what it must have been like to grow up so far away from everything and everyone else.

"Why did you leave?" I asked him.

He tensed, gesturing to his face. "My mother was ashamed of me."

"She kicked you out when you became an Outcast?" I asked, shocked.

"I was seventeen when the Revelations happened. I was homeless for a year before I finally found my way to Redenção."

A pang of sympathy went through me. "I'm so sorry."

He shook his head. "It is okay. I have done well, look. Someday, I will tell her I met with the great Prophet Grace, and she will not be ashamed of me anymore." I saw him glancing at his old house longingly. But we continued moving past it—his estranged mother would have to wait.

"I think she'd be proud of you," I offered hesitantly. "Her son is very brave."

He shook his head, seemingly unable to accept the compliment. "For the one true prophet, I would gladly risk my life. Anyone would." My stomach twisted, remembering all the half-truths Dawn had told him—that we were being persecuted by the other prophets for preaching on behalf of the *real* Great Spirit.

Before I could say anything else, Sousa pointed up ahead. "We are not far now."

About ten minutes later, Sousa landed our boat on a rickety dock, and we disembarked to discover a rustic but spacious lodge—several wooden buildings nestled into the greenery on a steep mound of forest. "Looks good to me," Dawn said in her usual, matter-of-fact way.

Zack marveled at the scenery around us, the peaceful sounds of nature. "This is pretty cool."

I agreed. All we could see and hear was the wild roar of jungle. As I looked up at the towering treetops, Zack took my hand, and a rush of excitement flowed through me. Maybe exile wouldn't be so bad after all. Immediately, I regretted that excitement, thinking of the friends we still needed to help and the strangers I'd professed to prophesize for. Though I was relieved we'd found a safe haven, I was determined to find a way to use this place as a base to help them, to rebuild the resistance. Worries nagged at the back of my mind . . . we were penned in here, on our heels, just trying to survive. How could we ever go back on the offensive, when our defenses were so flimsy?

We'd find a way, because we had to.

Sousa's accommodations were less than luxurious, but we had the necessities—a fan to deflect the sticky tropical heat and mosquito nets over our beds to stave off tropical diseases. We'd brought some dry goods with us, but it quickly became obvious that we'd need to forage for additional food if we were going to subsist out here for long.

Luckily that wouldn't be a problem; despite his outwardly dapper and urban persona, Sousa was a jungle kid at heart. He hadn't forgotten the skills he'd used to survive for the first seventeen years of his life. Our first night, he showed up at dinner with freshly caught fish, which we devoured ravenously. The next morning, I saw him scampering up a forty-foot tree with just his bare hands—one minute he was on the ground, the next he was at the top, gathering fruit and nuts for our lunch.

During meals, he insisted we speak in Portuguese. "When my prophet leaves here, she should speak the language of her people." The Outcasts of Redenção, he meant. Though I doubted very much if I'd ever leave this hideaway and actually talk to any of them, I did appreciate the distraction. Dawn and Zack took poorly to the lessons, but my high school Spanish helped me pick up the vocabulary quickly. After a few days of intensive practice, I felt quite comfortable speaking simple sentences.

But even our Portuguese immersion wasn't enough to take my thoughts away from the troubles of the outside world. To protect our location, we'd brought no phones, and this place had no internet, no communication lines at all. No way of finding out what might be happening to our friends. I felt safe, but trapped. Alone.

At the end of our first week, Zack noticed I was growing antsy, and after lunch he pulled me away from the others with a comforting smile. "Let's go for a walk."

There wasn't much space to move, since the jungle was flooded all around us, but Zack and I traced a zigzag path through the trees. "I'm scared," I admitted, finally feeling free to air my fears. "Aren't you? Of the prophets finding us?"

"Less scared, more frustrated," he confided. "I was terrified before, that your mother would figure out I was protecting you. Working against Esther, that was the scariest thing I've ever done. Now, I just feel powerless."

"No one to punch," I said, poking fun at him.

He laughed. "I would have really enjoyed punching a prophet or two, yeah. And now . . ."

"I know what you mean," I said. "I don't like living in hiding. I want to get back out there, do something."

He shrugged. "Even in hiding, *you* are one of the most powerful people in the world. You just have to figure out how to use it."

The thought of wielding that power still left me gutted, terrified. "Yeah, easy-peasy, no problem," I muttered. "Even if I do figure out how to use it, I don't know if I want to. I don't want my strength to come from lies."

Zack took my hand. "I'll help you. Dawn will help you. We'll find a way."

"Thanks." His reassurances left me feeling stronger. Like I could handle anything.

We emerged on the other side of our temporary island, at the edge of the river. "You want to go for a swim?" he teased.

I remembered all Sousa's warnings about what lurked beneath the surface. "With the piranhas and the giant alligators? No thanks."

"Come on, it'll be fun!" He hoisted me up, playing like he was going to throw me in. "Water's warm!"

"Stop it!" I warned him, and he obligingly put me down. My adrenaline rushed, being so close to him, and even once I was back safely on the ground, I found myself clinging to him, not leaving his embrace. I wanted to ask him a thousand questions, to crawl inside his brain and see what things looked like through his eyes. How I looked. Did he like me, did he want me? With his confident swagger, that playful grin, I'd be a fool to think I could hold his attention for long. My eyes bored into his, like I was drilling that hole to excavate his thoughts. But he held my gaze, looking back just as fiercely, and I knew.

After all the worry, the doubt between us, I could feel it. I knew that he cared about me, that what was between us wasn't all in my head. Our attraction was more than skin deep— months of spending time together, even under contentious circumstances, had bonded us in a way that was unshakable.

My heart raced with the sudden thought that everything I'd been hoping for, fantasizing about, might be about to come true. And in an instant, he was leaning in and I was leaning in and there we were in the hot, humid jungle, even hotter as he pressed against me, the warmth and sweat of his body, his lips brushing my lips.

Zack was all mine, and suddenly, though every other piece of my life had fallen away into a heap of disaster and despair . . . one thing was going perfectly.

5

The next few weeks were surreal, like living in suspended animation. For all I knew, everything outside our little bubble had hit pause. I was immersed in the symphony of animal sounds that filled the air, with all the new sights and smells and tastes, and . . . Zack. Zack was everywhere, even when he wasn't; he consumed my thoughts so completely that it felt like he was following me, his words echoing in my dreams.

Meanwhile, actually following me everywhere: Eduardo Sousa, attempting to attend to my every need. Though I kept insisting I needed "private prophet time" to rest and reflect, he'd find me to interrupt with anything he thought might be helpful. New kinds of fruit for me to try, new Portuguese slang to teach me. Once he even appeared at my door holding a tarantula. "Do you want to pet it?" he asked in all earnestness.

I nearly slammed the door on him, shrieking and retreating deeper into my room. Realizing his mistake, he released the spider into the jungle and apologized profusely every time he saw me for the next several days. "Don't worry," I reassured him each time, worried he might be Punished for any guilt he felt. "I don't mind. But no more spiders, please."

I knew why he shadowed me; that much he said outright, once a day. "I want to learn from you," he'd tell me. "I am so blessed to spend this time with a prophet. Please, tell me all your wisdom, so I may pass it on to others."

I wanted to brush him off, tell him I didn't have any wisdom, and that he certainly shouldn't be trying to enlighten anyone else based on the random things I said. But I thought of our cause, our safety, and I tried my best to play my part. Said benign things about being good to people, anything that might sound wise. He nodded and drank in every word, and it made me feel sick. Though Dawn just listened with an amused grin, tickled by the whole thing, I could see Zack starting to feel uncomfortable, too.

The next time Zack saw Sousa ready to ambush me, he grabbed my hand, pulled me away. "We're going for a boat ride."

"Be careful," Dawn called out, ever nervous that someone might spot me and discover our location. But I also saw a little smile on her face—though we hadn't told Dawn a word, she'd immediately picked up on the vibe between me and Zack, and watching our budding romance seemed to be the one thing that cheered her up during our exile. It felt like we had a fan, someone rooting for us, someone else invested in seeing this relationship work.

And I couldn't think of any place more beautiful to get to

know someone. As Zack and I rowed down the river, I was overcome by the cacophonous stillness. We couldn't see another human anywhere—just him and me and the sound of our oars cutting through the water.

"This was your plan, wasn't it?" Zack teased me as our boat drifted farther into the jungle. "Recruit me to join the resistance. Put my life in danger. Strand me a million miles from civilization so you could have me all to yourself?"

I grinned. "You figured it out."

For a moment we both stopped rowing, and we let our craft float. Let everything else fall away, and it was just us, looking into each other's eyes, sharing this moment.

"As evil plans go . . . I guess I don't mind," he said, reaching over to play with a wisp of my hair.

"You wanna get stranded with me?" I asked him.

"With you? Anytime, anywhere." There was an easy comfort to being with him. Even in the midst of all this chaos, he made me feel safe.

I moved over to sit next to him on the tiny wooden seat. Held him close as the boat swayed from side to side. An image of Jude flitted through my mind, wondering what his reaction to this gorgeous scene would have been. He'd always marveled at natural beauty . . . I knew he'd love it here. Did some part of me wish I were sharing this view with Jude, not Zack? The thought scampered off just as quickly as Zack leaned over and kissed me, so passionately, so perfectly, I was sure this must be a dream.

But all dreams end, and this one was more fleeting than most. Still clutching Zack, I heard an ominous sound in the distance—the rumble of a motorboat engine. He froze, hearing it, too.

Who is that? I mouthed to him.

He shook his head—he didn't know either.

As quietly as we could, we rowed ourselves behind a thicket of trees, out of view, as the other boat chugged into our line of sight. I ducked my head, hiding my face, and Zack watched warily out of the corner of his eye.

"Who is it?" I whispered.

He shrugged his shoulders. "Tourists maybe?"

I snuck a glance to see a few well-dressed Brazilians idly chatting in Portuguese, gazing around the jungle. What I gleaned from their conversation did seem to be touristlike—they complained about the heat and the bugs and admired the beauty of this place. I took a deep breath in as they passed—they hadn't seen me, so all was well.

"We should go back," I whispered, now nervous that Dawn's fears might have been an omen.

But as we returned to the dock, my stomach flip-flopped. The tourist motorboat we'd seen earlier was sitting in our spot. My usual fears rocketed to the surface—we'd been discovered. Before we could make any moves to flee, I saw Dawn emerging from our lodge, walking to the shore, waving to us. Zack and I glanced at each other, then rowed in. As I gestured to the motorboat, I could see Dawn shaking her head, her face a mix of worry and frustration.

"What's going on?" I asked as we disembarked.

"Sousa has invited friends," she said through pursed lips.

And indeed, a few dozen of those friends streamed out of the lodge after her. Up close I could see they were fellow Outcasts, all of whom stared, disbelieving, when they got close enough to recognize me. "Prophet Grace!" they called out, running to the dock, clustering around me. One look at Dawn's face made the problem clear. Our location was compromised.

Though I knew I should play my part and humor these strangers with my prophetlike words, I was too worried. I pushed past them, looking for Eduardo Sousa, eventually finding him in the dining hall, preparing our next meal. "What's going on? Who are all those people?" I asked. Dawn and Zack trailed behind me, listening in on our conversation.

Sousa seemed confused. "They are my friends. And your most loyal followers."

"And you invited them here?" I was done trying to hide my anger. "While everyone's searching for us, when our lives are over if word gets out about where we are?"

"These are people we can trust, and this is my home," Sousa said defensively, looking to Dawn and Zack. He was clearly horrified to have angered a prophet.

"We can't trust *anyone* right now," I said, trying to keep my tone as calm as possible.

Sousa considered me carefully. "You are a prophet, but you

do not want to see any people? Talk to anyone? What good is it to speak directly to Great Spirit if you keep all your wisdom to yourself?"

Though I was still furious, I knew what he was getting at. From his perspective, I was a pretty useless prophet. All the platitudes I'd been spouting couldn't have been very inspiring. If he was starting to lose faith in me, even just a little, maybe this was his gambit to prove to himself that I wasn't so useless after all: forcing me into an impromptu sermon.

I wasn't happy about it, but I knew our options were limited. "Take all their phones," I told him. "Anything they can use to communicate with the outside world."

"Already done," he said, proud to have anticipated my request. "I met them on the water, and I confiscated all electronics before they arrived." A bit of relief went through me.

"Good. No one leaves unless we say so," Zack piped in from afar, and I nodded my agreement.

This stipulation left Eduardo less happy, but he acquiesced. "Fine."

He left the room to pass on this new information, leaving the three of us alone.

"I guess he isn't so trustworthy after all," Dawn muttered.

I shook my head. "Like you said, we're out of people we can trust. People we can manipulate are our next best option." As terrible as that made me feel, I knew our survival depended on it. And I hoped I'd turn out to be any good at it.

Eduardo passed on our new edict with as much gusto as he could muster, and everyone nodded along, their faith still strong. My stomach sank, realizing that helping to nurture that misplaced faith was the only thing that could truly keep us safe. I took a deep breath and stepped over to meet this crowd of strangers, who fell silent as I approached.

"Prophet Grace," Sousa said nervously. "These are some of the most respected members of the Redenção community. Julianna is a fashion designer, whose clothes are the height of Outcast fashion." The woman he gestured to was dressed in an avant-garde style, a tunic clearly designed to hide her Outcast imperfections, disguising her neck and half her face. Sousa then turned to a pale man, who struggled to support his larger frame on his spindly legs. "Felipe is one of the best chefs in the world; he owns restaurants and nightclubs all over the city."

As Sousa spoke, I found myself growing frustrated by his motives. He simply wanted to show off a prophet to his famous friends. To ease the insecurities of being cast aside by his own family, he sought validation from anyone who would make him feel important and accepted.

Julianna, the designer, stepped forward holding a shopping bag. "From my newest collection. I can take your measurements, adjust it to the correct size."

"Thank you," I said politely, taking the gift. "And I appreciate that you came all this way just to see me. But I have to warn you, as I'm sure Eduardo has already mentioned, just how important it is not to give away our location."

Everyone nodded along, as I repeated my speech in the bit of halted Portuguese I'd learned—helped out along the way by Sousa correcting my grammar.

Just as I thought I'd found a way to wrap up, Dawn stepped forward, interjecting. "I'm Dawn, a guru of Prophet Grace," she explained, giving herself the highest possible nonprophet designation. While it annoyed me to have her take on that role without consulting me, I knew that giving Dawn authority and credibility was important, so I nodded along.

The crowd turned to Dawn, excited to realize they were in the presence of a second important figure, as she continued in a menacing voice, "If you do reveal our location, even inadvertently, you will face a Punishment more horrible than death."

My breath caught in my throat as she issued this blistering proclamation on my behalf. Since Punishments were caused by feeling guilty, and threats of Punishment made people feel guilty, those threats were tantamount to death warrants. But I couldn't contradict Dawn, not now that she'd given herself guru status.

So instead I simmered in my anger and signed off to my followers with a polite wave, gesturing for Dawn and Zack to join me. As soon as we were out of earshot, I pulled Dawn aside.

"What the hell was that?"

Dawn showed no remorse. "The more people who know our location, the sooner the prophets will find us. The clock is ticking now. I was doing what I could to slow it down, keep us safe."

"You didn't make anyone safer, you turned me into some kind of fire and brimstone prophet, just like all the others."

"To a few dozen people. It's fine." I hated how Dawn refused to listen, how she spoke with the air of someone who was always right. Though she'd been our leader for so long, and had years of additional wisdom and experience, the religious stuff wasn't her wheelhouse. For once, all my time spent immersed in the culture of worship was finally useful for something.

"What if it isn't?" I pushed back, frustrated.

"You can't be so focused on saving every single life, you have to remember the big picture. All those people out there, all the Outcasts you've never met who are counting on you."

"If they die, do you think Sousa will keep helping us?" I shot back. "My message has to be consistent, and it has to be different from the other prophets' . . ."

Zack put a hand on my shoulder, and it calmed me instantly. "Look, what's done is done. Grace, I get it, Dawn and I won't make any more Proclamations without consulting with you. Right?" he warned Dawn. She nodded grudgingly. "And let's all agree to let this one go. There's nothing we can do about it now. If you take it back, you make it more likely that someone thinks it's okay to compromise our location."

"I know," I muttered through gritted teeth, then took a deep breath. "We'll let it go."

Zack saw tensions were still simmering, and he tugged on my arm. "Let's go for a walk." I nodded, glad to leave Dawn behind. The way he spoke with confidence put me at ease. I felt like I could handle anything with him by my side.

"Where do you want to go?" I asked as we stepped away.

He gestured to the package from Julianna the designer that I still held in my hands, a sly glint in his eye. "I want to see you try on whatever's in that box."

The way he said it sent a little thrill through my body. And what he wanted . . . I wanted it, too.

7

Back in my room, I tore open Julianna's gift, unboxing a lacy, embroidered dress, which I discovered was nearly twice my size. "This Julianna is quite the designer," Zack said, laughing.

"She said she'd adjust it to fit my measurements!" I said, defensive of this stranger who'd been so kind to me.

Zack grinned, playing with the masses of fabric around my waist. "Maybe she can make you two dresses. Or better than that, zero." He kissed me again, and this time the kiss was a suggestion, an offer. I knew where it led—across that room, to that bed beneath the mosquito netting. I was drawn in, I wanted to follow, but . . .

Don't trust him. That stupid voice. I almost shouted back at it—I was certain by now that I could trust Zack, that he was staunchly in my corner in every possible way. But still, I was left on edge.

After all these weeks together, on the boat and out in the

rainforest, we still hadn't gone much further than a kiss. Zack had wanted to, that was plenty obvious, but each time we got to that point, I hesitated. Even though I knew it was all fake, that Great Spirit wasn't going to Punish me for having sex, wasn't going to Punish me for anything, since Punishments were just brain chemistry . . . it didn't matter. That long-ago instilled fear still held me back.

It tried its hardest, at least. Zack kissed me again, and as his hand moved from my waist up to my breast, I found myself regretting being covered head to toe in this tent of lacy embroidery. I wanted to be closer to him, to feel his skin on mine. That aching, yearning feeling . . . I wanted to let it take over, to give in to it.

But something inside me wouldn't budge. Maybe it was that stupid voice in my head, whispering and manipulating my thoughts. Or . . . maybe it was just me. Maybe I wasn't ready. Maybe it was some responsibility I felt as prophet, not to get too attached to anyone. Maybe it was all those things, mixed together in a toxic stew of maybes.

But as that kiss bellowed Zack's offer louder and louder, I pulled away, whispering, "What will those people down there think? You know, that you're in my room."

"That you're a person?" he said softly, brushing aside my concerns. "You're their prophet, you can proclaim whatever rules you want about sex. The male prophets have plenty of sex; you think the rules are different because you're a girl?"

I only knew what I'd been taught growing up, through a thousand silent cultural clues—that the rules on paper for men and women might be the same, but the unwritten rules, the ones people judged you on . . . those were still different. I forced a smile, knowing it was impossible to explain any of this to Zack, who'd never been in my shoes as a woman, much less a prophet. "You're right, I'm a prophet now. If I want to change the rules, I'll change them."

But now, the spell we'd been under was broken. We regarded each other carefully, trying to find a way forward. Before we could, a knock at the door interrupted us. We separated, and Zack opened it to reveal Dawn.

"We have a visitor," she said with a knowing smile.

My heart soared—could it be Jude? Had they finally gotten word from Turkey? But instead, a different familiar face walked through my door: Dr. Marko, the scientist who'd first told me the true cause of Punishments—the nanotech residing in our brains. Since I'd had some part in both his capture and subsequent rescue from Prophet Joshua's hands, and also because he was a genuinely delightful human being, I was deeply relieved to see he was still alive and well.

Marko smiled when he spotted me, bowing with a regal flourish and putting on a fake southern accent. "Prophet Grace, as I live and breathe."

I hugged him. "What are you doing here? Are you in danger?"

"My safe house was raided not long after you gave your sermon in South Africa. Only two of us made it out. I had a satphone, but I couldn't get in touch with my usual contacts in the resistance once our networks went down. Thankfully I saw the coded SOS Dawn sent once you made landfall in Brazil, so I came here to help."

"Help?" I asked, hopeful.

"You know, chop some wood, catch some fish, what else do you do in the rainforest?" he joked. I was relieved to see that his time in hiding hadn't dulled his sense of humor.

"Or maybe, you could make more pills, to save more people?" I asked hopefully. If he could do that, we could restart the resistance.

I was disheartened when he shook his head. "I'm not sure we have the supplies here to do that. Most of the resistance's drug manufacturing resources got taken out when our safe houses did. But I did learn one piece of information, which I traveled across two continents to bring you."

"What?" I asked, breathless.

"Last year, I know you traveled to Israel-Palestine to help the resistance acquire a code that would help us remove the nanotech in our brains for good." He held out a slip of paper with that familiar code.

"It's no good without the machine to input that code into," I reminded him, shaking my head. "And the last one we found, in that stadium in South Africa, wasn't operational."

He flipped over the slip of paper to show me another set of numbers. "GPS coordinates."

I took the slip of paper, heart beating wildly. "To a new machine?"

He nodded. "An even better one." Now we just had to get it.

8

It wasn't going to be an easy feat. For one thing, the new nanofabricator device was almost twenty-five hundred miles away, in Rio de Janeiro. For another, the facility it was housed in was incredibly well protected, owned and secured by Prophet Daniel himself.

"Why there?" I asked. "If one of these things was hooked up to the stadium in South Africa, maybe there are others in other stadiums. Those must be easier to get to than this one."

Marko nodded. "You're absolutely right. The problem is, any device that big is going to be impossible to transport. You want to get one into rebel hands, you need a smaller one, a newer one. The device at this facility is only five pounds, and a fraction of the size."

"How do you know all this?" I asked, nervous.

"Back when we were hacked into the prophets' computers, before they discovered us, we were able to access all their confidential files. Locations of important items. Even a few hints about some of the technology they've been developing." Despite himself, Marko lit up when he talked about this new tech—though he'd discovered weapons to be used against us, the science geek in him still found them incredibly cool. But cool meant dangerous. My stomach flip-flopped, thinking about what the prophets might yet have in store.

Dawn pulled up a map of the location, a massive military compound just outside the city. "I wish we had blueprints of the facility."

"It's silly to think we could sneak in and get it, right?" I asked.

"There's no way," Zack muttered. "This is going to have to be an all-out assault."

"An assault?" I asked, voice quavering. "If this place is really so well protected, wouldn't that just be a slaughter?"

"Waiting around is its own kind of slaughter," Dawn said pointedly.

"Would we even have the numbers to mount an assault?" Dr. Marko asked bluntly. "We still haven't heard from Turkey, have we?" My insides felt hollow, reminded of Jude, and Dawn turned her head away from us, hiding tears. It shook me to watch that strong woman overcome with such grief and fear. I knew she must be thinking about her wife, Irene, who was still missing along with all the others. My heart went out to her, knowing she had just as much at stake as I did; more even.

I tried to find a solution. "Couldn't we plant someone on the inside, a spy who could get past all that security?"

"That would take months, to place a double agent with the right clearances," Dawn said.

"So we turn someone who's already working there," I insisted.

"That's too risky . . ." Zack said dismissively.

Dawn nodded in agreement. "Even if we could figure out who to target . . ."

"One of my followers," I interrupted. "Someone working there must trust me. There are some non-Outcasts who liked my message, too. If you still have that satphone, we can use it to get on the internet, do some research, and then call them up."

The others looked at one another skeptically. Zack was the first to speak, hesitantly. "I thought you didn't want to use your influence that way."

"I don't," I admitted. "But with just one person, in a situation this important . . . of course I'll do it."

"We'd be risking our location by reaching out right now . . ." Dawn said, considering.

I nodded, validating her concerns. "You said yourself, every moment Sousa's friends are here, we run that risk. 'Waiting around is its own kind of slaughter,' right?" Dawn tensed a little, hearing her own words repeated back to her, but I knew she was listening now, as I continued, "We can't hide in the jungle forever, we have to make a move at some point. We just need to pick our moment. And I think this is our moment."

Marko nodded, seemingly in agreement with me. "I can get us a call out that'll be encrypted. I think the risk is worth it."

Zack shook his head, staunchly defensive, arguing only to Dawn. "There's too much danger it'll backfire. We have to protect our position here." His dissension irked me; I'd been so reassured by his support before, which made it more frustrating that he wasn't taking my side now. Some paranoid part of me worried this might be a sign of Zack's wavering affections. But I put those fears away. This was a tactical decision, which of course he'd have his own opinions about, and I appreciated that Zack wasn't blindly agreeing with me just because we were romantically involved.

Everyone looked at Dawn—though it was unofficial, all power still rested with her. After a moment of consideration, she nodded, too. "If Grace is willing to take this risk, we should do it."

My heart raced with excitement, then skidded to a stop with dread. Dawn was putting her trust in me, and I wasn't sure I'd earned it. Judging by the skeptical look on Zack's face, I could tell he had his own doubts. As he sullenly left the room, I wondered if a rift was forming between us.

I had moral concerns as well. I was already a false prophet. Was I really willing to abuse the trust of the people who believed in me most, for my own selfish needs?

Not *my* needs, I reminded myself. I was doing this for Jude. For Irene. For Layla and Mohammed and everyone we'd left behind in Turkey. For them, I'd cross this line. I'd have to.

It didn't take us long to find our mark. Using Dr. Marko's satphone connection, Dawn accessed the internet and hacked a list of the facility's personnel. A cursory sweep of their social media profiles quickly pulled up an engineer with the right clearances: a Rio native named Paulina, whose beloved sister was an Outcast. Paulina had eagerly embraced my message, posting video after video of people preaching in my name.

"And I thought *I* was obsessed with you," Zack teased, and I was flattered to hear him use such complimentary language.

"Looks like Paulina's single, you better watch out," I joked back.

I took the computer from Dawn, under the guise of re-searching Paulina, but was quickly drawn in to the videos Paulina was posting: tons of real-life clerics, all preaching my fake truth. The religion I'd created wasn't just me now; a thousand strangers had taken my one tiny speech and extrapolated a million unrelated ideas. Whatever they wanted to see in my sermon, they'd found a way to see it—found ways to make my words fit their agendas.

As had my opponents—loyalists to the original prophets dissected my phrases in their own videos and articles, trying to prove that I couldn't be communicating any kind of divine truth. The more I watched and read, the more I wondered if anyone had listened to my actual speech, or whether they'd just taken my words and rearranged them to form new sentences with completely different meanings. Though all these misinter-pretations made me sick, this access to the world outside was a drug, and after so many weeks without it, I wanted to drink it all in at once.

While I'd gone silent, in my little bubble, everyone else I knew was speaking for me. Back home, half my former class-mates had somehow found their way to news cameras or selfie confessionals to relate stories about me, most of which I didn't even remember. The time I'd given someone half my dessert in fourth grade, the time I'd worn my shirt inside out. I cringed as they said embarrassing and unkind things, and I glowed with pride as they heaped praise. Now that I was religious royalty, everyone wanted to associate themselves with me—for better or worse.

There was one notable exception, one person whose absence from the spotlight made my heart heavy: my own father. According to the news, he'd taken a sabbatical from our worship center, become a recluse; no one could find him to comment on my prophetship. What they didn't say, but I knew, was that he was still furious; he believed I was undermining real divine leadership, that I was worshipping the devil.

"Is there any way to find my dad?" I asked Dr. Marko.

"Did you put a GPS chip in him?" Marko joked.

"Didn't think of it," I muttered back.

"I'm sure he's okay," he said, trying to reassure me.

The thought gave me only a little relief. "I'm sure he is, too. Alive, he just hates me."

"No parent hates their child. Ever," Dr. Marko promised.

"You haven't met my parents," I grumbled.

He softened, putting on the kind of fatherly tone I'd sorely missed. "We may not see eye to eye with our parents—I never saw eye to eye with my dad—but they love us, in whatever ways they can. He'll come around, eventually," he promised. Though I wanted to believe him, I was afraid of getting my hopes up. As long as I challenged his deeply held beliefs, my father would only see me as a threat, not a daughter.

While I might not have converted my father, it seemed I'd made a disciple out of my oldest friend; Macy was making the rounds preaching in my name. From what I could glean online, she was giving a sermon a day, traveling all over the world. "She's been my best friend forever," Macy gushed into a microphone at a podium, explaining her devotion. "Grace was always so pious, I knew if someone was going to be the next prophet, it'd be her." It was strange and twisted, seeing how I'd manipulated even the people closest to me.

"What are you watching?" Zack asked, curious, as he entered my room.

I showed him. "Your sister's a guru now. She's going to hate me when she finds out the truth, isn't she?"

Zack smiled widely. "You can ask her yourself."

"What do you mean?"

"She's here. With us. In the rainforest."

9

What do you mean, she's here?" I asked, incredulous.

"Macy was being targeted by the prophets, for speaking out on your behalf. A lot of people were. The resistance rescued a few of them, got them to safe houses . . . before the last of our safe houses were raided. Like Dr. Marko said, only two people made it out—him and Macy. So when he got our SOS, he figured he'd bring her along. She was pretty sick when she first got here. We didn't want to worry you. After a couple good meals, she's doing much better." The way he said "we" irked me, like he and Dawn were talking behind my back, making decisions on my behalf about what was best for me.

"She's my best friend, you should have told me," I said, annoyed. And hurt to be excluded from his circle of confidence. Once again, I doubted the depth of his feelings for me.

"We don't have any medication to stop a potential guilt spiral, so we can't tell her the truth yet," Zack explained. "We didn't think you'd want to have to lie to her." I'd certainly felt plenty guilty watching Macy preaching in those videos . . . I had to admit, Dawn and Zack had correctly predicted my apprehension.

But now that I knew she was here, I couldn't keep hiding. I hopped out of bed, pushing past him. "Where is she now?"

He showed me to a nearby bungalow, where Macy ran out to greet me with a hug. "Grace! I missed you so much!" She paused. "Sorry, can I hug you? You're a prophet now, maybe you aren't supposed to hug a prophet."

I hugged her back just as tightly. "Of course you can hug me!"

"Okay, good. I knew you'd be, like, a cool prophet. I can't believe you're a prophet! How did it happen, how did you know? What does Great Spirit sound like? I want to know everything!"

Her effusive excitement gave me pause—facing my best friend was as difficult as Dawn and Zack had expected it would be. "I'll tell you everything soon. I'm just glad you're safe."

As Macy and I found a quiet patch of not-flooded forest to walk through, she excitedly peppered me with questions. "What happens when we die? Why did Great Spirit tell the other prophets the wrong things? Or did they just misinterpret His message? Wait, is Great Spirit a He, or like an It? Or like a He/She/It all-knowing combo? Also are you and Zack like . . . a thing? He wouldn't tell me."

I wanted so badly to come out with all of it—that this whole religion had been a sham, that it wasn't Great Spirit changing our appearances, but nanotech inside our heads. I wondered if hearing those words from a "prophet" might make them go down easier, might protect her from getting a fatal Punishment for doubting. But I stopped short. Macy's life was too precious to gamble like that.

"I only know what Great Spirit tells me, so I don't have all the answers. But the other prophets have been lying, for their own gain, and we're trying to stop them," I explained.

She seemed excited to be at the center of some kind of cosmological battle. "How amazing is it to be, like, the embodiment of divine perfection?" I wished she would stop saying things like that.

"We're all the embodiment of divine perfection, aren't we?" I joked, playing her off.

Macy nodded. "Even Outcasts, right?"

I smiled. "Even Outcasts."

"Okay, now tell me about you and my brother. Not the gross stuff. But, like, you're dating or whatever, right?"

I remembered the way he'd questioned my tactics earlier, and I wondered if a distance was growing between us. There was something about Zack's stoic confidence that left me constantly terrified I was going to lose him. "I don't know."

"He wouldn't stop talking about you earlier. He's really such a dork sometimes." A grin overtook my face, and I allowed my insecurities to slip away.

I put a lid on our girl talk as I heard branches snapping, someone approaching—Zack emerging into our clearing. "Dawn wants to see you."

"Seriously?" Macy said to her brother, annoyed. "I haven't seen Grace in a thousand years, give us five more minutes."

I nodded to Zack, knowing what he really meant—it was time to call Paulina. "I'll be back soon," I promised Macy. As we left,

Zack touched the small of my back in a way that felt reassuring, and I hoped more than ever that he was mine to keep.

Zack and I returned to my room, meeting up with Dawn and Dr. Marko, and the importance of this mission sobered me. "You're sure you can convince this lady to steal from her employer?" Zack asked one final time, as Dawn typed away on the laptop, extracting Paulina's number from her hacked employee file.

"I don't know," I said honestly, growing nervous at his skepticism. "I've never done this before."

"Neither have any of us. You'll be great," Marko reassured me, as he dialed the satphone.

Dawn continued with her warnings. "If this woman tells anyone, if she's Punished before she can get there . . . we'll lose the element of surprise. Don't give any clues about our location. If you get the sense that she's wavering, hang up."

"Got it," I said. As she pointed out all the potential pitfalls of this plan, my brash confidence dimmed. I hadn't had much time to build a successful track record as a prophet. Paulina might love me from afar . . . but when she actually spoke to me directly, I worried she'd be disappointed.

My stomach churned as the dial tone clicked, connecting us. "Hola?" an airy voice answered on the other end.

"Is this Paulina?" I asked in Portuguese, grateful for all of Sousa's language lessons.

"Yes . . ." she said warily.

"This is Grace," I said, not quite sure how to introduce myself.

"Grace . . . ?"

"Prophet Grace."

There was silence on the other end. "Is this a joke?"

"That's a fair question," I admitted. "But no, it's really me."

"Why are you calling me?" she asked, confused, still not quite believing me.

"Great Spirit said you could help me. That because of your sister, you'd be sympathetic to our cause."

Silence answered on the other end. She still didn't believe me. Dawn gave me a knowing look—she'd expected this from the beginning.

"You need me to prove myself. I hear you. I will at midnight tonight, and I need you to listen, and follow my word to the letter. But please, between then and now, keep this conversation between you and me."

I quickly hung up the phone, trying to seem mysterious, as Dawn and Zack regarded me skeptically. "Well, that went well," Dawn said.

"No, I have a plan."

"A plan?"

I hesitated. "You're not going to like it."

10

My plan: to send a video message to my followers. "You're right, I don't like this," Dawn confirmed.

I stood firm. "It's the only way."

"You can't just send Paulina a little private note or something?" Zack suggested.

"Then she'll show it to people, to check and see if it's really me. If we do it this way, we distract the prophets. We convince them that the video itself is the point, and they won't even be thinking about the facility."

Dawn took that in, considering. "You know what this means. You're putting yourself out there again. You saw what everyone did with that one speech. You really want to give them new words to misinterpret?"

In truth, I had to admit, that was the secret, real reason I wanted to do this—to give myself a chance to set the record straight, to reclaim my own narrative from those twisting it.

Paulina was a good excuse to steer the ship of this religion I'd accidentally created. To clean up a tiny bit of my own mess. But even if I had an ulterior motive, I still thought it was the right call. "If it doesn't work, we try something else."

As the clock ticked down to midnight, Marko pulled up the video function on the satphone to use as a camera. "Let's hope this works," Dawn muttered as she uploaded the file to an anonymous YouTube account, encrypting our location.

Prophet Grace's second sermon was live.

At first, we got only a few scattered hits. But soon, news outlets in Europe and Asia took notice. "Has Prophet Grace re-emerged?" they asked with bated breath. And then, our views began to skyrocket.

"My beloved followers," the video began. "I'm so sorry for my absence. As you may have noticed, the other prophets have not welcomed me with open arms. I knew I would encounter resistance to my message, and so I've needed to stay hidden, for my own safety. But I know that isn't fair to you, to declare myself and then disappear. And if there's one message I want to convey to you, it's that it's okay to be wrong sometimes. It's okay to make mistakes, and then work to make them right. Even when you're a prophet.

"So this is me trying to right my wrongs. I owe you all something. Proof that I haven't forgotten you. And I will offer that proof as often as I can. But in return I ask for one thing: stay faithful to Great Spirit in my absence. He will ask much of you, especially in the face of those who don't share your faith. But when He calls on you, answer. Listen. And follow his word to the letter." Those final words, I intoned exactly the way I'd spoken them to Paulina on the phone.

The next morning, I called Paulina again, and she burst into tears. "It really is you."

"I don't blame you for being skeptical," I assured her.

"I always knew, even if I was afraid to admit it. I didn't tell anyone, I swear," she blubbered.

"Thank you," I said, relief washing over me.

She was beside herself. "Why me? Why have you chosen me, out of everyone?"

"Like I said, I need your help. And your confidence. Can I trust you?"

"You can trust me with anything," she said breathlessly.

I inhaled deeply, hoping this would work. "I need you to borrow something for me."

I was sure I'd encounter more resistance. After years of being inundated by a culture of black-and-white morality, the idea of stealing wasn't glamorous, it was horrifying. I remembered how shocked I'd been, before I knew the truth, the first time I saw Ciaran rob a store. On our first date, he'd claimed he was protected by Great Spirit, that his transgressions were sanctioned somehow. But I'd still felt in my bones that what he was doing must be wrong; that even though he wasn't being Punished, he should have been. And I was right after all—it turned out that his "protection" came from being a sociopath, someone whose brain was incapable of feeling guilt in the same way mine was.

But surprisingly, Paulina had no such suspicions about me. By projecting a message to her for the world to see, I'd earned her trust completely. Within hours of our call, she sent a secure message with diagrams of her building and pictures of the device itself, which was in storage deep within the facility's vault.

"That's it!" Dr. Marko exclaimed when he saw the photos.

"So she's found it . . . she goes and grabs it, easy," I said, feeling quite proud that my plan had worked so well.

"She still has to get it to us without being detected," Zack pointed out.

"I'll meet her myself," Dawn said immediately. "I'll wait as close as I can to the building, make sure everything goes according to plan."

"But if you're recognized . . ." I said nervously.

"There aren't many of us left," Dawn reminded us. "Like you said, this mission is too important. We have to make sure it's a success."

I felt a pang of worry as Dawn packed up to depart. She was my friend, my mentor, and I hated watching her march into danger.

She left at midday, with Sousa as her guide to ferry her south. As she sailed off, my nerves set in. I hadn't realized until that moment just how much I'd been leaning on Dawn. She was the one who always had a plan, who always knew the best thing to do . . . or at least acted like she did. As much as I'd been chafing at her controlling attitude, deep down a part of me liked that someone else was steering our ship. Without her, I felt rudderless.

And realizing that made me nervous . . . I'd put myself in

a leadership position, as a prophet. Whether or not anyone in the resistance took me seriously, millions of other people did. And the truth was, I wasn't a leader; it wasn't how I'd been raised. I'd always been told my job was to defer to my spiritual elders . . . I'd never trained to *be* one.

But now that Dawn was gone, I was the one calling the shots. I was going to have to figure out how to lead, whether I wanted to or not.

11

The next night, I burrowed into Zack's arms, finding comfort nestling my head beneath his chin. "How am I supposed to act all-knowing when I know nothing? I'm just making things up as I go along."

He nodded, understanding. "Don't feel like you have to be 'Prophet Grace' all the time. Be you. You get to decide what a prophet's like. Who says you have to know anything? That's when people seem to really respond to you. When you're honest, when you show your faults. People aren't used to that."

"But I can't show all of them," I pointed out. "If people start thinking I'm a bad person, they won't think I'm worth listening to."

"Luckily you aren't a bad person," Zack said, kissing me. "And you've got friends to help you."

"What if I fail?" I asked, feeling vulnerable.

Zack didn't miss a beat. "At least you'll look hot as hell doing it."

Lost in an ocean of self-doubt, I grabbed on to Zack like a lifeline, pulling him toward me. His kisses weren't enough—my hands were drawn to him, magnetically taking on a life of their own. They found his body, as his found mine, and still nothing was enough.

Soon, the only thing separating us from the sticky, sweaty Amazon was that mosquito netting around my bed. The humid air hung around us, as Zack's whispers filled it with the words that warmed me up: "I love you, Grace."

"I love you, too," I whispered back. More than love, I needed him. In that moment I needed him more than I'd ever needed anything. Needed the security, surety, of his embrace.

As I pulled him closer to me, he whispered, "Are you sure?"

"So sure." He reached into his bag and pulled out a condom, and I had to stifle a laugh. "Really, of all the things to bring with you from civilization, that's what you picked?"

"It's coming in handy, isn't it?" As he tore it open, a surge of nervousness went through me. But one look at his grin, crinkling up a face covered in two weeks of Amazon scruff, made my body feel electric.

This will end in heartbreak, my brain whispered, but I pushed that stupid voice aside. It had been put there to hurt me, and this time I wasn't going to let it. I wasn't going to let any of the stupid anxieties in my head stop me from following my heart. No matter what happened next, I needed this now. And nothing would ever make me regret it.

12

The heat inside that room was sweltering all through the night, but I didn't care: I wanted to stay entwined in Zack's arms forever. When he finally awoke the next morning, he smiled when he caught sight of my face. "Good morning, Amazing."

"Me, amazing?" I asked.

"Yes, you. Also that ceiling fan, but definitely you."

"Why?" I whispered back, feeling insatiably needy all of a sudden.

"You have to ask why?" he asked, laughing. "Seriously, you don't know that you're charming and insightful and kind . . ."

"Go on," I teased.

He sobered up a moment. "You think one day I just decided, I'm going to put my life at risk, give up my career, everything I've ever worked for, 'cause I guess this girl's all right or whatever . . ."

"Also it was the right thing to do," I reminded him.

"You're the one who showed me it was the right thing to do," he admitted. "Watching you, I realized I couldn't be a coward anymore. I couldn't keep doing all the things I knew were wrong. I saw you being brave, and I thought, that's who I want to be, too."

His vulnerability touched me—he loved me for something other than my looks, after all. "And here I thought you were the brave one," I said quietly.

"I thought I was, too. Until I met you."

We lay there, fingers interlaced, and in that moment, I forgot that there was anything outside that room. That is, until the satphone by my bed rang. Zack and I both bolted upright, staring at it.

"You want me to answer?" Zack offered.

I shook my head and picked up. "Hello?" Zack wrapped an arm around me, comforting.

"Prophet Grace?" Paulina's voice shook on the other end.

"Paulina," I said, to clue Zack in to who was calling. "What's going on?"

"I'm sorry. I'm scared." I could hear her resignation.

"Where are you, Paulina?" I asked nervously.

"In the vault." I breathed a sigh of relief that she wasn't already at a prophet's office or police station reporting us.

"Why are you scared?" I asked, keeping my voice calm and comforting.

"I know you said I could steal and it would be okay. But normally stealing is wrong, right?"

"Normally, yes. But this is life or death. Great Spirit understands."

"Then why am I being Punished?" she asked, voice shaking. "I saw my reflection in a mirror just now, and it scared me."

This was what I'd been most afraid of. I took a moment to think—how could I save her life and still get the device? "You're in a facility run by the other prophets," I explained hastily, trying to concoct a lie that would convince her. "They've made a pact with the devil, to Punish anyone who threatens their power. And right now, because you're helping me, they must be targeting you. I'm so sorry, for putting you in danger like this. But I will die, your prophet will die, if you don't go through with this." The look on Zack's face as I spoke gave me pause. I knew I was guilt-tripping her, and making anyone guilty was dangerous. But I pressed on. "You have to steal that device, and then I promise, once you're out of there, once you pass it on, you'll be Forgiven. All the guilt, all the pain, it will all go away, I promise. You'll be a hero, and Great Spirit will reward you."

There was silence on the other end for so long, I wondered if she'd hung up, but finally she squeaked out, "Okay," and the line clicked dead.

"What happened? Is she doing it?" Zack asked.

I shook, racked with anxiety. "I hope so."

Our postcoital high had faded into a nervous waiting game. I could tell Zack was working through something in his mind, trying to find a solution.

"You might as well have told her the truth," Zack said as he reached outside the mosquito netting to grab his pants. "You've taken enough of a risk by telling her in the first place. Better she knows the real reason she's doing this."

"Knowing the real reason might have killed her. And if she knew the truth, she'd know I wasn't a real prophet, and she'd have no reason to do *anything* for me," I pointed out. I hated arguing with Zack, especially right after we'd finally connected like that. I took his face in my hands and kissed him. "It'll be okay," I reassured him.

"I hope you're right," he said skeptically, but he kissed me back.

As we dressed and headed back downstairs to meet the others, a strange kind of silence settled in between us. We sat among our Outcast friends as Felipe, Redenção's restauranteur, served everyone breakfast—our smallest portion of eggs yet. Supplies were running low. But Dawn would return with more when she came back with the device.

Unless Zack was right, and our plan was about to backfire; then maybe she wouldn't return at all.

As the minutes ticked into hours, my hopes began to dwindle. I knew exactly how big that building was, how Paulina planned to smuggle the device through the mailroom. If she lost faith in the plan, if I hadn't been convincing enough, then everything would fall apart. We wouldn't get the device, and Dawn would be a sitting duck; instead of Paulina showing up at their meet point, it might be agents of the prophet, informed about our plan.

How could I think I was as convincing as the "real" prophets, who'd been hand selected for this job as the most charismatic people in the world? Sure, I'd said a few things that resonated with people, but any idiot could do that, especially given the tools I'd had at my disposal—a whole stadium full of uppers to heal the crowd. Now that Paulina had talked to me in person, of course I should have expected her to lose faith.

That was exactly what Zack had been trying to say, even if he'd been too polite to say it to my face. I was a novice, playing in the big leagues, and I was flailing. My frustration at him mellowed into sympathy, and regret. I wished I'd listened to him when I had the chance.

Then, the satphone rang again. As my stomach swirled with nerves, I picked it up immediately, averting my eyes from Zack—I didn't want to see my own insecurities reflected in his eyes. "Hello?"

But it wasn't Paulina or one of her friends this time, it was Dawn, voice triumphant. "We got it!"

"The device?" I asked, hushed, knowing that every ear in this room was listening in on our call.

"I'm on my way back now," she said. "Good work, Prophet."

As I hung up, I found a smile involuntarily winding its way up to my ears. Zack clocked my expression and smiled in return. "She got it?"

"Yeah," I said, buzzing with a kind of pride that I'd never felt before. I'd gone toe-to-toe with the prophets once again, and somehow my words had won. I felt powerful, unstoppable. It reminded me of the first time I tried the pills, the moment I realized I wasn't bound to all the rules I'd thought were Great Spirit–given. But this was different, intoxicating—I was truly the only one in the world with this kind of power. What could I do with it?

Zack, for his part, was just happy we'd succeeded. "How

great will it be to get this crap out of our heads, after all these years?"

But we weren't in the clear just yet.

When I came into my room that night, I overheard Zack streaming a news broadcast, which he worriedly shut off as I entered. "What's that?" I asked him.

"Nothing," he said suspiciously enough that I immediately grabbed for the computer.

"Hey!" he protested, but I ignored him. "Don't watch that, Grace, I'm serious . . ." he warned, but I clicked anyway.

"A break-in at a facility owned by Prophet Daniel was discovered to be the work of an Outcast terrorist, who professed her allegiance to Prophet Grace. She claims Grace has been communicating with her and asked her to steal from her employer." On-screen, I watched Paulina defiantly being led away in handcuffs, her face now marred by Punishment, lined with anger and resentment. My lies, my manipulation, had ruined her life.

Before I could watch any more, Zack pulled the computer away from me. "Don't do this to yourself. You did a good job, you managed to get that tech out without losing any lives. Remember that."

I did remember, and his kind words gave me comfort. But I couldn't stop myself from feeling the guilt: the overwhelming sense that the earth should swallow me whole, that I deserved the same fate I'd given Paulina. "I think I need to lie down," I said, and I could hear in my voice how the Punishment was affecting me. It was swift and all-consuming, as though all the guilt I'd felt over deceiving billions of people was hitting me in one crushing wave.

Zack made room in the bed so I could collapse under the mosquito netting, and before I knew it, the world was black around me.

13

The night passed in a haze, like watching the world in fast-forward. One minute I was sure Zack was sitting right next to me, the next he was on the other side of the room, pacing. I heard Dr. Marko's voice, whispering, "It's bad, very bad." My breathing slowed as my windpipe constricted; I was getting very little air.

"Am I dying?" I tried to ask, but I couldn't speak, and that was answer enough.

When suddenly it was morning, I felt something touching my palm—and realized it was Zack's. He'd fallen asleep, sitting on the floor next to me, hand squeezing mine. When I moved, he jolted awake. "Grace, can you hear me?"

I couldn't speak, so I nodded weakly.

He gripped me so tightly it hurt. "Hold on. Dawn's on her way back. Just another day, just a little longer." I could see the fear, the desperation in his eyes, the grief thinking he might be about to lose me, and it terrified me.

I wanted to thank him for sitting with me like this, wanted to confess everything I'd been feeling. I made a list of all the things I wanted to tell him once Dawn got here and cured me, gave me back my voice. That I loved him, how grateful I was that he'd chosen to give up everything to fight alongside me. I repeated it like a mantra in my head, memorized the words, but the more I thought them, the more they blurred together. In my sickly haze, I wasn't sure they were even words, or just feelings that sounded like words.

I blinked and it was night again. Maybe this was all a dream. It felt like one.

Though it was dark outside, the room filled with a strange, bright light, cascading in pinks and purples up from the floor. I was alone, until I wasn't. Through the strange, colorful haze, a figure moved toward the bed. Jude.

"Hold on. Just another hour," he whispered. He looked so young, with that awkward stilted walk he'd had in high school. An innocence about him still. "Stay with me, just focus on the sound of my voice." I longed for him, ached to pull him close. I missed him more than ever before, even now when he was right in front of my face.

I blinked and Jude was Zack again.

"Just hold on," Zack repeated, with Jude's voice.

I'm holding on, I wanted to tell him. And suddenly, I found my voice again. "What if I can't do this?"

Zack leaned over to me, and suddenly his features swirled into a jumble—one minute he had Jude's nose, Macy's eyes, my father's smile. At once, he managed to be the personification of everyone who loved me. "I've got you." I stared at the mishmash of features in front of me, all urging me to "Forgive yourself."

I wanted to, but something dark nagged inside of me. "I'm supposed to be telling people how to be better," I whispered. "But every word out of my mouth is a lie. I'm manipulating people, I'm a monster. If I forgive myself, I'm saying that's okay. I'm saying it's okay that I haven't found a way to do this more honestly, that it doesn't matter who I've hurt along the way."

"You're right, you did make mistakes," the voice next to me said in its strange, ethereal way. "And you'll make more. But you'll learn to do things better, too. You'll show people a better way, you'll help make a better world. But you won't be able to do that unless you survive. Nothing will be better until you stop defining yourself by the sins of your past, and start defining yourself by the good you're about to do. Your journey is just beginning. Forgive yourself, Grace."

Without even trying, I could feel it inside of me, the healing beginning. "Thank you," I whispered. I reached out to touch my ever-changing friend, blinked again, and—

Everything was gone, black. There was something over my face. There always had been, I realized. Everything I'd just seen, those lights, the people—they were indeed some kind of dream state.

"Just take deep breaths." That sounded like Dr. Marko.

Another voice, that familiar echoey chorus, the voice my mother had planted in my brain, shouted at me. *Give up, give up, give up!*

But I took a deep breath, and the air rushed in, cool and

thick—I hadn't realized how little of it had been making its way into my lungs. As I gasped, enjoying each breath, Marko removed a gas mask from my face. The room was back to its normal, non-neon coloration, as Dr. Marko and Zack huddled around my bedside.

Zack put a hand on my back to support me sitting upright. I tried to remember all the things I'd wanted to say to him when I was delirious, but I felt them all slip away. I could see on his face that my appearance must have improved significantly. "Are you okay?" he asked.

I opened my mouth and found words coming out—less smooth than they had in my dream. "I think so. What was that?"

Dr. Marko grinned, proud. "Since we didn't have any uppers, I brewed you something new to boost your serotonin levels. A little pleasant hallucinatory experience. Think of it as an emergency anti-guilt serum."

"What do you mean, you brewed it?" I asked, confused.

"The nanofabricator, it can make just about anything," Marko explained. "Including very powerful and precise neurological manipulators."

"The nanofabricator . . . you mean we got it?" I asked, thrilled, and in that moment, I noticed Dawn across the room, walking over to my bedside. The sight of her filled me with deep relief. "You're back." I hugged her, thankful she was alive and that our mission had succeeded.

"I used the nanofabricator that your buddy Paulina stole to create that gas that blissed you out," Dr. Marko explained. "I'm looking forward to playing around with this device later. It can make just about any kind of small particle . . ."

Including the nanovirus that would destroy the bugs inside our heads. The reality hit me. "We can end this."

"One person at a time," Zack said, trying to temper my excitement. But the potential of this new tech was too tempting . . . my hope was now getting ahead of me.

"And it works, to remove the tech in our heads? You've tried it?" I asked.

"On myself," Dawn said. "My brain is liberated. You want to be next?" I nodded. I was about to be free, finally, for the first time in over a decade.

14

The nanofabricator looked and behaved totally differently than I'd expected. The massive contraption we'd seen in South Africa had been industrial, complex. This device was palm-size and digital, heavy but smooth like a large metal pebble with only a few buttons. Dr. Marko used those buttons to enter the code we'd stolen in Israel-Palestine, and the device beeped and lit up. "You ready?" Zack asked.

My heart fluttered with excitement. "I've been ready for nine years," I told him.

"Ten in July," Dawn pointed out.

Dr. Marko seemed less interested in parsing the exact number of days I'd been ready. "Press this button, wait for it to beep, and then inhale through the gas mask."

Don't do it! the voice in my head screamed. It knew that I was about to destroy it, and I relished the joy of finally killing my nagging, miserable sidekick.

I followed Marko's directions, breathing in as deeply as I could. The gas filled my throat, and it weirded me out to think that steamy substance contained tiny little computer chips, which carried the virus that would cause the bugs in my head to self-destruct.

"Okay, you can exhale," Dr. Marko instructed, and I let my breath go. Instinctively I grabbed for a mirror, excited to see the results. I could hear the screaming voice in my head fading away, which meant the process must be working; the nanotech was disintegrating.

To my surprise, what happened next didn't look like a traditional Forgiveness. In fact, the way my face changed looked unlike anything I'd seen before. I wasn't getting prettier or uglier . . . just different, somehow. "What's happening?" I asked, a little freaked out.

"The nanotech changed your appearance when it first lodged itself in your brain," Dr. Marko explained. "To operate, it sets itself up inside your cells, and everything changes just a little bit. You're going back to the way you would have looked before the Revelations, your real face, without any Punishment or Forgiveness."

I'd never considered that the beautiful thing I saw in the mirror every day might be its own kind of artifice. As my features settled, a shot of recognition went through me—the eyes staring back at me were the ones I remembered from childhood photos. I hadn't even realized they were gone until I saw them now, all grown-up.

There was a certain endearing familiarity to my face now,

an approachability—my cheekbones were a little more promi-
nent than I was used to, and my eyebrows had a different arch.
But I was *me* in a way I hadn't been in a long time.

But was I pretty? The mechanical whisper inside my head was
gone, but my own insecurities still dogged me. The face staring back—what would the world think of it? What would *Zack*
think of it? I could no longer do good deeds to be seen as more
beautiful. Was I beautiful enough? My skin was still dewy and
youthful, but when you put my features together, I worried they
were kind of a jumble, like a car put together with spare parts.
Perfectly nice spare parts, but still. I'd defined myself for so
long by my appearance, and now I was just . . . me. I was who
I was, and the rest of the world would judge me accordingly.

But maybe it didn't matter anymore. Now that we could
remove the nanotech, show people the truth, the resistance's
numbers would explode. We wouldn't need a prophet's fake
wisdom to win people to our side—we could give them the
real thing.

For a moment, I was afraid to turn and face Zack. Would he
be disappointed to see my exterior hadn't returned to the exact
same image he'd fallen in love with? As Zack caught my eye, I
analyzed every flicker of movement on his face, trying desperately to see what he was thinking, but his face didn't betray a
hint of emotion.

Dr. Marko took his turn next, and I was surprised to see his
face sink a little—like his skin had previously been pulled tight
in unnatural ways, and now it was loosening, giving away more
of his age. As the nanotech inside his head died, I saw a kind
of relief come over his features. He might not have been more

attractive in the conventional sense, but he looked more real somehow. Dawn, too, I realized, had lost some of her conventional beauty but had gained a kind of lightness in her demeanor.

"Your turn," I said tentatively to Zack. As he covered his face with the mask, I found myself silently praying for his handsome face to get just a little less handsome. So I'd feel more confident in our relationship, that I'd be able to keep him longer. *That's messed up*, I reminded myself. *You love him, you should want the best for him.*

"Is it working?" Zack asked, examining himself in the mirror. Inexplicably, his face wasn't changing at all—it looked like he was going to stay handsome as ever.

Marko examined the device. "Looks like it."

"How do you feel?" Dawn asked.

Zack grinned. "Great! Let's go sin up this joint. Stealing, murder, what should we do first?"

I threw him a suggestive look—I had an idea of what I wanted to do. But with a glance at Dawn and Dr. Marko, still in the room with us, I wasn't about to voice it yet.

And, unfortunately, I wouldn't get the chance; while we were still celebrating our victory, Eduardo Sousa burst in, in a panic. Dr. Marko quickly hid the device, but Sousa wasn't concerned with what we'd been doing prior to his arrival. "One of those drones just flew overhead."

We knew what that meant: Prophet Daniel knew our location. Panic surged through me. Our little rainforest bubble had just popped.

BOOK
TWO

Where can we even go?" I asked, hurrying down to the docks with Dawn and Dr. Marko. The morning sun was just beginning to peek through the canopy, and I had to strain to see where my feet were stepping.

"We need to move away from this location. The Amazon is big, so it'll be hard to pick out individual boats on satellite. We can use trees for cover and find shelter eventually," Dawn explained.

"So nowhere, that's a polite way of saying nowhere," I pointed out.

Our Outcast friends were already piling into boats as we approached the water's edge. "Prophet Grace!" they shouted, gesturing for me to join them as they piled onto the two good boats—the one they'd arrived on and the small craft Dr. Marko had brought. But I could quickly see there wouldn't be room for all of us . . . and more importantly, if Prophet Daniel was coming specifically for me, I didn't want to put these innocents in any more danger.

I shook my head, pointing to the wooden rowboat we'd arrived in. "I'll take this." The rag that had plugged the hole in its hull was missing, and it barely looked sturdy enough to keep one person afloat, much less all five of us.

As Zack approached with a confused and terrified Macy in tow, he eyed the boat warily. "Is that thing leaking?"

"Not very quickly," Marko joked.

"You guys go with the others," I said as bravely as I could muster. "If they're looking for me, I want you all as far away from me as possible."

Zack shook his head, squeezing my hand. "You're crazy if you think I'd leave you behind."

"Cool, so we're going in the good boats?" Macy asked, looking longingly at the motorboats.

Dawn shook her head. "We're harder to spot in something smaller. They won't expect us to take the slowest one." She'd already started using a cup to remove the extra water at the bottom of the boat. "Put on a life jacket and grab an oar, we need to move."

Macy delicately settled into her seat, glaring at Zack. "If I get eaten by piranhas, I'm blaming you."

"Better piranhas than a caiman," I told her playfully.

"Or a giant anaconda," Dr. Marko added, teasing.

"Stop naming scary animals!" she cried out, covering her eyes.

Dr. Marko handed Macy a black plastic case, which he'd wrapped carefully in two life jackets. The device, for which we'd sacrificed so much, was our only hope of winning this war. "This little box is worth more than any of us are," he warned Macy. "Your job is to keep it dry, and make sure it doesn't fall out of the boat." She clutched it, some of her fears seeming to subside as having a job calmed her, gave her purpose.

But not for long—as we backed away from the dock, I heard a faint whistle from afar, which quickly blossomed into a full-on roar. "What's that?" I asked. Before anyone could respond, the answer appeared in the form of a missile, flying overhead, then slamming into the dining hall we'd walked past moments earlier.

Prophet Daniel had found us already. More rumbling sounds in the distance left our boat silent—more artillery approaching.

"Let's get moving," Dawn said quietly, and we began rowing away with all our might.

2

never would have thought that a few oars could propel a boat so quickly. By the time the next explosion rocked the shore, we were already around the bend of the river, watching the flames grow from afar.

"They knew exactly where we were," Macy gasped. "This can't be the prophets, can it? I know they're wrong, but I thought they were still sort of good, right?" The rest of us exchanged glances, as our arms strained with the effort of pushing against the water. Macy's introduction to our world was going to be swift and devastating.

Zack leaned over, taking the device from Macy and punching in a few numbers. "I'm getting that stuff out of her head right now."

"We don't have time . . ." Dr. Marko protested.

Zack shook his head forcefully. "What she's about to see? I'm not letting her face it vulnerable."

Macy glared at her brother, annoyed. "Hi, I'm right here. Can you talk to me like I'm a person, please?"

I knew Zack was right—we couldn't risk Macy going into a guilt spiral in the midst of our escape. I leaned over and put a comforting hand on Macy's arm. "Just take a deep breath from that tube. It'll be okay."

"Okay," she said reluctantly.

"We need to get to the river," Dawn said nervously, watching the missiles fly overhead. We continued to paddle away from the island as Macy breathed in, and the gas worked its way into her lungs. Her face began to change rapidly, as her body began to look more like the Macy I'd always known. Macy clung to the device, white-knuckled, as our boat whizzed through the water, toward the horizon.

"Grace, will you . . ." Marko nodded to the cup at my feet, and I saw that our boat was taking on water quickly. I nodded back, siphoning the warm, brown liquid from beneath our seats as best I could.

Up ahead, I could see one of the motorboats, stuffed to the brim with my Outcast followers, all earnestly looking back at us, worried about me. "If the prophets found our location at the camp, they must be tracking where we're heading, right? All these boats, we're hard to miss."

Dawn nodded, grim. "That's why it's good we took this smaller boat. We can break off from the rest of the group, go down smaller waterways, hide places they can't."

"So we're using them as decoys," I said, not feeling great about this. In trying to protect my followers, maybe I'd put them in greater danger. But, though I felt guilty, my face didn't change—and it never would again. I felt a strange, sickening kind of power: I could hurt the people who loved me most and suffer no Punishment of any kind. What kinds of torture might they be subjected to on my account? What evil might I be capable of, might any of us be capable of, unchecked?

It looked like I was about to find out firsthand. As we turned the corner, emerging out onto the river, we saw a fleet of Brazilian navy ships, a dozen lightly powered crafts, lean and swift and populated by soldiers with guns. There was nowhere we could run, no way our little boat could outpower, outmaneuver, this military. We were trapped.

Guns? They have *guns*?" Macy cried out, flummoxed, as the rest of us dove into crisis mode.

"We need to find a place to hide," Dawn said, urgency rising in her voice.

"There's no way we can outrun one of those ships," Zack protested, but she ignored him, doggedly rowing onward.

"That crevasse there. Our little boat is smaller than theirs, they won't be able to follow us if we make it in time."

We all hesitantly rowed along with her, as Zack continued, "I don't know if *we* can fit. If we get stuck, we're screwed."

Across the river, I saw three navy vessels surrounding the boat of Outcasts. My heart filled with anguish as I watched soldiers raise their guns at my new friends. "We have to help them," I said urgently.

To my utter lack of surprise, Zack shook his head, darkly voicing the outlook of the rest of our boat. "There's nothing we can do. We have to focus on saving ourselves."

From a distance, I heard a gunshot, and screams. Birds fluttered out of trees, startled by the sound, and I whipped my head around, trying desperately to see what was happening. "Row, Grace," Dawn said, frustrated.

Zack gave me a sympathetic look, which doubled as a reiteration of Dawn's statement. *Row*. Indeed, the swift boat chasing us was closing in—we didn't have much time to escape.

But I didn't row. I had a different idea. "Macy, hand me that thing in your lap."

As she did, Dr. Marko looked at me, confused. "What are you doing?"

"Grace, we don't have time for this," Zack said tersely.

I ignored him, looking at Marko. "What's the code to make that gas you used on me earlier? The gas that made me get all blissed out?"

Marko quickly understood what I was after, and he entered the code. Dawn watched us skeptically. "You want to weaponize his invention against the soldiers?"

Zack shook his head, still against the idea, then shoved my oar in Macy's hands. "Someone needs to row," he said, annoyed, and she dutifully picked up my slack. Meanwhile, the device was humming—it seemed to be working. I unhooked the gas mask and pointed its nozzle directly toward the boat as it closed in on us.

"They have guns. You're not going to be able to get close enough," Zack warned, and I could see he might be right. As the navy ship barreled down on us, fear shot through me—I didn't know if I could direct the stream of gas effectively enough. We'd all had our nanotech removed and would no longer be susceptible to the gas' effects . . . but would the gas be able to reach the soldiers from here?

We were mere feet away from the edge of the flooded forest when a soldier on the boat spoke into a megaphone: "Stand down, and prepare to be boarded."

"They want to board this rickety thing, fine, we'll all go in the ocean," Marko muttered.

"They're going to shoot us," Zack warned.

Dawn remained focused. "Keep rowing, we're almost there. If we make it deeper into the forest, we can get away."

Our situation was futile, I could see that clearly. The break in the trees was too small for even our tiny boat to wind its way through. We were cornered. On the navy craft, I heard a menacing shout. "*Profeta!*" Prophet. Me. They'd found what they were looking for. And judging by their expressions, it seemed they thought the best place for Prophet Grace was at the bottom of the Amazon River.

Desperate, I knew we only had one way out. I pressed a button to release the gas and hurled the device directly at the navy ship, sending it sailing across the river between us. "Grace, what are you doing?" Marko cried out, protective of the machine we'd sacrificed so much to acquire. It clattered onto the boat, scattering the soldiers, who expected a grenade. I tensed as a few fired, bullets spattering the water around us. When the device didn't explode, they stopped and stared, not sure what to do with this strange contraption before them.

One soldier leaned down to examine it, but a second pulled him back, shouting in Portuguese, "*You idiot.*" The second soldier pointed his gun at the device—but before he could pull the trigger, the invisible gas enveloped the boat. That finger on the trigger slowly went limp, as the soldier smiled.

All of them smiled, safely in a haze like the one I'd experienced earlier. Surrounded by the comforting voices of those who loved them, urging them to be their best selves. Helping them process their darkest traumas. My plan was working.

In our boat, everyone exchanged tentative glances. Dawn leaned toward the navy ship, calling out hesitantly, "Let us pass."

The soldiers looked at one another, not sure what to do. They remembered that their orders were to kill me, but in this state, they couldn't imagine doing anything violent. Weren't even sure what was real, what was hallucination.

Finally, one soldier casually waved us aside. We took that as our cue and started rowing away as fast as we could.

"The device . . ." Marko whispered anxiously. Dawn and Zack exchanged nervous looks then steered our boat toward the navy vessel. As we passed the dead-eyed soldiers, Dr. Marko hesitantly leaned out, pulling himself onto the edge of their craft. I tensed, terrified the soldiers would react, but they just seemed confused. Dr. Marko scrambled toward the device, snatching it, then quickly returned to our boat. As he sloppily sat back down, our boat nearly overturned with his unexpected weight. But we all breathed a sigh of relief as we rowed off, out of harm's way.

"Good work, Grace," Marko said quietly, inspecting our precious cargo to confirm it was still in one piece, as we chartered away from our almost captors. I felt a pang of guilt watching the soldiers float there, confused and incapable of doing much more than stare into space. But we had bigger concerns than helping our enemies, and I knew they wouldn't be disarmed by a state of bliss forever.

"We need to get as far from here as possible," Dawn said, and Zack nodded in agreement.

I shook my head, taking the oar from Macy and using it to fight the strokes of the rest of my party. "We need to save our friends first." I pointed to the motorboats, full of the innocent people I'd convinced to follow me. More enemy ships were converging on them—they had no escape. But I wasn't going anywhere until we made sure they were free.

Hey, I was using that," Macy said, grasping at the empty air her oar once occupied, as the others stared at me, incredulous.

"We barely escaped one boat. You want us to head straight toward two more?" Zack asked with a hint of anger in his voice.

I wasn't going to be deterred. "But we did escape. We figured out how. We use the device again, on the rest of the soldiers, and we save everyone else."

The others shared hesitant looks. "And then what?" Dawn asked. "The prophets know our location. They'll send more forces."

"And now we know how to fight them. We can't keep hiding forever. Eventually we have to fight back."

"You're telling *me* we need to fight?" Dawn asked, an unexpected fury rising in her voice, and the others went silent. "You've been in this thing for a few minutes, you've gotten lucky over and over again, and you think that qualifies you to tell me when we should fight?"

"I didn't 'get lucky,' I was smart," I shot back, then caught myself, remembering all the huge mistakes I'd made leading up to South Africa.

"Smart enough to get yourself out of the messes you made for yourself. My wife might be *dead*, because you didn't take precautions, because you outed our most protected stronghold." Her voice was quaking now, and the force of it hit me like a freighter. I realized now just how much anger Dawn had been hiding. She secretly blamed me for what might have happened to Irene.

I wanted to apologize, knew I should apologize, but I was too angry. I spat back, "You're the one who made me go into that hospital, where I got infected with that stupid voice in my head. Blame me all you want, I deserve it. But you know you're to blame, too, for not figuring out sooner what was going on with your own subordinate. For nearly getting me killed in the first place."

My words clearly stung her more than I'd intended them to, and she went quiet. I felt bad—I knew there was nothing crueler I could have said than accusing Dawn of putting her wife in danger. Cruel because it cut straight to her worst fears, to her own guilt. The silence in our boat was punctured by the sound of gunshots from across the river. We looked over and saw our friends' boat was emptying out, that my Outcast followers were going willingly onto the navy ships. We were running out of time to save them.

Dr. Marko hesitantly spoke up, trying to keep the peace. "It's not a good strategy to let them take prisoners. They might give up dangerous information."

Everyone looked to Dawn. This boat wasn't going anywhere unless she said yes. With a sharp look at me, eventually she nodded. "We should preserve our operational secrecy. But that's it. We take no more risks than we need to."

I nodded, trying to put her at ease. "Understood."

My stomach tied itself in knots. We'd barely escaped capture and death just moments earlier. And we were heading right back into the prophets' clutches.

5

We rowed toward the navy ships in silence, our anxiety pulsing in time to the sloshing of the oars. Up ahead, we could see that our friends' two motorboats were encircled by an intimidating fleet of five navy vessels. Soldiers were pulling Outcasts off their boats, roughly taking them into navy custody. The motorboats were nearing empty—we didn't have much time.

As our rickety boat glided up, a few soldiers turned, confused—why the hell was this little rowboat moving *toward* them? They raised their guns, expecting an attack, and I realized we weren't going to have the element of surprise this time. I quickly lifted my hands in surrender, as the others around me followed suit.

I caught the eye of one soldier who seemed to be a lieutenant of some kind, with many gold stars across his broad chest. I directed my statements to him, as calmly and nonthreateningly as possible. "I'm Prophet Grace," I called out in Portuguese, and my voice echoed through the night as everyone went still. "If you let everyone else go, I'll come with you peacefully. I don't want anyone to get hurt in my name."

My followers looked to me gratefully, but I kept my eyes fixed on the soldiers. The lieutenant regarded me skeptically. "We will take you and all the others in your boat. Let these ones go." He gestured idly to the Outcasts.

"Good. The rest of us will come willingly," I promised.

"He's not going to cut you a deal," Zack whispered, a warning. "He'll go back on his promise and take the Outcasts anyway."

"Doesn't matter," I whispered back. "I just need to get this device on that boat." I gestured subtly to my waist, where I'd tied the device, hidden beneath my life preserver, ready to deploy.

"How long will the gas take to disperse?" Zack asked.

Dr. Marko did a few calculations in his head. "A minute? Then we have another ten before its effects start wearing off."

"What happens if the gas wears off before we can save everyone?" I asked, nervous.

Dr. Marko shrugged in his usual deadpan way. "Then they'll probably kill us."

"This was your plan," Zack reminded me. "Don't second-guess it now."

Our boat slowly floated along with the current, landing in the middle of the opposing fleet.

"We still believe in you, Grace," Julianna called out from one of the motorboats as a soldier helped me into the largest navy command vessel.

I was close enough to see the name badge on the many-starred lieutenant—Lopez. He stared me in the eye, barely believing his luck, and sarcastically sneered, "Welcome, Prophet Grace."

This was it. I stared him in the eye, as with my elbow, I nudged the switch on the device, knowing it wouldn't affect me or my friends, now that we no longer had any nanotech floating around our brains. "Thank you. Great Spirit thanks you for your hospitality."

The soldiers right next to me were the first to feel the effects. Their eyes went droopy, their bodies lax, as silly smiles covered their faces, none sillier than the smile of the once stern Lieutenant Lopez. Just like the soldiers on the first ship, the gas left them nearly immobilized, like happy, confused statues.

My followers on the boat next to me, unaware of what was happening, also breathed in the gas and were soon giddy. "Prophet Grace is fixing everything," I heard one say happily. In their blissful hallucinations, it seemed I was reassuring them.

I addressed the soldiers on the boat with a regal flair. "You're going to let us leave." I glanced at the lieutenant, hoping to see if my words had been effective. His eyes were glazed over, like his brain had been frozen . . . ready to unthaw at any moment. The gas was working. Now we just needed to get our friends off this ship, and to a safe distance for when these soldiers regained their wits.

I watched our enemies nervously for any signs of antagonism, but they just stared at us impassively. I tried to imagine what they'd be trained to do under normal circumstances. Did they know the truth, the whole truth? Or like Zack and his colleagues at the CIA, were they trusted with only the bare minimum of secrets? He'd known about the existence of pills that could change your appearance, but nothing else. Maybe these soldiers were the same way? If that was the case, they'd be endlessly loyal, devoted to the prophet they'd sworn to serve— willing to kill me if they were told it was what Great Spirit wanted. Either way, we needed to make sure we were very far away when they realized what was happening.

Dawn jumped onto the navy vessel. "Let's go!" she called out to the Outcasts who'd already been taken into captivity, but they didn't move. "Get back onto your boats, we need to get to safety." Still nothing.

"We could switch boats," I suggested. "Take the navy vessel."

Dawn gestured to the dozen soldiers still dumbly staring into space. "And what do we do with these guys?" Her words were still pointed—laced with the anger of our previous fight. I nodded, acquiescing, and helped her to usher our Outcast friends one by one back to their original boats.

As we moved through the stunned soldiers, it felt like we were tiptoeing around a sleeping dragon. At any moment, these trained fighters might regain their senses, remember their mission, and turn their weapons on us. I saw Dawn eyeing a rifle, considering whether to grab it, but perhaps deciding the reward wouldn't be worth the potential risks.

As I helped Felipe into a seat on his boat, he smiled up at me. "I knew you wouldn't leave us behind." My stomach twisted at the thought that we almost had.

Once we'd filled the first Outcast motorboat, Zack jumped

into the captain's chair, revving up the engine to pilot people to safety. "Where are we taking everyone?" he asked.

"Wait for us a mile down the river," Dawn replied. "If we don't meet you in ten minutes, keep going, as far as you can."

Zack nodded, grim, and looked at me. I knew he wouldn't leave until I gave my okay, so I nodded goodbye. "I'll see you soon," I promised.

As Zack drove away and we started loading the second boat, I noticed a soldier on the edge of the fray watching me closely. Based on his position, farthest from the device, he was one of the least drugged and therefore most likely to awaken early. Judging by his expression, it looked like that might happen at any moment. "Guys, I think we're running out of time," I said as calmly as I could.

"Got it," Dawn acknowledged, ushering the final Outcast toward his boat, moving as quickly but calmly as possible. I followed behind her, trying to steady my breath, as that half-unfrozen soldier slowly moved toward us, eyes on me. He weaved through his still-frozen comrades, eyes boring into my skull, but not speaking. Maybe he wanted to speak but couldn't yet. I saw him clutching his gun, and I wanted to run, to launch myself into one of our boats, but I steadied myself—sudden movements would be more likely to startle the others into action.

Dawn ushered the last Outcast into a motorboat and jumped inside herself. Now it was just me on the navy craft, with that foot soldier trailing behind me, gaining on me. I sped up; I was still ten feet in front of him, and almost at the edge of the boat, in the clear, when—

A hand grabbed my arm. I cried out, terrified, and looked up to see the owner of the hand: Lieutenant Lopez staring back at me, his grip strong and unrelenting. Though the intensity in his eyes startled me, there wasn't anger behind them . . . but awe. "Prophet Grace," he said in a breathless whisper.

I struggled to get away from him—my fear surprised him, and he let go. Unsupported, I stumbled backward, my feet finding only air beneath them. I toppled into the Amazon with a booming splash. The water was warmer than I expected, and a surge of fear went through me—I'd been so focused on the threats above water, I'd forgotten all the threats that were still lurking below.

"Grace!" Dawn cried out. But before she could reach me, Lopez grabbed my hand, pulling me back up onto the navy boat before the caiman could get to me.

He seemed unconcerned, smiling, embracing me. "You are not afraid, I know this much is true. Great Spirit is here, with you." A surge of relief went through me. He thought that what he'd just experienced was some kind of religious miracle.

I stood taller, wiping the wet hair out of my eyes, trying to play my part. "Yeah, of course, always."

He nodded. "You have shown me the truth."

A few other soldiers bowed their heads—coming to life not ready to kill me, but to worship me. One kneeled to kiss my feet, and others gathered around, lining up to do the same. As they did, I saw waves of Forgiveness go across their faces—they believed in me now, more than any follower I'd ever encountered. My mere presence was causing spiritual experiences inside of them.

"The things we do," one of them murmured to me, and I

knew what he meant. He was asking for redemption, Forgiveness, for all the things he'd been asked to do in war.

"Listen to me, and I will help you find true Forgiveness," I told him. "No more pills." He nodded, as though I'd read his mind.

"How?" the lieutenant asked us.

I looked to Dawn, who nodded—she knew what I was going to ask next. "Can you help us?"

Lieutenant Lopez nodded, humbled. "Anything for you, Prophet."

And that's how we ended up sailing off with the protection of Prophet Daniel's navy.

S ee if you can get us safe passage out of the Amazon," Dawn instructed, as the navy vessel escorted our Outcast motorboat down the river. "And a secure place to take all these people, if they're feeling generous."

"I'll see what I can do," I said nervously. Glancing at the weapons held by these military personnel, I was reminded of the stakes of my lies. If these hostile officers discovered I'd been deceiving them, their revenge would almost certainly be deadly.

Dr. Marko, meanwhile, was fidgeting with the device that had been around my waist when I fell into the river. "Will you be able to repair it?" I asked, worried that my stumble might have cost us something so precious.

"I hope so," he said, his tone not reassuring.

I retreated to find Lieutenant Lopez standing at the bow of the navy ship. I smiled, putting on my most charming face, hoping to use our new allies to gain some informational advantage. "What forces will Prophet Daniel send after us?" I asked him.

"Everything he has," Lopez responded gravely. "But we will help you evade them."

"How?" I asked. "Not to say you can't, just wondering what your plans are. Since there aren't many soldiers on this boat . . ."

He looked at me quizzically. "Great Spirit does not have a plan?"

My stomach lurched. He wanted me to provide the plan? "Great Spirit isn't always direct, you know," I said, dancing around the question. "He led me to you and your unit."

The lieutenant took that in. "I see. Then you must show my superiors what you showed us."

I could feel my insides freezing up. So long as Dr. Marko's nanofabricator device was broken, I was out of magic tricks. I wondered if on some level, the lieutenant guessed that was the case. After all, he'd seen that cloud of smoke—perhaps he assumed I had some mirrors to go along with it. Could he be testing me?

Whether he meant to test me or not, I was going to fail. Without Dr. Marko's supernatural cloud of bliss, I couldn't make my case as a prophet. But I knew this army must have access to the pills, in order to be effective . . . which meant for once, this was a group of people I could reveal the truth to.

"Can you do me a favor?" I asked him tentatively. "Radio ahead, tell everyone to take a pill. You know, the ones you need in case of war?"

I saw on his face that he knew exactly which ones I meant. "Why?" he asked skeptically.

I knew what he was thinking—was I going to ask them to do something immoral? There was no other reason in his mind that one might need those pills.

"I don't want them to hesitate to kill me, if that's what Prophet Daniel has asked," I bluffed. "I want them to choose not to kill me because they know I'm right."

He nodded; my gambit was working, for now. I returned to Dawn and explained the conversation I'd just had. "We have to recruit the rest of the Brazilian military to join the resistance."

"No," she said immediately. "It's not worth the risk. Get Lopez to help us into hiding, and that's it."

"And then what?" I asked, voice growing urgent. "We can't hide in the forest forever. This army has a whole supply of uppers. We recruit them to our side, suddenly we have a fighting chance again."

"Or we're all dead."

"We're dead either way," I retorted.

"You want to go, I can't stop you," she said stubbornly. "But if you go, you go alone."

I nodded, knowing I'd get nowhere by arguing with her. "Fine. Take our friends somewhere safe. If I succeed, I'll come find you."

Dawn gave me a sorrowful look, then a surprisingly firm hug. "Good luck."

"Thanks," I said, knowing I'd need it.

As Dawn motored away from our navy vessel, taking the

rest of our allies, I found Lieutenant Lopez and informed him of my plan.

"I look forward to meeting the rest of Prophet Daniel's army."

He nodded, excited. "Seeing you in person, that would convince anyone. They will be converts very soon."

I knew my presence would convince no one. I just hoped the truth would.

7

As we disembarked onto the dock, walking toward the barracks, I felt all eyes on me. Every soldier on this base was awaiting my arrival. I tried to steel my confidence. This was the easy part—no more lies. All I had to do this time was speak the truth. If even a few of these people were ready to hear it, I might survive another day.

We entered the main room of the barracks, and hundreds of skeptical faces turned toward mine. I quickly picked out the leader here, Lieutenant Lopez' boss—General Feliciano, the Brazilian minister of defense, a well-dressed military officer with so many decorations on her jacket I worried she might fall over. She approached our unit, glancing at me with disdain, then turned to Lopez. "You captured the rogue prophet. Well done." I wondered whether, like Guru Samuel, she might be in on the lie. She might already know exactly why I'd turned on the establishment—not for religious reasons, but for political ones.

"Thank you, ma'am," the lieutenant said humbly. "But before we notify Prophet Daniel, I think you should hear what she has to say."

The general looked at me carefully. "And what does *she* have to say?" she asked, My skin pricked as Feliciano nodded away from the crowded dining hall, ushering me somewhere private, but I held my ground. I needed to stay in the same room as all these soldiers, to convince as many of them of the truth as I could before the general locked me up.

"That it's all a lie," I said as loudly as I could, getting the attention of the rest of the room. Conversations hushed as people turned to listen. "This whole world. The prophets have been lying to you for ten years. Think about it: the secret pills you get to take, the ones no one else gets to have. Why would the prophets let people die out there, be Punished to death, when the solution to save them is so simple? Why are they hiding the cure? And why are they using it to weaponize you, so you can do horrible things in their names? Does that seem like a religious figure to you? Or a dictator?"

"Clearly you missed your history classes," the general mocked. "Do you think we'd live in the world we do if brave people hadn't fought on the side of good?"

"What side?" I asked. "How do you know it's good? A whole mess of folks out there think I'm the side of good—is it okay for *them* to kill in *my* name? If you really believe in Great Spirit, do you think He's happy you're defying His rules, and cheating to get out of being Punished?"

I saw faces around the room begin to change, struck by feelings of guilt, by the truth of my words—clearly my instructions to prepare for this meeting hadn't been heeded by everyone. Those faces looked down, reached in their pockets for pills. I nodded to one of the soldiers. "Hurry up, take it. You think that pill magically takes away your sin? Or does it just mask the symptoms?"

"You're saying we shouldn't take them? We should just die?" one soldier called out.

"Take them to save your lives. But stop believing the lies Prophet Daniel tells you. Stop mindlessly following orders. The truth is that the Punishments are a trick, to keep you on the prophets' side. They're using you, and you're letting them. Listen to your own hearts. You know what the truth is, deep down."

I looked to the brooding general, nervous. I remembered to state my goal—"Please, just let us go. Stop following us, let us hide away in peace." *Call a truce, and I'll stop fomenting insurrection*—that was what I was really trying to tell her. And maybe I could grab a few pills and reinforcements on my way out.

"And why would I do that?" she challenged.

"Because you know what's right," I said defiantly. "The prophets are using you to maintain a system that controls people, exploits them. You're killing for them, oppressing people for men who see you only as disposable pawns." Her stoic expression filled me with dread. The longer this conversation went on, the more I regretted my decision to come here. Dawn had been right—I'd gotten cocky and overplayed my hand.

I saw a few soldiers stand, look to the general. One leveled his gun at my chest. "The prophet said to kill her on sight," the soldier reminded Feliciano. Lieutenant Lopez' face fell, realizing I wasn't going to provide any new miracles. That perhaps his faith had been unfounded.

"So kill me," I dared the soldier, walking toward the gun. Panic sparked in my chest, but I did my best to dampen the flames. "That's what Prophet Daniel told you to do, so do it. You take your prophets at their word, don't you?" I gave him a sly, knowing smile. "Or do you think you know something they don't? Do you have some sense, deep down, that their orders are morally wrong?" I saw the shooter hesitating, and I seized on it. "We all have moral intuition. In your bones, you don't want to kill me. Even though you know you're supposed to. You can't do it, because you're a good person. A better man than Prophet Daniel, and you know that. Why would you fight for a man you know you're better than?"

The soldier's face twisted cruelly, and I was startled to hear a loud bang—his gun firing. I did my best not to flinch, let the bullet whiz past my ear, lodging itself in the wall behind me.

My heart was racing but I did my best not to show it. "Do you feel like a good man?" I asked him. Though I knew I'd gotten lucky that his shot had gone wide, I hoped it wasn't just luck . . . perhaps his hand had shaken due to his own doubt, his wavering convictions. "Or are you relieved that fate spared you from becoming a murderer?" The soldier lowered his gun, humbled.

I returned my gaze to the general, the one person who could still save me. "Just look the other way. Let us be."

She smiled, baring her teeth, and for a moment I worried she was going to eat me up. "You know I can't do that."

I shook with fear, trying my best to stay unyielding. "We're all that's left," I begged her. "If we die, the truth dies with us. Any chance at true justice in this world, it's gone. Do you really want to be the one responsible for that?"

She hesitated a moment, and I glanced at the exits, knowing I had nowhere to run. Finally, I could see her weighing a decision in her mind. "We have a responsibility, that's true. Our responsibility is to the chain of command, to respect the authority of the prophets. To do as Great Spirit wills. And right now, it is clear we are needed more than ever before." Her face lit up, full of fiery resolve. "We will protect you, Prophet Grace."

The room hummed with excitement and confusion. I realized in that moment that I hadn't said a word about nanotech, about guilt and serotonin, nothing that would have given away the scientific truth of what was happening to us. Despite my best efforts, I'd failed to reveal my true identity as a member of the resistance, and I'd failed to lift the veil of lies over anyone's eyes.

But somehow, I'd replaced Prophet Daniel's shroud with my own. These people still believed I was a rival prophet, preaching my own gospel. And it seemed like I'd inadvertently converted half the Brazilian military.

Most importantly, I'd converted their leader. My first instinct was to correct her, to tell her the truth—that I was part of the lie she'd been believing in. But as I looked around that room, I realized the risk. I might not have accomplished my goal in the way I'd planned, but I'd accomplished it all the same. I couldn't afford to make this woman look like a fool in front of the troops she commanded. She'd offered to protect me, and I knew I needed to accept that with grace. "Thank you," I squeaked out.

She eyed me carefully. "We control the largest cache of weapons in South America. Tell me, who would you have us point them at?"

This time I knew it was a test. But luckily, I had the right answer. "No one," I told her boldly. "A true prophet doesn't need to fire a shot."

"But how . . . ?" the lieutenant asked.

I could hear my father's preaching style coming out of me, unbidden. "Let the other prophets think we're like them. Let them think we'll fire. Let them know we could destroy them if we tried." I remembered enough from my history classes about pre-Revelation geopolitical strategy that I was pretty sure that tactic would work if we used it. "We have Great Spirit protecting us. We don't need anything else."

The general nodded, and the room began to whoop and clap.

I could barely believe it was happening—that in just a few moments, all these people had come over to my side. But at the same time, I recognized the precariousness of my position. As quickly as these soldiers had turned toward my camp, I knew they could turn away. *Would* turn away, eventually. "Thank you," I said softly. "Great Spirit thanks you."

The general nodded. "We must move quickly to lock down all munitions in the area, before the prophets realize what's happening. Where would you like us to take you?"

I knew I needed to meet up with Zack and Dawn, but I had no idea where we could go that would be safe.

"You tell me," I said carefully. "Great Spirit brought me to you. I believe you're the one who can tell me where is safest."

She considered a moment. "The Outcast city, near the coast. You'll be welcome there, and there should be enough resources to house our forces."

I smiled, remembering its gleaming silvery towers. We were on our way back to Redenção.

8

We left the barracks at midday; I rode in the lead vessel with the general and lieutenant, a few other ships cruising behind us. I was desperate not to blow my cover, but thankfully, these two tough military brass seemed to be fully converted, hanging on my every word. By now I'd learned I could get away with a lot as a prophet through silence, by listening with compassion instead of talking, a skill I'd learned by watching my dad. The more I made the people around me feel special, the less likely they were to notice I wasn't special at all.

As we approached the meeting point, a small recharging station in a rural village, I saw Zack and Dawn waiting with two boats full of nervous, shaking Outcasts. The size of our approaching fleet was clearly scaring the pants off my friends. I gave them a *we're okay* wave and they visibly relaxed.

As Zack hopped onto our military vessel, he pulled me aside with a hushed tone. "What happened?"

I whispered back, a little sarcastically. "Need a nuclear weapon? I've got one."

His jaw dropped. "What?"

"As long as they're believers, we've got an army."

Zack's face took on a troubled look, but I wasn't in the mood to deal with his concerns. The Outcasts from our camp were trying to swarm the military boat to see me, and the soldiers were instinctively wary, trying to fend them off—still in their old mind-set of Outcast equals Bad. I hurried over to play referee.

"Ride along behind us," I told my followers. "We'll meet you in Redenção." They acquiesced, and we were off.

The farther we traveled down the Amazon, the more boats joined our pack. Military ships from all over the country, all under the command of General Feliciano, along with civilian craft: Outcasts who'd heard about us and simply wanted to travel along.

I felt simultaneously protected and vulnerable. Clearly word was spreading of our movements, and our giant party must be easily visible from any satellite. As the days ticked by, my nerves frayed more and more. By now, the prophets must have noticed all these unscheduled troop movements . . . were we about to encounter some opposing army? And if we did . . . would I have to talk these soldiers into using violence after all?

My stomach churned thinking of the kind of weapons we might be traveling with. Chemical, biological, nuclear. What kind of havoc could I wreak, if I really wanted to? The general seemed assured of our safe passage, so I tried to stay calm as well. If she sensed my fear, it might make her suspicious and put us in more danger.

I'd gotten used to the adoring looks of all the strangers aboard this ship, so I was thrown to see a face scowling at me in the galley as I ate my dinner. Macy. "Hey," I said, greeting her warmly, though her expression stayed cold.

"I've come to hear more about Great Spirit," she said with mock adoration, her voice dripping with disdain.

My stomach swirled into an anxious knot. "Zack told you the truth. I'm sorry . . ."

Feelings of betrayal seeped from her pores. "You lied to my face."

"To save your life. He told you that part, right?"

She was not placated. "I went on TV, saying how great you were . . . You convinced me to lie to the whole world . . ."

"I get it, I bought into the Revelations, too. We've all been lied to . . ." I protested.

"Not by our best friends," she said forcefully.

"I'm almost done lying, I promise," I insisted. "Once we can remove the nanotech on a worldwide scale, we can reveal the truth."

"No, you can't," Macy blurted out.

"Why not?" I asked, furrowing my eyebrows.

She stared me down, pity in her eyes. "You really think you can tell people and they'll just be, like, 'okay, cool'? Especially these guys?" She gestured to the army around us. "I heard what kind of weapons they have."

"I know, I've been worried about that, too," I admitted. "I'll wait till we're out of the line of fire, if I can."

Macy was unrelenting. "*No one* will understand. I was your best friend, and I don't understand. Everyone thinks they would have been strong enough to survive learning the truth. The world will literally crucify you, and no, I am not trying to say you're an actual messiah. You're a liar."

Though my guilt at deceiving Macy had been weighing on me for weeks, I hadn't expected her reaction to be so strong. It bowled me over, knocked the breath out of me. "A liar for the greater good . . ." I said defensively. I hated having people be mad at me, especially my closest friend.

"Why are you the one who gets to decide what the greater good is?" she spat back. "Or maybe you do think you're the messiah after all . . ."

"I don't think I'm the messiah. I'm sorry . . ."

Before I could say anything else, she picked up her tray and left me alone. Seeing an opening, a group of nearby soldiers swarmed my table, eager to ask me questions. I smiled politely at them, sinking into my shame. Macy had only confirmed all the emotions that were already haunting me. I knew that lying and manipulating people was wrong, but I kept doing it anyway.

I tried to put those feelings away. We'd sacrificed lives for the sake of our cause . . . I should be prepared to sacrifice friendships, too. But still, I watched Macy leave the room with heaviness in my heart, wondering if she was right.

"Prophet Grace, why do bad things happen to good people?" a stranger asked me.

I put on a smile, and I kept lying.

A few days into our journey, Dawn boarded my ship and cornered me alone. "I have some bad news."

We'd had so much bad news already, I couldn't bear to hear more. "What now?"

"The device is broken."

The horror overwhelmed me. "Broken?"

She shrugged. "A swim in the Amazon will do that."

My face burned with the shame of knowing I was the one who hadn't been careful enough with it. I was the reason it was broken—another mistake, another burden that was mine to carry. "I'm so sorry . . ." I began.

Dawn interrupted me. "It was a good trade. You got us an army. Now we just have to keep them on our side." She smiled at me tentatively, a peace offering after our earlier quarrel. An admission that maybe I was in fact contributing to our cause.

"I could try again to tell them the truth," I ventured. "They have the pills."

"Which is good. We can restart our manufacturing facilities when we get to Redenção. But we won't be able to remove anyone's nanotech until we fix the device. Or acquire another one."

"Another one?" My mind swirled—how on earth were we going to find another device like that? Without it, we were back to where we'd been before—rescuing people one at a time, with a long-term diet of pharmaceuticals.

Dawn saw my concern and squeezed my hand. "It's okay. You're doing good. Just keep playing Prophet Grace for now, we'll figure something out." Her reassurance gave me hope. We had to focus on the battle still ahead.

Before I knew it, the river gave way to ocean, and I marveled at the great expanse of blue stretching out before us like a dimpled marble. The water out here was choppier, tossing even our big boat enough to make me nauseated.

But early the next morning, the shimmering beacon of Redenção on the horizon made my heart soar. As we pulled closer, I could see dozens of military ships in position already. The city was ours.

9

Before we'd even disembarked, the mayor arrived at our ship to greet us once again and offer his assistance. "We are so grateful for and blessed by your speedy return," he crowed, kissing my hand. As he did, I saw his face change, just from the natural high of brain chemicals, after coming into contact with a supposedly divine presence. I hoped as many military officers as possible had seen our exchange; I needed to perform as many "miracles" as I could to keep these guys on my side.

The apartment the mayor provided us was luxurious: three floors and seven bedrooms, meant to fit the ever-growing ranks of the resistance. I hoped someday we'd fill it to the brim. It was just a few blocks from where my navy had taken up residence— which meant General Feliciano was right around the corner if we needed a cup of sugar, or to call for a nuclear strike.

As my friends and I entered our palatial apartment, we spread out through the massive halls, trying to get our bearings. Every room was packed full of gifts—clothes, electronics, anything the citizens of Redenção thought might curry favor with the prophet.

Macy ran up and down the long halls like a gleeful little kid, slipping and sliding on the marble floors. "Being in the prophet's entourage is the best," she declared.

I laughed, glad the ice was finally thawing between us. "One fancy house, and all's forgiven?" Her stony expression implied it wasn't time to joke just yet, and certainly made it clear that nothing was forgiven.

As Macy retreated to claim a third-floor room, the rest of us converged to make a plan. "The mayor has cut off all communications from inside the city," Dawn explained. "No one needs to know we're here."

I cleared my throat nervously. "Actually, I think you should tell him to take that back."

Dawn looked at me like I was crazy. "Do you have a death wish?"

I stood my ground. "No, but I have an army. I think we should broadcast our location. The prophets must know by now anyway, and we need to show a strong face. Bluff that we can't be taken down."

"And if they call that bluff?" Zack warned.

I turned back to Dawn, resolute. "We finally got what you wanted—a safe haven for the resistance to operate from. Only this time, we don't just have the truth on our side, we have nuclear weapons."

"That you won't fire," Dr. Marko pointed out. I'd certainly made my peacenik views clear to the general.

I shook my head. "We'll never need to fire a shot, so long as everyone else thinks we will."

"Mutually assured destruction, 2035 style," Zack muttered.

Dr. Marko spoke up, "My old partner Dr. Smith might be able to help me replicate the broken nanofabricator, if she can find us."

I looked to Dawn eagerly. "Wherever Dr. Smith is, if she sees we're here and safe, she'll come. Everyone will."

"Maybe even Irene," Dr. Marko said, trying to help, but I wasn't sure invoking Dawn's missing wife would win me any goodwill.

"And Jude," Zack said pointedly. Was that jealousy in his voice? Would he really be jealous of me trying to rescue the rest of the resistance? Just the mention of Jude's name hollowed out an empty spot in my heart . . . the longer I was apart from him, not knowing his fate, the larger and more painful it grew.

Dawn looked me dead in the eyes. "You need to be very careful about what you say from now on. Everything you do will be broadcast to the world, every detail scrutinized."

I grinned. "So that's a yes."

She looked around the room for a consensus. Zack seemed skeptical, but he shrugged along with the rest of our nods. Dawn's voice was grave. "Let's bring our friends home."

10

I stared into the camera Dawn pointed at me, imagining the prophets on the other end who would be listening to my message. "We're here," I told them. "Anyone who believes in us is welcome in Redenção. And to my supporters who can't make it all the way to Brazil, know that I'm watching over you. I will do everything in my power to protect you from those who seek to harm you." And to the prophets, an unspoken threat—*don't mess with us*. My heartbeat felt out of control, like I'd just run a marathon, even though I was just sitting in our living room.

"We'll get this posted right away," Dawn promised.

As she moved off, Zack took my hand. "I guess we'll see if this works," he said. I could tell he was trying to hide his skepticism for my benefit, though not as well as he thought.

I expected messages to pour in right away, and they did . . . but not from anyone I cared to hear from. We quickly had to disable the comments on our video because of all the hateful rhetoric from devoted adherents to the other prophets, directed both at me and at those supporting me. We also received plenty of positive feedback from my little cult, but I forced myself to ignore that, too. I couldn't answer every response, and I was afraid to put too much out there for people to analyze and misinterpret. So I ignored everything, and we waited. Where was Jude? Where were the rest of our allies? Hours ticked by, and then days.

And that was when the flood began.

On the edges of the city, Outcasts from around the world began to converge: pilgrims attracted by the news of my presence. Tents popped up like weeds, and unfamiliar faces roamed the streets, eager and gaunt from the journey. Some had traveled hundreds, thousands of miles. Quit jobs, left families. They believed they'd been called here.

With soldiers flanking me, I roamed the streets of Redenção, examining the faces of these newcomers. Could any resistance members be hiding among the pilgrims? But achingly, I saw no one I recognized—our friends were still missing in action.

"Where is everyone?" I asked Dawn as we canvassed block after block. "Shouldn't they be contacting us?"

"They will," she said confidently. But I knew we were both thinking the same devastating thought. If anyone was still alive in that underground city in Turkey, we should have heard from them by now. The hollow space in my heart felt raw . . . I wasn't ready to mourn Jude, not yet. I still had to hold out some hope he'd find his way back to me.

Meanwhile, my video had ignited Redenção. The location of our apartment had been discovered and publicized, leading hundreds of people to camp out, day and night, waiting for a glimpse of me. As I returned from searching for our friends, they nearly tackled me, grabbing at my hands, shouting their love.

I recognized one of the camped-out Outcasts as Felipe, the restauranteur who'd joined us in the rainforest. He saw me looking at him and pushed through the crowd. "Grace, you remember me?"

"Yeah, Felipe, I remember you," I said, and he beamed with joy.

"I have a club, many clubs. Any night you want to come by, everything is free." He pressed his business card into my hand, as my bodyguards pulled me away from him. "You see," he called out to his friend, "I know her!"

I retreated back into the safety of our living room, stunned and shaking. "They're hounding us, everywhere we go," I stammered.

Dr. Marko went to the window to inspect my ever-growing fan club stationed outside. "Maybe they're just here for me."

"What do we do?" I asked.

Dawn just smiled wryly. "Enjoy it."

"Enjoy it?" I asked, incredulous.

"The more they love you, the more protected we are. Go, prophesize, play the part. And have fun."

Once again, I heard the dark undercurrent in her voice. *Have fun now.* Bad news might be coming.

11

After just a few days of exploring, I decided Redenção was my favorite place on earth. It had once been a sleepy beach town, catering mostly to wealthy Brazilians. But after the Revelations, as Outcasts started to set up camp along its beachfronts, tourists got skittish, worried about crime and scandalized by the black markets cropping up. That was just fine with the town's new residents—as their neighbors fled, my new friends saw an opportunity to build a city all their own. And as word had spread of the thriving Outcast community on the northeast coast of Brazil, others from all over the world had poured in.

As the population grew, the city became more self-reliant; they no longer had to import architects and doctors and plumbers from the outside world: plenty of Outcasts had held those professions before the Revelations. And the more the city thrived, the harder its residents fought to improve it, and to protect it from non-Outcast outsiders. By the time I arrived, more than two million Outcasts had clustered into gleaming silver skyscrapers—*and every single one of them worshipped me.*

Once I got used to the constant, ever-rotating entourage of devotees following behind us, the city opened up to me. Everyone was eager to show me around, to make sure I was having a good time. Little girls handed me homemade paper jewelry, while college kids guided us to the most popular nightlife in town, where we could dance till dawn with a few of our two million new best friends. Felipe wasn't the only club owner willing to roll out the red carpet for me and my entourage. Though Macy initially refused to leave her room, still annoyed with us for lying to her, eventually even she was drawn in by Redenção's charms.

During the day, every block pulsed with dance beats; different immigrant cultures had fused together to make new styles of music—Jamaican drums mixed with lyrical Balinese melodies. The buildings were simple, practical, adorned with quirky street art. And everywhere we went, I got the prophet's treatment: food was free, entertainment was free—it was like a paradise built just for us.

And next to me, through it all, was Zack, who had taken somewhat uneasily to our new life. He seemed restless; while initially he had just been relieved to be alive, safe from the clutches of his former employers at the CIA, it was increasingly clear that he hated being penned in, not being in control of our destiny. When he'd imagined himself working with the resistance, it had been as a double agent, a fighter, a hero . . . not playing house with me in a city full of strangers.

The one task that seemed to give him purpose was protecting me from the constant onslaught of outside affection. He appointed himself my bodyguard, following me around any time I chose to leave our protected enclave. In some ways, this made things harder—even if I did manage to evade my crush of followers with some kind of disguise, Zack's presence immediately alerted people that I must be nearby. But I liked being with him—and not just for protection. Despite everything that had led to this moment . . . I couldn't stop myself from *liking* him.

We hadn't discussed our feelings at all since we'd had sex in the Amazon, and the tension that followed. When we arrived in Redenção, I worried that the physical and emotional intimacy we'd shared in the rainforest had been left behind there, somehow. As we settled into that apartment together, I found myself constantly tracking Zack's movements—now he was taking a shower, now he was making himself a sandwich, now he was glancing at me and looking away when I met his eye.

I kept waiting for him to bring up everything that had passed between us. Maybe he was waiting for me to do it—now that I was back in the public eye, I arguably had more at stake. But though I was revered at every turn in Redenção, there was still only one person in this city whose adoration I desperately wanted. And the more time passed, the more worried I became that I might not get it.

Until, one rainy Wednesday, morning coffees in hand, Zack and I ducked through a series of alleys and found ourselves alone near the water, at the outskirts of the city. "Where are your minions?" Zack asked, looking around for the posse of Outcasts that usually followed me.

"I think we're alone." We'd been alone at the apartment

plenty of times before, but now saying those words out loud was a turn-on, an invitation.

He grinned. "Hurry, before they find us." He grabbed my hand and pulled me onto a rocky outcropping, overlooking the ocean. The water shone bright like flecks of glass, as herons circled above our heads.

"How long do you think we have?" I asked.

"Shhhh, don't jinx it." Zack put his arm around me, a bit of protection against the stiff salty breeze. His face nuzzled against my cheek, and I could feel his breath on my neck.

"About what happened," I started, but before I could finish, he peeled back my hair, blowing around me like a wild mane, and he kissed me. His kiss was salty, too, soft and wet, as his lips found mine over and over again.

As we separated, his eyes were bright and giddy as he asked, "Sorry, were you asking me something?"

"You answered it." I grinned.

He laughed, staring deep into my eyes. "I can't believe there was any question. I love you. Every part of you, every little cell in your brain. And I always will."

For all I knew, I'd be assassinated tomorrow. So I decided to take Dawn's advice and enjoy myself.

I spent that night in Zack's room. And the one after. It felt too good to be true, and in some ways I knew it was. While I knew Zack was worried about the safety of the resistance, he wasn't close to any of them like I was. He did his best to console me when I got anxious about their safety, but still I couldn't quite express what Jude meant to me . . . not to him.

And then one night, we returned home from dancing to find Dawn and Dr. Marko still awake in our dining room, huddled around the long table like it was a boardroom.

This must be it. "Did you hear anything?" I asked nervously.

"We got a message," Dawn said, voice shaking. "They're still alive."

I didn't even notice the tears pouring out of me until they started dripping off my cheeks. Hearing good news about Jude was like waking up from a bad dream. And I had a strange pang of guilt, knowing that my bad dream had included so many good moments with Zack. That I'd been happy and falling in love while Jude was suffering. "Where? How?"

"They're still underground. Their supplies are running low."

"Do you have a plan to get them out? Or get them some food, or pills, at least?" Dr. Marko had restarted the manufacture of uppers in a small factory near Redenção, so I knew we could provide them with a small supply.

"I don't know what we can do. All our resources are here," Dawn said, shaking her head.

"What if they weren't?" I asked tentatively.

The others stared at me like I was crazy. "You want to take our army to Turkey?" Zack asked. I knew it was a risk, one that might potentially alienate the only useful ally we had right now.

But what risk wasn't worth it, to save my best friend, and Dawn's wife, and so many others? I insisted, "There are thousands of people in that underground city, who have knowledge and experience we desperately need. If we save them, we have a fighting chance again. It wouldn't be just a few of us sitting around in an apartment. We'd have a real resistance." I desperately needed Zack to know there was more to this than just saving Jude. "I can't think of a better option, can you?

They couldn't. I glanced at Zack, who was simmering in the corner. Unhappy with the perilous odds we faced, or jealous of whom I was going to rescue, I wasn't sure. But as Dawn's face filled with a new kind of hope, the weight of it fell heavy on my shoulders. I hoped I wouldn't let her down.

braced myself as I walked into the military's outpost, an old police station converted into an industrious base, efficiently crammed with personnel. A deputy escorted me in to see General Feliciano, who'd taken up residence in an old kitchenette, placing her desk next to the refrigerator. "Prophet Grace. I hope my men showed you the security precautions we've taken around the city. Twenty-four/seven watch, and algorithms monitoring satellite footage for any potential invasion or projectiles headed toward us."

"Thank you," I said carefully. "But I'm actually here to ask you for another favor. Outside of Redenção."

"Another favor?" The general's wariness set me on edge. She'd done so much for me already, despite only knowing me for a few days . . . might I stretch her goodwill too far by asking for something else?

I tried my best to project strength, though my voice cracked with emotion. "The prophets are threatening the lives of some of my friends. They're going to slaughter thousands of innocent people."

The general stood up straighter: the invocation of saving innocents seemed to win her over immediately. "Where?"

"In Turkey."

"The country Turkey?" Her disbelief gave me pause. I wanted to explain the whole story, tell her the truth finally, but fear nagged at me. If she knew the truth, she had no reason to follow my orders. Might she pull out her troops and leave us with nothing? I tried to scale back my request. "We don't need to take the whole army. If you could just get me a plane, a few soldiers . . ."

"I will take you myself," she said immediately.

"I . . . thank you," I said, surprised by her easy acquiescence.

"Of course," she said, fixing me with a respectful but critical gaze. "I would love to meet the friends of Prophet Grace." The way she said that, I wondered if she'd fully made up her mind to trust me. She could always turn me in to the prophets, couldn't she? If she handed them the most dangerous agent of the devil, her insurrection might be forgiven. I was sure the thought must have crossed her mind.

I not only had to do the impossible and save my friends, I had to do it without outing the truth to the woman who could destroy me. I smiled, hoping she couldn't see my fear. "Thank you."

We were on our way to Jude. I just hoped we'd get there in time.

BOOK

THREE

1

The engines' roar filled my ears as I boarded the plane behind General Feliciano. Dawn trailed me, expression grim; she'd insisted on coming, and I wasn't going to say no to someone so desperate to save her wife. Zack, too, had invited himself along. Though I worried about taking more people than we needed, I appreciated his comforting arm around me as we took our seats.

"Think we can convince the general to give us a layover in Paris?" Zack joked.

I appreciated his attempts to lighten the mood. "Ooh, or Rome," I said, playing along.

"Yeah, forget Turkey, let's do Rome."

"I'll see what I can do," I teased. It felt so warm and familiar, bantering with Zack . . . but coldness seeped in as I remembered our mission.

As the plane took off, I glanced around at all the soldiers, solemnly buckled into their seats. None of them would make eye contact with me—afraid of being disrespectful perhaps? Or maybe just afraid of what I might ask them to do. They'd seen plenty of prophets outwardly preaching nonviolence while secretly sending soldiers to do the worst kinds of crimes. Why should they think I was any different? *Was I different?*

Eyeing the general across the plane, I whispered to Dawn in hushed tones, going over our strategy, "When we land, I'll try to broker a truce. Failing that, I'll start the rescue op." I hesitated, the task in front of us feeling too massive to conquer. "What if all that fails?"

Dawn's voice wavered only a little. "Then Guru Dawn will send in your army to pick up where you left off."

I eyed the wary soldiers. "And if the army won't go?"

"You mean, if the general loses faith in you?" Dawn rephrased, a little less gently.

"Yeah."

Dawn tried her best to contain her dread. "Then we've lost Cappadocia and Redenção and everyone we love in one fell swoop." My heart was heavy. We had to succeed.

I saw fear breaking through Dawn's mask of strength, and I squeezed her hand. "We'll save Irene. I promise." She squeezed back, and it was an odd feeling, being the one to reassure someone who had spent so much time supporting me. Someone who'd so recently scolded me for my own mistakes. But I'd put all of us in this position, and I knew it was my job to get us out of it.

I noticed the general watching us and quickly broke eye contact with Dawn, staring straight ahead. I couldn't show fear. I couldn't let the general see through the thin façade I'd pulled over her eyes.

Fourteen hours later, we landed in Turkey, at a tiny rural airport not far from Cappadocia, which the resistance had once used to secretly transport its members and refuel their supplies. I hoped it would be as secure now as it had been a few months ago.

As we exited, I remembered we were alone, in enemy territory. All we had were a few dozen soldiers and a few empty planes to ferry resistance members home. How on earth were we going to defeat the rest of the prophets, with their much grander resources?

"We take the rest of the journey on foot," the general commanded, and the soldiers dutifully stood to follow her.

"No," I said quickly. "We'll attract too much attention as a group. Let the two of us go alone." I gestured to myself and Dawn, and the other soldiers breathed a sigh of relief that I wasn't sending them to their deaths quite yet. The general nodded, glad to accede to my supposed divine wisdom.

Zack pulled me aside. "Let me come, too," he whispered.

I shook my head, whispering back, "Keep an eye on our troops. Make sure they're still here to take us home." He shifted uncomfortably, clearly resenting being given the supporting role. But he nodded, acquiescing.

We waved a goodbye to our entourage as we headed off, trekking over a ridge to spot a familiar sight—the strange jutting rock formations of Cappadocia. The last time I'd seen them, I was with Jude, and this city had been an oasis of safety, after all my escapades evading Prophet Joshua in New York and D.C. Now, it was compromised, and we were walking straight into the prophets' clutches.

"You ready for this?" Dawn asked me as we drew closer.

I took a deep breath. I was ready to get Jude back.

When Jude had first taken me to the underground resistance stronghold, I'd been surprised to find its cavernous entrance in the midst of a seemingly empty expanse. I never would have been able to find my way back there on my own. Unfortunately, this time, that entrance was impossible to miss—it was at the center of a mass of Turkish military vehicles. Our small army was greatly outnumbered—even with the help of every soldier we had back in Redenção, it seemed impossible for us to take this place by force.

I looked at Dawn, but her face betrayed no fear, only determination. She'd always seemed superhuman to me, strong in a way I never could be. But finally I saw the source of that strength—it wasn't callousness, like I'd always assumed: it was love. She was going to get her wife to safety if it killed her; she couldn't imagine a world where she failed, and therefore she was certain she wouldn't.

"Look over there," Dawn whispered, pointing to a pair of

Turkish infantrymen taking a break, lounging away from the main group.

"I'll do my best," I said, knowing exactly what she wanted me to do—isolate them away from the pack and work my usual magic, converting them. I'd done it twice before—walked into the prophets' clutches and come right out again. Why shouldn't she expect I could do it a third time? I tried to summon Dawn's courage. I was going to save the people we loved, because I had to.

As I walked up, those two soldiers immediately stood on guard, calling out in Turkish. I immediately regretted every moment over the past few months that I'd spent learning Portuguese instead of Turkish, the language that might have saved my friends. Though I didn't understand the specific words they were saying, I knew what they meant: "Get your hands up!"

I threw my hands in the air, indicating surrender. "I'm not here to hurt you," I called out, hoping they understood enough English to get the gist.

They kept their guns pointed at me but didn't shoot, as I came close enough to see their faces—the smirks of victory. They couldn't believe their luck, that the rogue prophet had walked right up to them. One of them turned to me and sneered, "We know who you are."

Upside, at least one of them spoke English. Downside, these two seemed to be strong adherents to the mainstream prophets' faith, as expected. "I'm here to tell you the truth," I began, ready to launch into my usual speech, the one that had worked so well so many times before.

Before I could get any further, the second soldier grabbed my arms, pulling them behind my back and handcuffing me. My speech wasn't going to work this time.

But it didn't need to. Moments after touching me, the soldier recoiled, dropping to the ground, clutching his throat. His partner looked at him with horror; without lifting a finger, I'd delivered a Punishment more swift and terrifying than either of them had ever seen.

I knew what they didn't—this particular Punishment was the work of Dr. Marko, not Great Spirit. Using our newfound resources in Redenção, he'd whipped me up a transdermal salve, a poison that would seep in through the skin and cause deadly Punishments. I could now use these "downers" to fell anyone who laid a hand on me.

The soldier writhed on the ground, skin turning blue, and I averted my eyes, not wanting to watch him squeak out his final breath. Though my brain no longer contained the nanotech that would make me die of guilt, I still felt that guilt. Still felt the horrifying weight of what I was doing—killing a foe in order to save my friends. Though it was a calculation I'd made before, this felt more intentional than the guard who'd died in the hospital explosion, or Prophet Joshua, torn apart by a crowd of my followers. This was cold-blooded, premeditated murder.

I was shocked by the simplicity of it. *Anything to save Jude.* This man was bad and in my way . . . and now he was gone. The decision itself had been easy, but its aftermath left me feeling disconnected from myself. Who was this dark Grace who could so callously take a life? She certainly wasn't someone

I identified with, someone I'd ever wanted to be. But she was powerful, and she was going to get her way. I stared the other soldier square in his terrified eyes. "You will do what I say now."

He clearly wanted to bolt, but stayed frozen in place, nodding helplessly.

I continued, "Good. You're going to help me rescue everyone who's trapped underground."

He nodded again. *Hold on just a little longer, Jude*, I thought to myself, as though he could hear me. *I'm coming for you.*

3

The one surviving Turkish soldier led me through the circle of tanks as I threw a scarf over my head to hide my face. "Keep your eyes down," he whispered. I was happy to acquiesce. If too many more of the prophets' loyalists spotted me, I might not make it to my friends. I could Punish anyone who touched me, but I couldn't stop a stray bullet.

Staring resolutely at the feet of the soldier walking in front of me, I made my way toward the city's entrance. The soldier made small talk in Turkish with a few men as we passed—explaining away my presence well enough to put them off, it seemed.

As we descended those familiar stone steps, the sounds and smells were eerily different than I remembered from my first visit. The bustle of a hundred thriving, intersecting cultures had been replaced with an odd, echoey silence. There were still people inside—I could hear the heaving breaths, the creaky bones of all those bodies—but they were still. Fearful.

The dozens of soldiers patrolling otherwise empty hallways told me why. My friends weren't just trapped in a standoff—they were prisoners. These rock walls had become cells overnight.

"Clear this place out," I whispered to my terrified guide. "Get everyone to safety."

"How?" he asked, genuinely confused.

Luckily, Dawn and I had already made a plan. "I'll create a distraction," I told him. "I'll lure the rest of the soldiers toward the main entrance. Then everyone else will sneak out the back." We'd learned that the Turkish army was already aware of the back entrance, a tiny rock tunnel that was meant to serve as an emergency exit for situations such as this.

The rescue plan was in motion, but we were going to need help. Though every cell in my body wanted to run to Jude's old room, to see if he was still there, still alive, I needed to do something else first. I pressed on past the Jewish quarter, toward the Muslim quarter, to the big familiar suite where I'd once spent an unpleasant election night.

The soldier rapped on the door, and a stunned and gaunt Mohammed, Layla's father, exited. Initially his eyes filled with apprehension, then confusion when he finally recognized me. I was elated to see he was alive, and I smiled, trying to let him know I was still on his side. "Long time no see," I said. "We could use your help."

The realization landed heavy on my chest. I'd gotten this far. Which meant my time was almost up. I finally admitted to myself what I'd been unable to admit to Zack, or to Dawn: more likely than not, I wouldn't be making it out of Turkey.

4

I haven't been much help to anyone in a while," Mohammed said darkly. The former leader of the resistance looked so small now. His politician's charm and confidence had withered, leaving behind a broken shell.

I let myself into his cell, closing the door behind me to give us privacy. "I have an army," I told him. "Maybe you've heard, out there they think I'm a prophet."

Mohammed chuckled. "I heard rumors, but I did not believe they could be true."

His pure amusement lightened the mood, for just a moment. I played along, joking, "I guess you didn't know, I'm very wise."

He nodded, serious for a moment. "I believe it."

I couldn't help but be touched by the compliment. "I converted Prophet Daniel's army in Brazil, and they flew us here. We brought empty planes we can use to rescue everyone. We just need to find a way to get everyone into them."

"A distraction," he surmised.

"That was Dawn's idea, yeah."

He looked at me, understanding more clearly why I was in his cell. "You want me to be the distraction."

"Both of us," I said quickly, making sure he knew I was willing to put myself in the line of fire. "Better distraction."

He eyed me carefully. "Will your army take my family home if you aren't flying with them?"

My stomach lurched. It was a fear I had as well. "Probably. Dawn told them she's my guru . . . I'm sure they'll follow her, too."

"A guru, not a prophet." Mohammed paced, deep in thought.

"Dawn had the same objections," I told him. "But I told her I wanted to do this."

He shook his head, resolute. "I can do it alone."

"No . . ." I whispered, knowing what he was offering.

"You did not really think I would let you go out there with me, did you?" Mohammed asked, a glint in his eye. "You knew what you were asking when you came here."

I stood my ground, insistent. "I made myself a prophet because I wanted to save you guys. It got us here. That was all I needed it for . . ."

Mohammed's voice grew grave. "You need it to keep fighting after this. For all of us. You have seen the power of faith by now. All around the world, people are looking for someone to believe in. Someone to give them hope, to make them feel safe. That desire is what allowed the Revelations to take hold. Perhaps that desire can end the Revelations as well. Instead of covering people's eyes to lead them away from the truth, lead them toward it."

"I might not succeed . . ." I warned him.

"But what if you do?" he said, covering his pain with a sad smile.

"Thank you," I said, not knowing how to properly express my gratitude for the risk he was taking.

"You will thank me by getting them to safety."

I nodded. "I'll do everything I can, I promise. I hope we have enough time . . ."

"You will," Mohammed said, grim.

"I appreciate your confidence, but . . ."

"No. There are not many of us left, that is what I mean. You will have time."

My heart sank. "Jude, Layla, Irene . . . ?"

His expression gave me relief. "My family, and Dawn's, have been well cared for. The prophets know they are leverage. Others have not . . ." He couldn't bring himself to finish the sentence. My insides ached, remembering the thousands of people who had once filled our massive meeting hall. Wondering how many were left.

I couldn't grieve just yet. We had a plan. Now we just needed to survive it.

5

"Tell your commander, the leader of the compound wants to negotiate," I told the terrified Turkish soldier who'd been helping me. He nodded and ran off as I hurried in the opposite direction. I had a limited time to find and free what remained of the resistance, while the Turkish army was distracted by Mohammed's gambit.

I moved through the halls in a blur, opening door after door and finding . . . no one. Mohammed hadn't been exaggerating. This place which had once been full of life was . . . empty. That silence wasn't just fear, it was death. Loss.

Though Mohammed had promised my friends were alive, I still felt a jolt of dread as I approached the Jewish quarter. My feet pounded the stone floor, almost ran ahead of me to reach Jude's door. I threw it open, my eyes searching the room. It was empty, I thought at first, as I scanned in a panic.

And then I saw him, leaning against the wall in the corner.

Thinner than I'd ever seen him before, with a distant look in his eyes, and a dirty grayness to his skin that camouflaged him with the floor. It was his movement toward me that made me notice him at all, and I blurted out instinctively, "Don't touch me." I couldn't risk him getting the same fatal Punishment as the last person who'd made that mistake.

He was surprised and taken aback, but he took it in stride. "Hello to you, too."

I'd built a picture in my mind of what Jude's experience must have been like while I was away. But seeing him staring back at me, I realized I knew nothing. For the third time now, he'd gone off and had a whole other life without me, emerging changed. He'd begun as an awkward teen, transformed into an angry rebel, and now . . . something else. Something calmer, clearer, surer.

I wished I could spend the next century just staring at him, being relieved he was alive, but we didn't have time. "Find Layla," I told him. "And Irene, and everyone you can who's still alive. Tell them to meet us at the back entrance."

"So you're my rescue party," he said, looking at me with a kind of relief and awe.

"Best you're going to get, unfortunately."

"Best I could have gotten." Jude grinned, that same boyish grin I'd once fallen in love with, the one that made me feel like everything was okay, even just for a moment. "I'll see you soon," he said, and we parted with the same ease and familiarity as always.

Jude was alive. Now I just had to keep him that way.

Somewhere out there, Mohammed would be emerging from the cave. Facing down the general of the Turkish forces. The prophets' men would be confused—why would a prisoner think he had the leverage to negotiate? He'd tried this before many times, to no avail. But now, Mohammed would have a plan: an incendiary device I'd given him, an elaborate, multipronged smoke bomb. The hope was that by using it, he could simulate an attack coming from the east, to distract our enemies, while the rest of the resistance escaped to the west. There would be only a small window for Mohammed to escape, and I desperately hoped he'd be able to slip through.

At least, that was how it was supposed to go. Down here in this dank cave, I could only guess how Mohammed was faring aboveground. I couldn't see or hear a thing; I had no idea whether our plan was working, how much time we had left. Whether, as I gathered these few survivors, one by one, I was simply leading them to their deaths. As I scoured the compound, my mission felt more and more futile. A dozen or so prisoners, that was all I found alive—the others, thousands, were already gone. We were too late.

But rescuing a dozen people was better than nothing. When I arrived at the back entrance, I was relieved to see Jude approaching with Layla and Irene in tow, both looking haggard and terrified. Layla's eyes flashed when she spotted me; clearly she'd pieced together what our plan was. "What is my father doing? Why is he not here?"

"He's giving us cover to escape," I said nervously. Though Mohammed had been eager to help, I knew how worried I'd feel if my own father was walking into the line of fire.

"I am not leaving without him," Layla said. "Where is he? Jude would not tell me."

"Risking his life to save the rest of your family. I promised him I'd get you out of here safely," I told her carefully.

"So you will lie to me to do it?" she asked breathlessly. "You think I am some kind of child, who needs to be protected with secrets?"

I knew exactly what she was—irrationally desperate to save someone she loved. I'd been in her shoes too many times to count. I knew what would happen if I told her the truth, but I also knew, from being in those shoes, that I couldn't lie to her. "He's at the front entrance," I said. "Creating a distraction."

"I'm going to help him," she insisted, walking in that direction.

"Layla, don't!" Jude called after her. He looked desperately at me as Layla disappeared into the darkness of the cave. Guilt came over me; Mohammed was making this sacrifice to save his daughter, and here I'd just endangered her life.

I turned to Jude. "Get everyone out of here. Dawn will be waiting to take people to the plane."

Jude's eyes trailed after Layla, reluctant to leave her behind, but he acquiesced, begging, "Get her out safe." I nodded, a promise I hoped I could keep.

Jude followed the few resistance members who were already climbing toward the bright crack of daylight in the ceiling. I hoped this wouldn't be the last time I saw him. But I knew I couldn't face him, face anyone, if I didn't get Mohammed's family, my friend, out of Turkey. Determined and terrified, I followed Layla into the darkness of the cave, not sure what I'd find when I emerged on the other side.

My feet echoed as I ran down the halls. It was even more eerily silent now that all the patrolling soldiers had been distracted by Mohammed's gambit near the front entrance. "Grace!" a voice hissed, and I saw Layla ahead of me, hiding behind a jagged edge in the rock wall. I moved to meet her.

"Who are you hiding from?" I whispered.

"There are soldiers up ahead. My father is just beyond them." Her eyes roved the blackness in front of us, and I could see her trying to formulate a plan.

"We can't save him," I urged her. "He has to do this alone. He would want you to go back, to get on that plane. The risk he's taking isn't worth it if he can't save you."

Layla shook her head. "He is my father. I will not leave without him."

I'd gotten used to my words having these magical powers, to people just going along with whatever I said. It was a strange change of pace to be ignored. I wondered if this was how Dawn had felt, all the times I'd impetuously gone off book, determined to do the "right thing," even if it wasn't strategic.

I heard heavy footfalls, growing louder, making their way toward us—a glance up ahead showed it was a guard, making his rounds, perhaps drawn by the sound of our whispers. Layla held her breath as I coiled myself up, ready to pounce. The moment the Turkish guard was within striking distance, I lunged, touching him with my toxic hand. He cried out, as his face quickly morphed into something twisted.

Remorse overtook me, knowing I'd taken another life. Intentionally, this time. Actively. It felt like my grip on morality was slipping, like I was tumbling deep into a dark realm I never thought I'd tread. *This is war*, I told myself, steeling my conscience against this harsh new reality. But still . . . I couldn't quell the sickness in my stomach.

My own horror was mirrored by the revulsion on Layla's face, but she didn't have time to judge me. The screams of the guard must have attracted attention—we could hear more footsteps moving toward us. Layla glared at me. "They know we are here now," she whispered angrily.

But I wasn't deterred. "You weren't going to be able to help your father, you were just going to get in the way. You have no weapons, no tools, no special knowledge. I do," I said, gesturing to my deadly skin. "I need you to trust me. I need you to go back to where Jude and the others are. I can save your father."

"You promise?" she asked me hesitantly. I knew if I said yes, it meant I could keep my promise to Mohammed to get her out of Turkey, even if it meant breaking a new one to Layla.

"I promise," I told her. "Go. Please."

After a moment of hesitation, she glanced at the now dead guard in front of us, listening to the echoing footsteps of more on their way. "Save him," she commanded me, and then she turned and ran.

As her footfalls disappeared into the shadows, the ones ahead of me grew louder. I braced myself, looking at the guard lying in front of me, filling with sick determination. I didn't want to have to kill anyone else, but I knew I would do what I needed to do to protect Layla's retreat. This kind of murder felt repulsively routine. I was becoming desensitized to my own cruelty.

A figure emerged, and as I prepared to strike, I made out his features in the dim light. It was Mohammed, running like a madman. The heavy feeling in my gut lightened, as I realized he'd made it out alive after all.

He spotted me, and I slipped into a brisk run next to him, both making our escape. "We only have a short time," he told me. "The soldiers are busy shooting into the smoke; your distraction is working. But it won't for long."

The winding hallways seemed lengthier than ever as I wondered when the soldiers at the front entrance would realize what was really happening. Finally, we rounded the last corner, and that sliver of sky was in sight . . . just as three guards approached us from the opposite side of the hall, guns raised.

"Don't move," they shouted, and I followed Mohammed's lead, putting my hands in the air. We'd come so close; I could see our escape path. I couldn't believe our mission would really end like this.

Before I could say anything, make my case . . . a gunshot rang out. I was sure it had missed, until I saw Mohammed crumple to the ground.

"No!" I screamed, dropping to my knees, watching the blood pool around his face. It couldn't be, not like this, not with one simple shot. His eyes were closed, his breath was silent; he was warm but unmoving. I wanted to shake him until the life reentered his body, wanted to rewind time, find some other path through these caves, some way to route my friend to safety. But I couldn't do any of those things, I could only stare at the husk of this once intimidating man, his lifeless form sprawled on the ground so casually.

"No," I whispered again, forgetting there were still guns trained on me. Forgetting my own life was still at risk, until three more gunshots rang out, deafening. I braced myself for the impact, before looking up to realize . . . my three assailants were lying dead on the ground. I twisted my head behind me to find a familiar face: the soldier who had been protecting me, the one I'd converted by killing his friend. His gun raised, shaking. He hadn't even hesitated; he'd shot his own comrades point-blank, one at a time.

A strange pallor came over my new soldier friend. "I'm sorry, Prophet," he whispered. He could feel himself being Punished—this time, from his own guilt at killing his friends. His voice shook. "I thought that was what you wanted."

I pulled a pill from my pocket, borrowed from my Brazilian military friends, and placed it in his hand. "It was," I promised him. He took the pill, and his expression returned to normal. One death averted, at least. For now.

Still, as I looked at the bodies of those three dead Turkish soldiers, my insides curdled. Those three deaths had saved my life, had protected the lives of the resistance members I was trying to rescue. I hated the way I kept doing the math like that . . . and I hated more how the math kept changing. First I could balance one life against all of ours, then two, then three more. How far was I willing to go, what was I willing to give up?

I looked at Mohammed's body, unmoving on the ground. It killed me that I hadn't been able to save him, that I hadn't been able to keep my promise to Layla. That a good man had borne the cost of this war. I didn't want to leave him behind, but I knew his sacrifice would be worth nothing if I didn't make it to that plane. I scrambled up the rock face, until my fingers touched the stiff blades of grass blanketing the world above. I emerged on the surface, where I could see the rest of the resistance at a distance, retreating toward the airstrip. I sprinted after them, hoping the prophets' military wouldn't find me before I was safely with my own.

As I reached the crest of the ridge, I saw Dawn, waiting where I'd left her, gesturing for me to hurry onto the planes. She handed me a sweatshirt. "Better not risk you rubbing up on anyone with that stuff on your arms."

"Thanks."

I put it on, but I didn't head toward the plane. "Mohammed's gone," I choked out.

Dawn looked at me with sympathy, upset though unsurprised. "You saved the others," she reassured me. As I boarded the plane, the guilt, the anguish followed me—guilt that I couldn't save Layla's father. Guilt that I'd allowed others to die in the process. All that guilt would follow me back to Brazil, I knew. It would follow me forever. Dawn was right—the guilt itself was Punishment enough for a lifetime.

While our engines were revving up, General Feliciano pulled me aside with a genuine, respectful gaze. "Thank you for keeping my troops out of danger. Prophet Daniel would not have done the same." So I'd accomplished one piece of my mission, at least. Whatever doubts the general might have once harbored, I'd managed to assuage them. For now.

"Of course," I said, putting on my wise prophet's smile. "I don't believe in violence."

I moved to sit next to Zack, who looked around the plane with concern. "I thought you were rescuing more people than this."

"So did I," I murmured.

As the plane lifted off, I felt my stomach tighten. We'd made it this far. I hoped we could get this plane back to Brazil in one piece.

8

As the plane reached altitude, I hazarded a glance at Layla, sitting across from me. Her eyes were red from crying, but she stiffened as she caught my eye. Staring daggers at the friend who'd failed to keep her promise, the friend who'd let her father die, who'd left his body behind while she ran to save herself. I looked away, but I still felt her eyes boring into me, as though trying to drill a hole through the side of the plane and send me thirty thousand feet down into the Atlantic Ocean.

"You should talk to her," Zack said softly and encouragingly.

Hesitantly, I got up and sat down next to her, trying to find the words. "I'm sorry," was all I could think of.

But she wasn't interested in my apologies. "It should have been you," she spat back. "Why couldn't you have been the one to stay behind?"

"I tried to," I told her. "I begged him to let me stay, too . . ."

"You don't deserve to be the one to live," she said through her tears.

"I'm sorry it had to be me," I said. "I really am." I wanted to shake her, to remind her that I'd saved her life, that I'd saved the rest of her family. But I knew right now, she needed someone to hate. So I stepped away, finding a seat on the opposite end of the plane, alone. I wasn't the person she wanted consoling her, and I didn't blame her for that.

I'd saved my friends. But I wasn't sure I was comfortable with the price I'd paid. I was still stewing in my regret, staring idly at the blue water below, as Jude moved to sit next to me. "I won't touch you, I promise. Dawn told me you have lethal cooties."

I smiled, just glad someone wasn't angry at me. "Thanks. How's Layla?"

His expression darkened. "You know." I did.

"I tried everything . . ." I swore.

"I know. And Layla probably does, too. It doesn't mean she isn't mad, doesn't mean she won't hate you forever."

"You won't though, right?" I asked him.

"Never," he vowed.

In that moment, I so badly wanted to wrap my murderous arms around him. "I was so worried about you," I said softly.

"Same," he admitted. "Little did I know you were living the high life while I was eating scraps."

"I would have traded with you in a nanosecond," I said honestly, feeling guilty for all the days he'd sat in a cell. "I think you would have done all this prophet stuff a million times better than me."

"Are you kidding?" He laughed. "Me? Public speaking?"

I remembered the speech he'd tried to give in sophomore history class, stumbling over the names of ancient gods and goddesses. "Aphromighty!" I teased him.

He laughed along. "I would have been outed immediately. Or lost my nerve, or something. You don't give yourself enough credit. You're doing great." I hadn't realized how desperate I was to hear someone say that.

"Yeah, well, you might be the only person who thinks that."

"I guess everyone else is an idiot, then." I held his admiring gaze, and it filled up a part of me I hadn't known was empty. Jude was the only person in my life who always saw the best in me, no matter the circumstances.

"Thanks."

"When you have to make tough decisions, not everyone will agree with your choices. You've always been someone who likes having people agree with you, so I get it, this isn't easy for you. But maybe you'll learn to be okay with pissing people off sometimes. Maybe you'll learn that being the one to make the tough calls is worth it, if they're the right ones."

I knew he was trying to cheer me up, to cheer me on, but his words still cut like a knife, reminding me of all the pain I'd caused. "What if you're the one I end up hurting next?" I asked tentatively. "Would you forgive me then?"

"Try not to hurt me," he said with a laugh.

Though Jude's words reassured me a little, I still stewed in my fears. How many enemies was I willing to make? How much guilt was I willing to shoulder, in exchange for how much good? Only time would tell.

I saw Zack watching our conversation from across the plane, and a strange feeling came over me. Did I feel guilty for talking like this with Jude? Why would I feel guilty, just for chatting with an old friend? Was I worried Zack might be jealous? Should he be jealous?

I moved to sit next to Zack again, deciding all that was in my head. "We're almost there," he said, looking out the window nervously.

Our landing in Redenção was bumpy, but the moment the wheels hit the ground, the plane erupted into cheers. We'd made it home to Brazil. What remained of the resistance was safe. But as I looked around the plane, I remembered—what remained of the resistance was barely anything: just a few scraggly, underfed former prisoners. A young woman and her two children; an old man with a limp. These weren't fighters, they were refugees. We'd saved a handful of lives, but we hadn't gained any strategic advantage.

We still hadn't heard from Dr. Smith. Our radios had been silent for days. We'd been holding out hope that there was some secret enclave of rebels left out there, but more likely, this was it. Everyone who hadn't been slaughtered by the prophets was right here in Redenção. As much as I wanted to celebrate this victory, I knew how precarious our position was. If we failed, if I failed, the prophets would win.

As we exited the plane, Macy was the first to greet us, running up to hug Jude. "You're alive!"

He seemed genuinely happy to see her. It had been years since he'd seen any of his old friends from high school, since he went into hiding. "Hey. Yeah, alive, who would have guessed, right?"

She gave him a deadly serious stare. "If anyone else needs to fake their death from now on, I want in on it. I can keep a secret, I promise."

"Same," I told him with a smile.

"I promise," he said.

The general moved to escort our allies to their own apartments in the city. They weren't going to be of much use to us militarily, especially Layla's family, who were furious with me for what had happened to Mohammed. All the rescued resistance members were under strict orders not to speak the truth to anyone they knew. Right now, we were still relying on the goodwill of General Feliciano, and telling her the truth seemed like a risky play.

Even if everyone kept perfect secrecy, I wasn't sure how much longer this safe haven would remain safe. Especially once we deplaned to see Dr. Marko waiting on the tarmac, grim. "What's going on?" I asked him.

"There's someone else here to see you."

For a moment, hope stirred inside of me. Maybe there were others left out there after all. "Who is it?"

He hesitated. "She's outside the city limits. The army wasn't sure if they should let her in. I said you'd go and meet her if you wanted to see her."

My heart stopped cold. I knew exactly who it was. I looked at Zack, knowing he was the only person here who would understand. "Come with me?" I asked. He nodded.

As we drove to the edge of town, I went over all the things I wanted to say to her, tried to figure out what on earth she might want with me now. I had it all rehearsed, but the moment I saw her, everything slipped out of my head.

There she was, standing next to her car, parked in the middle of an empty street. My army creating a human wall, protecting me from this innocent-looking middle-aged woman. "I can go with you," Zack offered, but I shook my head. This part, I had to do alone.

I walked across our defensive line, and there she was, waiting patiently. No longer wearing her burqa, her dark features watched me curiously. Valerie, Esther, Mom, her name as scrambled and confusing as her motives. The curves of her mouth, her expressions even, felt like looking in a fun house mirror—seeing my own face reflected back in a twisted, unpleasant way. I didn't want to see myself in this woman, especially not now.

"What do you want?" I asked, glad to be the first to speak, to set the tone.

My mother matched my gaze, defiant. "Believe it or not, I'm here to help you."

BOOK

FOUR

Believe it or not, I didn't believe her. "Why would you want to help me?" I asked.

She didn't blink. "We might disagree on the hows and the whys, but at the end of the day, we want the same thing. A world at peace. You've put that in jeopardy."

"I don't see how," I said, holding my ground.

"Then you haven't been paying attention. Fatal Punishments are on the upswing since your speech, did you know that? You're fomenting doubt. Tearing apart the very fabric that holds our world together. By contradicting the other prophets, you put everything I've worked for in jeopardy."

"Maybe everything you worked for is terrible," I retorted.

"I know you believe that, but I've come here to show you that isn't true. You're my daughter; I know that if you see the facts, you'll see things my way. Give me a chance to state my case, to show you what a big mistake you're making."

Though that old childhood hope surged inside of me, that maybe my mother was finally on my side, I forced myself to say what I knew I had to. "No."

She smiled, a challenge. "You said it yourself, being wrong is okay." My face flushed, thinking of her watching the videos of my "sermons." I'd imagined thumbing my nose at the prophets, I'd imagined inspiring strangers who didn't know better . . . but I hadn't considered the shame of my mother knowing I was lying through my teeth. "I'm giving you the chance to live up to your own words," she continued. "Make things better."

As she spoke, I wanted to believe her, wanted to find common ground. I'd inherited my mother's silver tongue, an ability to make lies sound better than the truth. But remembering that she was trying to con me made me want to tear her apart. I steadied my stance, reminded myself of her strategic value. Having Esther in our hands might be an advantage. "Okay," I said. "I'll listen. But we do it on my terms."

"Of course." She raised her hands in surrender, looking to the soldiers standing behind me. "I assume this is what you want me to do next?" she asked wryly.

I nodded to the general, and two soldiers stepped forward to take her into custody. As they handcuffed her, I asked, "What's your real reason for coming here?"

"You mean besides saving the world?"

I rolled my eyes. "Yeah, besides that."

Her eyes grew sad, and I wondered if it was another ploy. "You're still my daughter. You think I have anything other than your best interests at heart?"

In a strange way, I knew that was almost the truth. Whatever her ulterior motives might be, I knew that protecting her daughter was probably part of it. She'd saved my life, after all. But what she wanted for me, and what I wanted for me . . . those were two very different things.

As the soldiers led her off, she gave me a little wave—a slow, rhythmic, bobbling of her fingers that gave me chills. I remembered the last time I'd seen her do that, the morning of the Revelations, walking away from me. The tiniest little gesture that connected me to who my mother used to be. Who I used to think she was.

I felt myself holding back tears at that memory, as Zack reached out to take my hand. "You did great," he said, reassuring, and as he wrapped his arms around me, those tears came loose. Came pouring out, unhinged, as Zack pulled me tighter.

"I'm still her daughter," I whispered to him. "And she's still my mom."

"I'm sorry," he whispered back. No one but Zack had witnessed the full extent of her cruelty, and it helped to know someone else understood.

I tried to find my resilience again, to put aside these overwhelming emotions. "I hate that she's here. But she might be the best lead we have right now."

"Or she might be leading us into a trap," he warned, articulating a note of disapproval. While I was annoyed by his tone, I couldn't help but feel like this time, he might be right. Though that little voice had been out of my head for a long time now, my own intuition whispered nearly as loudly, as I watched my mother march toward a prison cell in Redenção: *This will end in heartbreak.*

Redenção's prison was a dank affair, smelling of mildew and sulfur and worse. I wondered if it had received a proper cleaning in years, if ever. Two soldiers led us down halls full of prisoners crowded into musty cells. I worried for their health—these were some of the most sickly-looking Outcasts I'd ever seen. As I passed, they looked at me with sad and hollow eyes, more confused by my presence than anything.

"Prophet Grace?" one called out hopefully. They'd seen my sermons, urging spiritual clemency for past crimes. Perhaps they wondered if I was there to help them. I kept my eyes fixed ahead, afraid to raise expectations.

The soldiers led my mother into a high-tech cell, with Plexiglas walls and an elaborate additional security system on the door. Zack squeezed my hand while they handcuffed my mother to a table and chained her legs to the floor. "She looks so much like you," he said in hushed tones. "I don't know how I didn't see it before."

My skin crawled, hating that comparison, but I had to admit, he was right. As I entered my mother's cell, she looked down at her garish orange jumpsuit. "This is all a little overkill, don't you think?"

I ignored her attempts at casual banter. "Tell me what you need to tell me."

She sighed, relenting. "When they took my real clothes, I told them they'd find a flash drive in the pocket of my blazer. They left it over there." I followed her gaze to a table in the corner and walked to pick it up. "I also told them to bring a computer so you could read it, doesn't look like they did."

"You really think we're going to let you plug some random flash drive into our computers? No way," I told her flatly.

Zack nudged me. "It's okay. They can air gap a laptop, keep it off any server, so even if she has the nastiest virus on that thing, she can't hack into the prison's system, no matter what."

He was speaking so confidently, I wanted to trust him, even though this whole thing still made me uneasy. "Sure, fine," I said, and one of the soldiers left to go track down an air-gapped laptop.

My mother nodded to Zack, a playful smile on her face. "So you two are still . . . ?"

I stayed defiant, not willing to engage with her lighthearted and belated attempts at parenting. "Still trying to save the world from you, that's right."

She saw I wasn't willing to play along, so she turned to Zack. "You're taking good care of her?"

Zack nodded, instinctively playing the good boyfriend for his girlfriend's mother. "Trying, at least."

In that moment I hated them both for acting like this was some normal meet-the-parents conversation. But my annoyance was thankfully short-lived, as the soldier returned with the laptop.

When I popped in the drive, it brought up just one Excel document. "What is this?" I asked my mother.

"Statistics. I know, who wants to sit and read a bunch of statistics. But they've saved a hell of a lot more lives than you know. Take a look."

I started reading. Projected versus actual deaths by year, stretching out a century into the future, from causes like war, famine, water shortages. "This was what you came here to show me?" I asked, a little miffed.

"This is what the world would have looked like without me, without what we did. Those numbers have faces and names. Billions of them, people who haven't even been born yet. And I saved them. I am saving them. I know what you're going to say; what about everyone else who died in the Revelations, everyone who died in the resistance."

"Friends of mine," I retorted, Mohammed's death still fresh in my mind. "Friends you slaughtered."

"To save billions more."

"You've made this argument before, and I don't buy it," I protested. "You can't say for certain that all these people would have died. But I know of actual people you *actually* killed, a billion of them."

"And I know that without our intervention, sea levels would have risen an extra inch. Hurricanes would be 4 percent stronger on average, resulting in billions of dollars' worth of damage and even more lives lost. That's not just one year, that's every year humans exist on this planet, and it would only be getting worse. You can fault me all you want for the crimes I've committed, I know I deserve plenty of blame. But you have to give me credit for saving those lives. Just because I can't put names to them doesn't make them any less human. Being passive and watching the world go by, leaving fate in God's hands . . . that doesn't make you pious, that makes you weak, that makes you cowardly. A brave, moral person steps forward and does the right thing. Even when it's hard, even when they get no credit, even when everyone hates them for it." Her words felt familiar, the same sentiments Jude had used to reassure me mere hours ago.

"The trolley problem, we get it," Zack muttered, then quickly explained to me, "There's an old thought experiment. If you saw a train about to hit five people, and you could divert it to hit only one person, would you do it? She's saying you should, that letting those five people die is worse than killing the one."

It was the same logic I'd used to justify saving everyone in Turkey, the logic I'd been using since I joined the resistance. "When you pull the lever, when you divert the train, you're taking responsibility," I finally said. "Maybe you're right, maybe it is the moral choice. But you still have to answer for what you did." I turned to my mother. "You're hiding in the shadows, deciding this for everyone without telling us that's what you're doing. How angry do you think people would be if they found out the truth?"

"How angry do you think people would be if they found out your miracles weren't so miraculous?" my mother retorted without losing a beat.

I shook my head, undeterred. "I'm just trying to fix the world you messed up."

"You think I *created* a world full of violence and death? This planet has been hell since human beings showed up on it. I'm just doing my best to save us from ourselves. The secrets we keep, we keep because we have to. Because to tell the truth is to kill innocents. And neither of us is willing to do that, are we?" I hated the way my mother got in my head like this . . . hated it more because some little part of me wondered if she was right.

Zack saw me floundering and stepped in. "Grace will take responsibility when this is all over, we all will. Including you."

I nodded, taking comfort in that thought. "And you'll sit here in this cell until then," I added.

Esther nodded, resigned. "I figured you'd say that. But Grace, I hope I won't be sitting here alone. It breaks my heart how little time I've gotten to spend with you, while you've been growing up. It may not be the ideal situation, but I hope you'll take advantage of this opportunity, however long it lasts, to finally get to know me."

Zack shot me a warning look. He knew she still thought she could convince me. But I knew exactly what my mother was capable of; I didn't need any warnings. "I'll visit if I can," I told her.

She smiled, as though she'd gotten the upper hand. This was a woman who'd spent years building her inner resolve, inoculating herself against the worst kinds of torture. But I had a feeling that the aching guilt of motherhood might be a type of leverage she wasn't prepared for.

As we exited the prison, Zack grew anxious. "Don't visit her again," he warned.

"What does it matter?" I asked, chafing at the imperative way Zack was talking to me. "She's locked up, she can't do anything to us."

His voice went cold. "There wasn't enough on that flash drive to justify her coming here, getting herself locked up like that. And she knows she won't convince you of anything. There's something else she wants, but I have no idea what it is."

I had no idea either. But whatever it was, we needed to find out, and fast.

When we arrived back home, we found Jude, Dawn, and Dr. Marko holding an anxious summit at the dining room table. At first I assumed they were discussing my mother, but the look on Dr. Marko's face told me it must be something even more urgent. "What's happening?" Zack asked, as I sat down next to Jude.

"We finally got a message from Dr. Smith," Marko said, voice a little unsteady, and I remembered that Dr. Smith had once been Marko's beloved business partner. Though I didn't know him well, it pained me to see him so worried. "The resistance cell she was working with in South Asia was wiped out by the prophets last month. She managed to escape, and she's hiding out in a monastery in Thailand."

"We're trying to find a way to extract her and bring her here," Dawn explained, and I felt the tiniest bit of hope sparking in my chest. If we saved Dr. Smith, she could help Dr. Marko repair the broken device and get us back on track to strengthen the resistance and end the prophets' reign for good.

"What can I do?" I asked. "I could ask my supporters for help again, or maybe there's someone inside the prison . . . ?"

"We're worried about exposing ourselves too much," Dawn said gently. "You have the trust of the Brazilian military for now, and we need that to survive. If you start allying yourself with random insurgents abroad, people might ask questions. Well, more questions."

"Protecting Redenção is the priority," Zack agreed, with a calculating tone that reminded me of the calculating mother we'd just left.

Jude looked at me. "If Grace thinks she could make it work . . ."

As antagonistic looks passed between Zack and Jude, I stepped in, eager to diffuse the tension. "What's the plan, without me?"

Dr. Marko explained, "We think we can send her a serum that will mimic the effects of death."

Jude chuckled. "I think I saw that play. *Romeo and Juliet*, right?"

Dr. Marko continued, voice hopeful, "Something like that. When they take her to the morgue, she pops up, alive, and manages to escape."

"And with any luck, she makes it here to us," Dawn finished.

I nodded, shooting an olive branch look around the table. "Sounds like you don't need me after all."

I stepped out with a polite smile, hoping to give the rebel

decision-makers space to make their decisions. But as I was heading up the stairs, trying to find privacy, I heard Jude's voice behind me.

"Hey, are you okay?" I turned and hugged him, happy to finally be able to.

"I should be asking you that question," I said.

"I'll be fine after a few more good meals and hot showers." His easy way of brushing off trauma worried me. I wondered what other horrors he might have seen that he wasn't sharing. "I heard your mom's . . . well, I've heard a lot of things about your mom."

"She's alive, she's here, she's evil?" I guessed.

"Yeah, those were the things." His smile once again gave me that reassurance I hadn't realized I'd needed.

I hesitantly told him, "She asked me to keep visiting her in prison. Zack doesn't think I should, but . . ."

"But she's your mom," Jude finished for me. He'd known her as a little kid, and he'd witnessed everything I'd sacrificed trying to find her just months earlier. If anyone would understand what I was feeling right now, it was him.

"She thinks that I'm just her without all the wisdom and experience, and if she keeps arguing her case, eventually I'll see things her way. But . . . I keep using that same logic. I keep thinking that she just hasn't seen what I've seen, and if I can show her . . . maybe I'll be the one to convince *her*."

Jude took that in. "Well, you've staked your reputation on knowing how to convince people of things."

"So has she."

"I'm not worried about her changing your mind," he encouraged me. "You know who you are, and you think for yourself. You're Grace." It had been so long since someone I actually knew had said my name with such warmth and affection. "But if she's like you, I bet she's just as stubbornly devoted to her values. Even if she does love you, even if she does listen, I don't know that changing her mind is necessarily in the cards."

I nodded, acknowledging, "You're probably right. I just wish I knew what the right move was."

"Tactics were never your thing." He caught himself and explained, "I mean that in a good way. Your strength is connecting, communicating, thinking on your feet. Leave the battle plans to Dawn. You just keep being the prophet that people can relate to. That's the big picture anyway. You were smart enough to make yourself a prophet, to get all these people on our side. You'll figure out what to do next, I know it."

"Thanks." His words felt so precious, like little jewels I had to hoard where I could. Because though he was my dearest friend, we both knew we had to maintain a certain amount of distance. He wasn't mine, and I wasn't his. Hoping to create a little of that distance, I tentatively added, "How's Layla doing?" I hadn't seen her in the conference room, and I knew she must still be reeling after her father's death.

Jude's expression darkened. "She hasn't gotten out of bed since we got here. I should probably check in on her."

"Tell her I'm thinking about her," I said, knowing I was probably the last person she wanted to be reminded of right now.

Jude hesitated, then said, "If she stops being angry at you, she has to be angry at herself. Because she knows, deep down, her father sacrificed himself for her and her family."

I remembered the deep, painful place I'd spiraled into as a small child, when I'd thought my mom was gone forever. I wanted to help Layla out of it however I could. "Let her stay angry at me. As long as she needs."

A smile passed between us. Even with the overt romance stripped away, talking to Jude still felt deeper, more meaningful, than talking to anyone else I knew. He'd seen me becoming who I was from start to finish, understood every facet of my personality in a way no one else could.

And maybe some piece of that was outwardly visible, because when Zack exited the conference room and saw us talking together, I saw a flash of jealousy cross his face. Jude must have seen it, too, because he took that moment to nod his goodbye. "I'll see you later."

Before he could go, I couldn't help but wrap him up in one more hug. "I'm so glad you're okay."

Watching him walk away left me with a kind of loneliness I'd forgotten about. There was something simple and pure about the love I'd had for Jude, about the love he'd given me back. There had been no expectations, no fear. I knew he'd always be there, as a friend even when he couldn't be more than that. With Zack, since the beginning, I'd always felt unsteady, unsure . . . both of my feelings for him and his for me. And being reminded of how simple and perfect love had once felt made my love for Zack feel even more precarious.

As Zack came up to me, kissed me, something nagged at my gut, but I couldn't quite put my finger on what it was. Or maybe I knew *exactly* what it was and just didn't want to admit it. No matter how close I'd gotten to Zack, no matter what I felt for him, I'd never stopped loving Jude. Never stopped hoping that maybe things could work out between us. I clutched Zack more tightly, trying to banish those feelings from my heart. Here was someone who loved me right now, in the best way he could.

But that night, as I lay in bed next to Zack, I found my mind wandering. Pretending it was Jude next to me, wondering what his body would feel like if he were in Zack's place. We'd never had sex before, but I'd spent plenty of time imagining it. And I couldn't stop myself from picturing it now. The guilt flowed through me, but nothing could stop the thoughts. The fantasies, flooding my brain.

You're involved with someone else, I reminded myself. *Someone handsome, and kind, and funny. Someone who loves you, who would do anything for you.* But for all the times Zack had said he loved me, I still knew, deep down, he didn't have faith in me the way Jude did. Unlike Jude, he didn't trust me to know what to do next—in fact, in that boardroom, Zack had spent every breath he could spare arguing against my ideas, questioning my judgment.

Being with Zack reminded me that I was a fraud. Every insecurity I felt about myself was magnified back through his eyes tenfold. At times, I couldn't help but feel like Zack was right when he pointed out my errors in judgment. Maybe Jude was too blinded by his childhood friendship with me to see the truth. That I was in over my head. That I was going to mess something up again, sooner or later.

The more my anxieties piled up, the more I wanted to seek out the people who couldn't see any of my flaws, the ones who only knew my lies. The love of my followers was like a drug, one that soothed my deepest fears. And slowly but surely, I was becoming addicted.

As Zack snored softly beside me, I pulled out a laptop and started searching my name. Before becoming a prophet, googling myself had brought up only a few academic awards and a middle-school soccer league. Now, there were countless news articles, videos, fan pages.

I'd gotten good at brushing past the sites that seemed like they might be critical, or skeptical—it was easy enough to tell what their tone would be from only a sentence or so. Instead, I focused on the self-proclaimed gurus of Prophet Grace, who were seeking meaning in my words; their unwavering praise filled me with purpose.

But once again, watching my words becoming twisted in strangers' mouths left me feeling twisted as well. Even though my whole prophetship was a sham, there was a part of me that still cared about my message. My purpose might have been a lie, but my missives could still be the truth, could still be meaningful, useful. My speeches had been an attempt to put good into the world, and hearing people distort those words into something hateful filled me with an obsessive revulsion.

I found myself creating fake online personas, commenting on the videos, trying to set people straight. I wished I could decry these false gurus without putting our position at risk. Unfortunately, I knew my job was to lie low, not to defend my reputation.

When I started to feel overwhelmed, I did what I'd done so many times—instinctively, I prayed to Great Spirit, hoping for some kind of guidance, tranquility. But this time, rather than the usual sense of calm that came over me during prayer, I felt a jolt of guilt. How could I expect my god to listen when I'd devoted myself to blaspheming in His name? The uneasy feeling in my gut just sent me deeper into the internet, looking for some kind of salve—hoping others' kind words would help me feel better about myself.

As I clicked around, I found a new adherent to my faith who was gaining popularity—a so-called Guru Sousa . . . our friend from the Amazon. He'd begun exploiting our personal relationship to build a hugely successful platform overnight. I was horrified to hear him repeating my sad little platitudes like they were real wisdom. He'd have done better to find a good greeting card and claim that as gospel. The way he described me, I sounded like a clichéd hack . . . because I was one.

In one video, I saw his mother standing next to him; apparently his newfound spiritual fame had helped them reconcile. So something good had come out of my deception, at least. I wondered whether their bond would survive once she knew he was preaching in the name of a false prophet . . . that he was just another Outcast after all, and a foolish one at that.

The more I read, the more the hollow feeling in my stomach grew. Not just because the words themselves were lies, told by people I'd tricked into speaking them, but because there was one glaring absence. My father was still missing in action. News reports assumed he was deep in contemplation somewhere in the woods—no one had seen him in months. I'd secretly hoped that once I showed my face to the outside world, *he* would have been the parent who showed up in Redenção. That he'd send me a message, at the very least. But wherever my father was, he was still too angry to speak to me, and that thought hurt more and more every day that went by.

Maybe it was that particular pain that drove me over the edge, that compelled me out of bed, toward the door. At least one parent wanted to see me, and the truth was, right now I needed a mother more than ever. I grabbed my shoes, quietly as I could, trying not to wake Zack. I knew what he'd say if I told him where I was going, and I knew I wouldn't go if I heard it. I was heading back to prison.

4

One of the soldiers standing guard outside our apartment accompanied me to the prison. Though visiting hours were long over, I knew they'd make an exception for me.

My mother's cell was coolly lit only by the fluorescent bulbs above us, and as I stepped inside I saw she was unrestrained—unprepared for my visit. "You want to call that guard back, tie me up?" she asked dryly.

"You won't hurt me," I told her. "If you wanted to, you would have already."

She nodded, somber. "You're right about that."

I stepped closer. We were alone in this cell, and with her CIA training she should have been able to overpower me. But I knew I was in control. "You didn't come here to show me statistics. And you've had ten years to find me and chat; I was your daughter for every one of those ten years you spent 'dead.' Tell me why you're really here."

Esther considered, weighed her options. I knew not to trust

whatever might come out of her mouth next. "I told you already, I'm here to recruit you."

The same thing I was trying to do to her. "You won't succeed," I promised her.

"So you're not a numbers girl. I get it. I wasn't either, at first. You think with your heart, I always loved that about you. That's what makes you so believable, as a prophet, it's the same thing that makes your father good at what he does. You connect with people, you empathize with them . . ."

"I'm glad at least one of my parents knows how to do that," I shot back.

Esther ignored me. "You have your father's good soul and your mother's brains, and that makes you the most formidable young woman I've ever met. It's also what makes you the solution we've been looking for."

"Solution?"

"To save the world, we needed a mechanism, a way to keep people in line. Punishments. We figured people would feel guilty, sure, but they'd learn from their mistakes, and they'd recover. We figured some people might stay Punished, but the number of Outcasts in the world now is far, far greater than we ever would have projected."

"Maybe you should have run the numbers one more time before you used mankind as the testing ground for your cosmic war," I grumbled.

My mother continued, undeterred. "But you, Grace, you're the answer. You did something we never figured out how to do. You spoke directly to the Outcasts. And it's working. The healing rates in Outcast Wards have more than quadrupled since you gave your speech in South Africa. You gave people hope. Tens of thousands of people around the world would have been dead, or still gravely sick, without your intervention."

I couldn't help but be moved by my mother's words. For all the pain and suffering I knew I'd caused, I hadn't really grappled with the breadth of the good I might have done, too. But I was afraid to show any weakness, so I stayed defiant. "They all would have survived, decades of dead Outcasts, if you'd bothered to intervene. If you'd given them drugs to stay alive, anything."

My mother nodded. "We considered that. But ultimately, secrecy remained the priority. Casualties were inevitable, but we knew they'd only increase if too much information ended up in the wrong hands."

The more I thought about my mother's explanation, the more skeptical I became. "If what I'm doing is helping, why are you here? Why try to stop me?"

"I'm not trying to stop you. Far from it, I want you to speak more. Correct your followers . . . I'm sure you've seen the trash people have been preaching in your name?" It was like she'd read my mind. "I want you to use your newfound influence for good. But right now you're just taking random shots in the dark. It's the same thing you just criticized me for—experimenting with your words on a global scale. You've had some successes, I can't deny you that. But you've had some misfires, too. Which is why I think I can help you. We can shape your message together. Stop this silly war with the other prophets and focus on helping Outcasts."

"You want me to be your little puppet?" I asked sarcastically.

"Not a puppet, a partner. We want the same things, Grace. I

know you think I'm some evil monster, but at the very least you know we're fighting for the same future. For peace. We've both made sacrifices in service of reaching that goal. But you and me, working together, instead of fighting against each other . . . together I think we could actually make it happen." She was so earnest, I wanted to believe her. But I couldn't. Even if her words were genuine, I'd never trust her. I knew what it would mean to give my power over to someone like her.

"You know I won't say yes to that, right?" I said quietly.

"I don't know that. I don't know *you* well enough to say anything for sure, and that's my own fault, I know it is."

I felt the gulf between us, an impassable ocean, and it swallowed me up. That loneliness reminded me of the only person who might be able to cure it. "Do you know where Dad is?" I asked tentatively. "You're tracking everyone, you must be watching him."

"You haven't heard from him?" Esther sounded surprised.

"No," I replied, hiding my disappointment.

"Last I heard, before you arrested me, he was in the Blue Ridge Mountains, deep in prayer and meditation."

I was relieved that the news reports were right for once. "So he's safe?"

"Samantha's never left his side," my mother promised. My mother, manipulating her ex-husband by providing him a girlfriend to protect him—it made the contents of my stomach curdle.

"Why were you ever together, you and Dad?" I asked. "What did you see in each other?" It was a personal question, one that served no part of my mission, save my own curiosity. And yet I was more eager for that answer than any other.

"Opposites attract, doesn't everyone say that?" my mother said with a rueful smile.

I pressed on. "Back when I thought you ran a battered women's shelter, it made sense. You were both pious, do-goodery people. But now that I know you were working for the CIA, keeping all these secrets . . ."

"I can't have been a do-gooder, too?" Esther challenged.

"You aren't one," I told her.

"I'm not," she admitted. "But I wanted to be. That's what I loved about your father. I saw in him the kind of person I aspired to be. But then I watched how hard he worked, and I saw how little it mattered. How I could devote my whole life to canned food drives, to helping the poor, and it was just a tiny dent in a world full of insurmountable problems. And then I found a job where I could change the world. I saw a way to do what your father was doing but on a global scale. His goodness inspired me to be great."

"And his religiosity made you think, people are dumb, this is a good way to manipulate them?" I asked, prodding.

"Not his. It was my own faith," she admitted. "Maybe I framed it as your father's, when I described it to people, but it was my own. The way the god I believed in influenced my life. I still pray, do you know that? You must think I'm a monster, praying to the very god I worked so hard to kill."

I thought of how I'd failed to connect with Great Spirit in the way I used to, before I became a fake prophet. "Does God answer?" I asked, genuinely curious.

"No more than He did before," my mother said with a shrug. "But for what it's worth, I do feel like I've made Him proud."

"I don't," I told her.

"Well, Prophet Grace, I guess you'd know, wouldn't you? You think God's on your side, really? The God I created for you?"

If I was honest, I wasn't sure, but I kept up a brave face. "He's gotten us this far. Me a prophet, you in a cell."

My mother snorted. "You're a prophet, hell, you're *alive*, because I protected you. That's not some higher power, that's the privilege of being the daughter of one of the most powerful people on earth." For the first time, I could see a hint of disgust peeking through in her expression. "Your whole life, even back before you knew the truth, I was watching. You were so smug. You thought that everything you had was because you'd earned it, by being perfect, and pious. You had no idea, you still have no idea, how much work went into giving you that world."

"That's what you wanted me to think," I said, face getting hot.

"Sure, the way a parent wants their kid to think Santa gave them their Christmas presents. Then they're supposed to grow up and realize all the hard work and sacrifice that went into that experience. There is no 'Great Spirit' watching your back, sweetheart. Trust me, I made it up. And the sooner you realize that this world runs on the blood and sweat of people like me, that you aren't magically protected or privileged because you believe in the right god, the better off you'll be."

Her words left me reeling, and I realized we'd talked this whole time without me getting in a single word I'd come here to say. I steeled myself and began, "You wanted me to listen. You wanted me to consider that I might be wrong. I did that, I did what you wanted. Now I want the same thing in return. I want you to hear me out. I want you to think about those numbers on that spreadsheet, and think of all the people who aren't on there. All the Outcasts. All the people who died in the Revelations. Maybe there aren't as many, but they're dead all the same, and that blood is on your hands whether you admit it or not. The trolley ran over those people, and you have to account for it. The blood of every Outcast who dies from a Punishment until the end of time will be on your hands, too, unless *you* help *me*. Because you're the only one who can stop this. You turn double agent, you help us find a safe way to tell everyone the truth, and this war is over."

"It's too late," Esther said, shaking her head. "Maybe we could have turned back a month, six months after the Revelations, but after ten years? It'll be chaos."

"Maybe it has to be chaos, for a while . . ." I pointed out.

"That's what I said about the Revelations themselves, and you called me a mass murderer," Esther retorted. "We are where we are now, and we have to do the best with what we have."

"No, we don't," I insisted. "We can push for something better."

Esther nodded to the door of her cell. "And all those people out there, they'd think your world is better? Right now, most people get to live every day thinking they're doing everything right, that bad things don't happen to good people. That all they have to do is live justly, and Great Spirit will magically make everything work out for them. They don't have to face any of the hard truths you and I have to deal with. They're happy. Like you were, until recently. And you want to take that away from them?"

My heart ached for that simpler time, when that had been me. But I shook my head. "That's not real happiness and you know it."

She smiled sadly. "The younger generation, you always want what's different. What hasn't been done before. You want to re-make the world in your own image, and you know what? Sometimes the young people succeed. I certainly made my mark, once upon a time. But once you change things, you can never change them back. You, my darling, will never be anything other than Prophet Grace. Whatever future you imagined for yourself before, it's gone . . . you only have this one now. You can never take back the deaths *you* caused. And you have quite a bit of power now, so take it from someone who has just a little more experience with that than you do. Be careful, sweetie, be very, very careful."

My insides boiled as she spoke. I wanted to tear her apart, rip out her condescending tongue, but I stayed calm. "I'll give you one last chance to help us, and then I'm not coming back."

Esther paused, considering. "Okay."

I was startled by the response. "Okay?"

"Sure, I'll do it." Her smile was bitter, ironic.

"You're lying," I said, frustrated.

My mother's eyes bore into mine. "You never would have gotten a yes that wasn't a lie, and you knew it before you stepped through that door. The same way I knew I'd never get one out of you."

"Then why are you here?" I asked her, begging, "Please, just tell me."

My mother sat down on her cot, looking at me sadly. "Thank

you for visiting. I'm sure it wasn't easy, but I'm glad I got the chance to talk to you again."

I felt numb. Empty. "So that's it, nothing? Goodbye forever?"

"I hope not," Esther said. She looked at me with love and pity, and I discovered all the hope I hadn't realized was still living inside of me. My desperate, impossible, secret wish that I'd get something from her I'd always wanted . . . That I'd get my mother back. And in that moment, I finally realized that I never would.

Holding back tears, I pressed the buzzer, signaling to the guard I was ready to go. "Goodbye, Mom."

Esther's eyes were wet, too. "Goodbye, Grace. I never wanted to hurt you. It kills me to know that I have, and I will." It felt like less of an apology than a threat. But I let it hang there—I wasn't going to stoop to her level.

The guard opened the door for me, and as I stepped outside, it closed behind me. My heart clenched, as I fought the urge to turn around, open that door again, go back in, hug her one last time. Ask her to say something mothering, something real.

But the hollowness in my bones told me that was it. That was the last time I would visit her cell.

Y ou went to see her? Alone?" Dawn was beside herself, as Irene gripped her hand, trying to calm her. When I'd arrived home in the early morning, I found my friends already assembled in our meeting room, a larger crowd this time, including Layla and a few other rescued members of the resistance. They'd heard about my late-night jaunt to the prison, and they were *not* happy about it. I was certainly not going to get any sympathy for my mommy issues from this group.

"Why didn't you tell me you were leaving?" Zack asked, pacing the room. His tone was colder and more condescending than ever.

Feeling everyone's eyes on me, judging, I got defensive. "Because I knew you'd react this way. I knew I'd get more out of her if I saw her one-on-one, if she felt like I was coming to her as a daughter, not an interrogator."

"And what did you get from her?" Layla challenged.

I struggled to think of something that would seem worthwhile. "She won't turn. We all knew that. But I think she'd believe me if we fed her false information. If we allowed her to communicate with the outside, maybe we could mislead the prophets."

Dawn shook her head. "She knows too much about our position in Redenção. We can't risk her being in contact with her home base."

"We should just kill her," Layla muttered.

"Kill my *mother*?" I asked her, pointedly.

Layla stared daggers at me, not backing down. The unspoken: *You killed my father.*

Irene stepped in, playing moderator, "No one wants to kill anyone. But I think we can all agree, Esther is the enemy. We shouldn't trust her."

I stepped in, defensive. "I never said we should trust her. I'm saying she's valuable, there must be some way we can use her."

"Torture her for information?" Zack suggested in a casual way that made me want to strangle him.

"My mother?" I asked again, incredulous.

"You're the one who said she was valuable," he reminded me.

Before I could answer, Dr. Marko entered, face grim. "Dr. Smith is dead."

The room fell into a devastated silence. Dawn put a comforting arm around him, as tears ran down his face.

He stammered out, "Someone knew we were sending the serum and spiked it with cyanide. She tried to fake her death and . . . well, she never left the morgue."

Dr. Marko's oldest friend, and our one chance at fixing that machine, was gone. My mind reeled. I wondered, was there some way I could have saved her? I knew Dawn was right, that one life wasn't worth compromising our position, but still, after the fact . . .

"How did they know we were sending the serum?" Irene asked. "If they'd just wanted her dead, they could have killed her a million other ways, but to intercept a package and contaminate it . . ."

"We have a mole," Dawn said, definitively. Instinctively, eyes shot around the room, inspecting the faces it contained.

"It's not anyone here," Zack insisted.

"Who else knew?" Dawn asked.

Dr. Marko shook his head. "I sent the package from Redenção, and no one knew what was in it except the people in this room."

"There are a million other explanations," I dismissed. "They might have tested the serum, seen what it was, and spiked it to make a point. Or even seen the label and gotten suspicious that it came from an Outcast city."

"Someone's acting a little defensive," Layla grumbled.

Was she really accusing me? "Me?" I blurted out, offended. "You think it's me?"

"You're the one who snuck out in the middle of the night to talk to the enemy," she argued.

"Hey, let's not attack each other," Jude said, stepping in.

"If Dr. Marko's right, we need to attack someone," Zack pointed out. "There are so few of us left, we can't afford to have anyone working against us."

Suspicious looks went around the table again. Finally, Dawn said, "I trust all of you. You wouldn't be sitting in this room if I didn't. There must be some other explanation." Her surety gave me comfort, even though I guessed it might be a simple ploy to put her secretly distrusted culprit at ease.

Irene glanced around. "There could be a recording device in here somewhere." My heart sunk imagining that the mayor might have betrayed us like that, but admittedly it felt preferable to thinking one of my own friends might have done the same.

Dawn shook her head. "We checked when we first arrived." But, seeing the tension in the room, she added, "We'll look again. If there is one, we'll find it."

Dr. Marko turned to me. "Your mother didn't say anything about Dr. Smith, did she?"

"Nothing at all," I assured him.

"We could ask," Zack suggested. "Throw her off guard, see if she gives anything away in her reaction."

I nodded. "We have her here, we should use her."

The others seemed less enthused, wary of any new idea now, not knowing if they could trust its source. I felt more than one set of suspecting eyes tracking me in their periphery, and I found myself casting my own doubting looks. Layla had been so distraught since she arrived, and so eager to cast blame on me. After the trauma she'd endured, had she buckled and cast in her lot with the other side? I saw Zack, hunched and imperious . . . he'd been growing colder and colder, the more he disagreed with my tactics. He'd once worked for Esther . . . could he have turned back toward his colleagues at the CIA? Maybe his time with us, our whole relationship, had simply been a long con?

As my eyes flicked around the table, I realized I could formulate a story about any person sitting here. They were all equally plausible and impossible, and I agreed with Dawn—doubting one another was getting us nowhere other than fractured. Maybe that was all our enemies had intended anyway . . . to manufacture a situation in which we doubted our allies.

I slipped away from all these suddenly wary eyes, escaping to my room, trying to decide what to ask my mother, how to trap her. She wasn't likely to give away much even if we did manage to catch her off guard, and if she *did* know anything about Dr. Smith's death, our line of questioning wouldn't have the element of surprise anyway.

Before I'd settled on a plan, Zack interrupted me, opening the door with a hollow look on his face. "I have bad news."

"What is it?" I asked, nervous.

He finally said, stunned, "Your mother's gone."

Gone?" I asked, not sure how it could be possible.

"Her cell's empty, so yeah, gone, I'd call that gone," Zack said, getting hot.

"How?" I asked. "I just saw her, she was surrounded by a million guards . . ."

Zack paced, furious. "The soldier I talked to said he reported for duty, and the room was empty. The other guards hadn't seen anything and had assumed she was there the whole time."

"So let's interrogate those guards then!" I insisted. "Clearly someone is lying."

"We've isolated everyone who had access to the cell. They'll be questioned thoroughly," Zack said.

"Whoever told the prophets about the plan to save Dr. Smith must have freed Esther, too," I guessed.

"Yeah, I'm with you," Zack said, mulling this over.

"Who could it be?" I asked, trying to hide any hints that I might suspect him.

But Zack was much more expert in this kind of deception, and his CIA training left him uninterested in playing my games. "Any of us," he replied bluntly.

We gathered around the conference table again, but this time all eyes were on me. Layla was the first to come out and say it, not hiding one speck of her ire. "Grace was the last one who saw Esther. You didn't see anything, any clue she was about to escape?"

I ignored the accusation in her voice and thought about the heart of her question. "She was strangely calm, it's true. In fact, she never seemed worried, from the moment we took her in. It was like she had her escape plan ready."

"She knew she had a mole," Layla said pointedly.

Dawn's voice carried a note of caution. "There's no reason to think these events are connected."

"But just in case, we should be careful about sharing information from now on," Zack added. "The whole group doesn't need to know everything anyway." His words felt pointed at me, whether he'd intended them to be or not.

I knew I was innocent, but if I'd been in anyone else's shoes, I'd have been just as suspicious of me. I tried to think how I could defend myself and came up short. Finally, I stood. "I don't need to be here. This isn't my area of expertise anyway. Just let me know if I can prophesize anything useful to the cause."

As I stepped out of the room, Jude trailed after me. "You didn't have to do that."

I shook my head, resolute. "If we do have a mole, I want to

prove it isn't me. Eliminate one suspect at a time, so we can find out who it really is."

Jude's forehead scrunched up, deep in thought. "There must be some other explanation." I knew he didn't want to imagine that our mole might be me, or Layla. Once again, looking into his empathetic eyes, I felt an undeniable ache. Whether I wanted to admit it or not, it was true: *I still missed him*. Though I was happy with someone else, and wanted Jude to be happy with Layla, I couldn't help but feel a tug toward him, a reminder of who we'd once been. Maybe I'd always be a little bit in love with him. It was simple, in a way: no one could ever measure up to my first love. And the way he looked back at me, I hoped . . . maybe he felt the same way.

Before I could say anything else, the door to the meeting room opened, and everyone slowly filed out, casting suspicious glances at one another. I'd never seen our group quite so gloomy or silent. As Layla passed us, I felt her eyes boring into me, and Jude stepped away, following her to their room.

Zack was the last to exit, hanging behind in the doorframe. "You okay?" he asked.

My frustration at his recent behavior boiled over into quippy resentment. "So you've decided I'm not the mole?" I said lightly.

His gruff tone eased for a moment. "I know you're not the mole. But since I don't know who is, until then, Dawn and I decided to limit who knows what." I was struck by the way he said "Dawn and I"—like the two of them together shared some position of authority. I wanted to remind him that he hadn't even joined us until recently, that despite his CIA training he had far less experience with the resistance than most of the people here. A brief thought flashed through my mind . . . the existence of a mole might actually help Zack climb higher within our ranks. A new enemy to fight, a threat that gave him license to push others out, to place himself in a position of trust and authority. Might it be worth it to Zack to fabricate this mole, to further his own interests? It was the kind of strategy my mother, the woman who trained him, might have employed. The moment I thought it, I dismissed it. Zack would never let someone die, would never let my mother go, for such petty, selfish reasons.

I stepped toward him, trying to lighten the mood, to bring us back to a happy place. "Maybe we can go out tonight?" I remembered the first few nights we'd spent here, the ones Dawn had told me to enjoy. I wished I could get a little bit of that joyful feeling back right now.

I saw the hint of a smile playing at his lips. "We could go out."

For a moment, all the stresses of the past few days began to slip away. "I'll go get ready."

It felt like playing dress-up—putting on a fancy outfit, stepping out onto the street with Zack, politely greeting all the Outcasts coming up to adore me. I'd always been playing a part, but now, especially, I felt the farce of it all. Trying to pretend like things were normal, while everything was falling apart.

As we walked up to Felipe's club, I tried to put all these concerns aside . . . but once we entered, the club seemed strangely morose. The music had gone silent, and the worried murmurs of the other clubgoers gave me pause. I found Felipe, pulled him aside. "What's happening?"

"You don't know?" he asked, incredulous.

"Tell me," I said. "Let me help."

His voice quavered. "We're under attack."

7

Felipe's words conjured images of missiles and bombers, but his phone conjured the truth. Our citadel of Redenção was just fine. My followers, his fellow Outcasts: they were in trouble.

He let me borrow his phone to read the disturbing headlines: "Clashes on the Streets of Redenção." A local Outcast pilgrim had been attacked only hours ago by true believers of the global, mainstream faith, left beaten and bloody. Then another in Spain, another in Japan. The incidents seemed to be increasing in number as more copycats popped up, committing more and more heinous crimes against Outcasts. The perpetrators were streaming their violence live on social media, receiving no Punishments for the assaults they were committing: visual confirmation of their "correctness" that inspired more and more others.

After a moment, Zack grew grim and pulled me into a cab—

driverless, thankfully, so we could talk freely. "Your mother's work?" he guessed.

"Maybe?" It would make sense. My mother could have sent instigators to accost Outcasts, to undermine my supposed power as a prophet. The more I thought about it, the more I was sure Zack was right, and those first assailants must have been CIA plants. But I doubted all the hundreds of copycats around the world could possibly be her doing. As long as ordinary people believed their violent actions were "righteous" in the eyes of Great Spirit, they would be just as safe as CIA agents taking pills—because they wouldn't feel guilty for hurting others in the name of their god. My guess was that most of these viral videos were simply normal people, who had seen the CIA instigators on the news and decided that this was what Great Spirit wanted them to do.

We were in the middle of a full-fledged holy war, the inevitable result of having two warring faiths. My mother had warned me as much—I just didn't expect her to kick off the violence. "I have to say something. I have to stop this."

"You could tell people to come to Redenção," Zack suggested.

"Millions of Outcasts all over the world? Even if they could get here, how am I going to protect them?" I pointed out, feeling helpless. Since it had gone public that we were staying here, Redenção's borders had been inundated enough. The flocks of pilgrims at the edges of town had now formed elaborate tent cities—poorly defended dwellings that left them vulnerable to exactly these kinds of attacks. "I'll tell them to defend themselves, I can do that much," I said.

"What if they go too far?" Zack warned. "Do you want a bunch of your followers committing murder, even in self-defense?"

My heart broke as I scrolled through images of people who'd been injured just for swearing an allegiance to me, and a seething anger burned inside of me. "I'd rather they live than their attackers."

Concern rose in Zack's voice. "You don't know what kind of people are following you. Maybe they'll start attacking in retaliation. You'd be giving them cover for who knows what kind of terrible crimes . . ."

"I'll tell them not to kill," I interrupted him.

"You can't control everything, and everyone," Zack insisted. "Whatever unintended effects your words might have, you're still responsible. You can only say so many things, people can only remember so many Proclamations. You need to be careful, make them count, make sure they help our cause."

I was incredulous. "You want me to just abandon the people who follow me? Only say the things that are helpful to the resistance, and screw any idiot who buys into what I say?"

"You're not a real prophet!" Zack said, a little louder than he intended to. "You're acting like this is a real religion you've created."

"It's real to them," I retorted. "I'm real to them. I have a responsibility . . ."

"And the moment you reveal the truth, they'll hate you. Your responsibility is to fix the world they live in, to give them freedom."

"And what if we can't? What if we don't?" I asked, finally voicing the fear that had been nagging at me for all these months. "We're not doing so well, I don't know if you've noticed. What's left of the resistance is living in a few thousand square feet of real estate. We've got no resources. The best thing we have going is this city, this military protecting us, and it's built on this religion I made up. And maybe that religion is fake, maybe I'm fake, but those people who believe in me are all we've got. And I'm going to protect them." As the passion in my voice rose, so did my conviction.

"So what, ten years from now, you're still going to be Prophet Grace?" His words reminded me of my mother's warning.

"It's better than being dead," I said definitively. "Than all of us being dead, than the prophets winning."

"You say 'the prophets' like you wouldn't be one of them. Like you wouldn't be the very thing we're fighting," he said with disgust.

My breath caught in my throat. "If you can't see the difference between me and them, I don't know why you're here."

"Some days, I'm not sure either," Zack said quietly.

His words filled me with a sadness and a rage I was sure would destroy him, if I let one word of it out. As tears welled in my eyes, I opened the door of the cab, which had stopped at a red light.

"Grace . . ." Zack said, a hint of apology in his voice, but I wasn't willing to listen. I hopped out, and I ran. Ran and ran until I found myself somewhere that felt safe. Somewhere that felt right.

I was at the gates of Redenção, guarded by my loyal soldiers. If I couldn't speak my truth to my boyfriend, at least I could speak it to the rest of the world.

"Tell General Feliciano to call the press," I told the nearest soldier, my voice sure and clear. "I have something I need to say."

8

As I approached the podium that General Feliciano had arranged for me, I trembled. Though Dawn had joined me to help write this speech, I was still nervous about actually saying any of it. Swarms of Outcast tents littered the expanse of land at the edges of the city, stretching as far as I could see in every direction. These were all followers of "Prophet Grace," strangers who had come from around the world to be close to me.

A whole makeshift economy had emerged out here—vendors selling goods, buskers playing music. The locals had jokingly begun referring to it as "New Redenção," a nickname I feared would turn into a postal designation if the pilgrims didn't find a more permanent place to stay soon.

As the crowd of unshowered devotees moved closer, their stench filled my nostrils, their voices muddling into a low hum. I was grateful for every single one of those soldiers, whose sheer muscle was all that protected me from the onslaught of adoration that made its way toward me.

True to her word, the general had called the press. A dozen reporters from in and outside of Redenção clustered near the podium, waiting for me to speak. I tried to put the massive crowd out of my mind as I stepped up to the microphone, hands crinkling the paper on which I'd written my speech. But though I was dying to, I didn't look at it. I couldn't seem like I was some stooge reading a prepared statement. I had to be strong, powerful, godlike.

So I tried, staring the reporters in the eye with a fiery vengeance. "Like you, I've seen the recent reports of violence against good people, attacked solely because they've chosen to follow me." So far my voice felt good, clear, confident. "I condemn these attacks, and I hope my fellow prophets will do the same. This is never what Great Spirit would have wanted.

"But I have one more thing to say. I want to ask my followers not to respond in kind. I want you to prove to the world that we are better. If not a single one of you lifts a finger in violence, the message will be heard loud and clear, around the world. We have moved past the Universal Theology to something better. This is the next step in religious evolution, and in time, the whole world will join us. The world will see the beauty in Outcasts, the power of your devotion. You'll be trailblazers—the ones who show the world the truth. Be patient, be kind, and keep the faith. Thank you."

As I finished, I saw a couple soldiers murmuring to each other. One finally turned to me, asking hesitantly in Portuguese, "So you want us to proselytize?"

I was confused. I hadn't said anything about proselytizing, but upon reflection, I could see how one might read that into my speech. "Not exactly," I responded nervously. "Hopefully you won't need to. Hopefully your actions will speak for themselves, to those who don't yet believe." But as he nodded, I realized that once again, my words had been heard differently than I'd intended. Rather than passively waiting for others to see the "truth" of our cause, my followers might actively try to convince their friends and family to join us. And I had a sinking feeling that their efforts might not go as smoothly as I'd hoped.

I looked to the mass of pilgrims, trying to glean information from the cacophonous sounds all around me. Would they heed my words? And then a familiar voice cut through the cheers, stinging and rich and terrifying. "Grace Luther. The Chosen One, never saw that coming."

I turned, trying to find the speaker, as the cadence of those words sent chills through me. Among the cavalcade of arms thrusting at me, I saw his face. The boy who was my first kiss, the one who'd nearly killed me. The sociopath I'd thought I'd seen murdered, only to discover him alive, incarcerated in West Virginia. The last person I expected to see among a throng of worshippers all the way in South America.

Ciaran. My skin crawled, and all of me shrank away from him, as he smiled wickedly. "I've missed you, Grace."

BOOK
FIVE

1

My mind swam. *Ciaran.* Visceral images shot through my mind: him pinning me down on our stargazing trip. Me just barely getting away. Zack emerging through the woods to incapacitate him. I'd survived Ciaran once, and I'd thought he was safely behind bars. What was he doing here? Last I knew, he'd been incarcerated by the prophets. How had he escaped from that Appalachian prison?

Ciaran moved toward me, slowly but confidently, like we were old friends. His sick grin made me feel like my insides had come loose. "You know why I'm here. Give this all up, and we can go our separate ways."

Throat dry, I choked out to the nearest soldier, "Him. Take him, capture him."

The soldier followed my gesturing finger with confusion. Why would I want to arrest this random, pious-looking young man? By the time she raised her weapon on Ciaran, he'd retreated into the crowd with a smirk. I stood on my tiptoes, trying to see where he'd gone, but he was concealed by the throng of worshippers.

"Find him," I choked out, and the soldier dutifully pressed herself into the crowd. Though I knew it was futile, I had to try to capture him. My body vibrated with rage, wanted to tear him limb from limb. I remembered the last time I'd felt this way— the time I'd watched a crowd devour Prophet Joshua, the man I'd urged them to hate. My rage could destroy people now, if I wanted it to. This time, would I let it?

The soldier returned a few minutes later, shaking her head regretfully. "I can't find him. I'm so sorry, Prophet."

"It's okay," I told her, eyes still scanning the crowd. I noticed two other faces watching me, with normal, non-Outcast features and strangely cool expressions. They both looked vaguely familiar, but I couldn't place them. Could I also have seen them in that prison in West Virginia? "Let's head back in," I said, trying to project a confidence and authority I no longer felt.

As soon as we were within the city limits, I retreated to our apartment, where Zack was the first person I encountered. He flew toward me in a quiet rage. "I can't believe you went out there and spoke without talking to me."

"I talked to Dawn," I said, dismissive. I didn't have time for Zack's admonishments right now.

"So my opinion doesn't matter?" Zack asked.

I found anger spilling out of me. "Your *opinion* mainly seems to be that I don't know what I'm doing."

"Because you don't!" he blurted out.

"I don't?" I asked, incredulous.

He backed into a defensive stance. "You're eighteen, you remember that, right? You have no life experience, you don't even have a college degree . . ."

"Oh, and with your extra few years of wisdom, you should be the boss of me?" I shot back.

"At least you should be asking for my help. You should have let me come to the compound in Turkey . . ."

"That rescue mission was a success . . ." I reminded him.

"People died!" he retorted in a way that cut a little too deep. "You really don't see how you're in over your head? It's infuriating, watching you make all these novice mistakes . . ."

"Everybody makes mistakes," I insisted, my resentment growing with each word. "You think you wouldn't make plenty if you were in my shoes? You've *made* plenty . . . Working for my mother?"

He didn't even flinch. "You're right, that was a mistake, one I learned from. You haven't had any time to learn from your mistakes . . ."

"Maybe this was a mistake," I said quietly, and I felt those few simple words shattering everything.

Zack seemed stunned. "Us. You think that was a mistake?"

Now that it was out in the open, everything came tumbling out of me. "Things have changed. You've noticed that, right?"

He nodded but didn't say anything.

"What is it? Is it just . . ." I couldn't bear to say *my appearance*.

Zack guessed what I meant and immediately shook his head. "You're as beautiful to me as you always have been."

I wanted so badly to believe him. "You say that, but I don't know if you mean it. It's like suddenly you want to criticize everything about me except my appearance. Like you're working so hard to be the good guy and not abandon me that you're finding all these other things wrong with me."

Zack took that in. "I didn't mean to criticize you, I was just trying to help you, to help the resistance. You . . . I think you're amazing."

"I didn't know that," I said softly.

Zack moved toward me, brushing a few sprigs of hair out of my face. "Well, I do. And yeah, we've been going through some tough times lately. Saving the world, that's pretty stressful. But we'll get through it."

Looking at Zack, I remembered how safe he'd once made me feel. But now he felt like an obstacle, like he'd taken the place of that nasty voice in the back of my head. Now, he was the one whispering all the things that made me doubt myself. Perhaps I'd have to learn to ignore him, the way I'd learned to ignore my old mechanical foe.

I tried to be put at ease by his smile. "I need you to support me. Let me back in that room."

He hesitated. "I thought you wanted to keep yourself out, to prove your innocence."

I summoned my strength. "I want to talk to everyone."

Though his expression conveyed a mountain of reservations, I realized I no longer needed his permission, or Dawn's. I'd spent all this time following the orders of a resistance that barely existed anymore. The power we had here in Redenção was mine, and wielding it was my responsibility. And if we were going to rid this city of Ciaran, I was going to need all the help I could get.

With Zack at my side, I entered the boardroom to find my friends whispering their wartime secrets. Eyes turned suspiciously toward me as usual, but I held my ground. "Ciaran's back." I could hear the gravity and conviction in my voice. I was speaking more like a leader now, less like the timid little girl who didn't know if she belonged.

Dawn's eyebrows furrowed. "Back?"

"I just saw him here, outside the gates of Redenção."

Jude stood, confused. "The sociopath kid from that prison in West Virginia? Why would he be here?"

My lack of additional knowledge left me feeling despair. "I don't know."

Dawn hesitantly volunteered, "I heard there was a breakout from that facility a few days ago." So perhaps those other faces I'd half recognized had been Ciaran's cellmates after all.

I looked to Dr. Marko, who'd once been imprisoned in that very place. "How could they have made it outside the perimeter without help? And how could they have gotten all the way here?"

"Well, call me crazy, but I think they had help," Dr. Marko said matter-of-factly.

The truth washed over me like a bitter wave. "Esther." My mother was using her prisoners as a resource. She'd unleashed my attempted rapist on Redenção as a last-ditch attempt to bring me in. I felt sick to my stomach, remembering the cryptic message Ciaran had delivered. This was her way of hurting me, of trying to coerce me into doing what she wanted—joining up with her.

"I told you we should have killed her," Layla muttered. I ignored her—I wasn't going to let her faze me.

"We'll develop a strategy," Zack promised me.

I felt my anger hardening into resolve. "We need to find them, before they hurt anyone else. We need to get those soldiers searching through every last tent out there."

Dawn nodded approvingly. "Muster your army, start the search. We'll let you know if we need anything else."

"I can help here," I insisted. Since I knew I wasn't the mole, I worried that the real mole might have more power without me present.

It was Dawn who gently said, "We haven't had any more breaches since you stepped aside. I think it's best you stay away for now." The others averted their eyes but cautiously nodded in agreement.

Their polite dismissal stung. I wanted so badly to argue my value, to force everyone here to listen to my ideas. But I knew if people here suspected me of being a mole, I wouldn't be much use. "Fine," I said, heading out to continue my self-exile, feeling the sting of isolation. I might have all the power in Redenção, but still . . . I was on one side of that door, and all my friends were on the other.

Well, not all of them. As I retreated into the hall, Macy crossed my path, munching on a bowl of cereal she'd just poured herself. "Isn't it a little late for cereal?" I joked. Our relationship had remained tense since arriving here, and I took any opportunity I could find to rebuild rapport.

Macy shrugged. "They always eat dinner in there, planning secret resistance things. I don't want to bother them, so I make do."

I smiled, trying to build a bridge between us. "Yeah, I guess we're in the same club."

Macy rolled her eyes. "Seriously? I'm out here because I'm not important and nobody cares about me. You're not in there because you're *so important*, everything would *fall apart* without you."

"I'm out here because my mom set me up," I said hotly. "That's probably why she came here in the first place—to make everyone suspicious of me."

Macy's anger eased for a moment. "Yeah, I'm sorry to hear about the evil mom. Your life got weird."

I couldn't help but laugh. "Yeah, pretty weird."

There was a moment of tense silence, until Macy offered, "All I'm saying is, it's no fun, watching all the drama and not being able to do anything to help."

"I'm feeling pretty helpless myself right now," I admitted. "I keep waiting for them to catch the real mole, so I can go back in there and do something again."

"That's dumb. Look, I've just been doing the watching-from-the-outside-and-eating-cereal thing, but from what I've seen, nothing interesting really happens in that little dining room. Everything that's actually helped? It's been you. And no, I haven't always agreed with you, you know, lying your butt off to everyone, but at least it's working. And if you're going to perpetrate this whole stupid hoax, you should keep making it work."

"Thanks," I said, taking that in. Macy was right. Everyone else could busy themselves with their battle plans. The real war was happening right now, outside the gates of Redenção, and I needed to go lead that fight.

Though the general was hesitant to label Ciaran as a suspect without any hard evidence, she agreed to distribute pictures of the escaped inmates to news outlets and circulate hard copies throughout the city. Anyone who spotted them was instructed to notify a patrolling soldier immediately.

"Bring them in by any means necessary," I told General Feliciano, unable to contain the venom in my voice. "Kill them if you have to. These are agents of the devil."

In her expression I saw hesitation—she'd never heard anything this violent from me before. "We'll comb the beach," she tentatively promised me. "Inspect every person. It should only take a few days."

But we didn't have a few days. Early the next morning, I awoke to a muted phone call from the general. "Prophet, I wanted you to be the first to know, before it hit the news."

Her grave tone gave me chills. "What happened?"

"There's been another incident."

I flew down to the barracks, determined to see for myself, but the general wouldn't let me anywhere near the pilgrim camps.

"It's not safe right now, Prophet."

I nodded, willing to trust her judgment, as a small council of Redenção's leaders, including the mayor, arrived to assess the situation. "We need to solve this, and solve it now," he said, pacing the room with his limping gait.

The general showed us footage taken by her soldiers, which sent my stomach into knots. The first few videos were taken at night, in the midst of chaos—pilgrims bloody and screaming for help. As the footage rolled on, the room fell into a desperate kind of silence.

"What is this?" I breathed.

"Late, while everyone was sleeping. Two dozen killed, no one saw the attackers. Everyone is pretty shaken."

I swallowed my horror. The scale was far worse than any of the previous attacks. More than twenty people killed, all vulnerable pilgrims with no permanent housing. Terrifying the thousands more still sleeping exposed in their tents. That was the point: to bring fear to the camp, to drive away my supporters.

"You haven't found any of the perpetrators?" I asked. "Anyone whose picture I sent you yesterday?"

The general shook her head mournfully. "We searched the area thoroughly, but never found them."

I had a hunch they must have taken downers—the same kind of drugs I'd used last year to see Macy in the Outcast Ward—and infiltrated the camp disguised as unrecognizable Outcasts.

But Ciaran had brazenly shown me his true face only the day before . . . why take that risk?

He wanted me to know it was him. He was trying to bait me . . . or rather, my mother was. She'd crafted a situation she knew would enrage me, in order to make me act the way a prophet never would, to prove to my followers that I was no better than Prophet Joshua or any of the others. I couldn't fall into her trap. But I couldn't let my followers die either.

"Maybe they won't return," the mayor said hopefully.

I shook my head, knowing Ciaran, and my mother. "They'll be back tonight, and every night. There must be some other way to protect people. Soldiers patrolling . . ."

"There were soldiers patrolling last night . . ." the general reminded me.

"And it didn't help," I finished for her. I tried to think of anywhere else we could put the pilgrims. "Could we keep them somewhere secure, away from the rest of the city. Like the prison even . . . ?"

As much as I dreaded the idea of forcing my followers into a prison, I dreaded the forlorn general's response more. "There isn't enough room for all of them," she said apologetically. "We're overfull as it is." I'd seen that firsthand, when I'd visited my mother. I knew jail capacities had been greatly reduced since the Revelations, even in Outcast areas, so having a military presence patrolling for petty crimes must have sent local prison populations skyrocketing.

I tried to think of any other option. "We could ask them to find shelter away from the city. At least for a little while."

The general raised an eyebrow. "You can try."

I nodded, definitive. "Take me outside." I silenced her caution with a firm stare, and she reluctantly gathered a posse of troops to protect me: three times as many as usual. Though I assumed Ciaran and his friends weren't reckless enough to strike during the day, I still broke into a cold sweat as we stepped outside the gates, nervous knowing he might be lurking somewhere in this crowd.

As I exited, the pilgrims flocked to me with newly panicked faces. Their worshipfulness had turned to desperation—hoping I'd ease their fears, take away their pain, and promise that nothing like this would ever happen to them again. I wished I could make promises like that. I'd never wished more that I was telling the truth, that I could use some supernatural power to protect everyone.

Thankfully, I noticed the crowd had thinned and was thinning further. A few skeptical faces, loaded up with bags, gave me the hint that perhaps last night's brutal attack had already convinced some of the message I was here to send: they needed to leave, now.

It seemed that this tragedy had caused people to question their faith in me. I wanted so badly to apologize and admit that they were right. But before I could reach out to any of the retreating pilgrims, I was stopped by a young grieving Outcast mother: an American about a decade older than me, whose young child had been killed in the attack.

The moment she saw me, she collapsed at my feet, asking, "Why, why?"

Her son's murder had been graphic, from what I'd seen. Not that there was much to see. By the time the cameras reached him, there was hardly anything left of his face. I cried along with her, taking in her pain, feeling the weight of my own responsibility for that death. "I'm sorry," I whispered as I held her.

"He was so smart," she told me, pride still beaming in her eyes. "He already knew his times tables. He had to go to the Outcast school back in Florida because that's all that would take him, but I knew he was meant for great things."

"I know he was," I said, the guilt building up inside of me.

She looked at me with a kind of desperate hope. "Maybe he was meant for this. To be a martyr for you." My stomach sank hearing her twisted logic. I knew she was grasping for meaning after such a tragedy, trying to give her son a purpose when all purpose had been taken away from him. I hated the role I had to play to give her some kind of peace.

I wouldn't play it. "No," I said, shaking my head. "He should have done so much more. I'm so sorry for your loss." The shame burned inside of me, that someone so young and innocent had died because his mother had made the fatal mistake of believing in me. And because *my* mother was using this child's death to pull on my heartstrings like a puppeteer.

The grieving woman grasped my hand, held my gaze. "We won't leave, even now. You told us to have faith, and we do."

"No!" I said, almost yelling it. "You have to go. Find somewhere safe, away from the city."

She shook her head, confused. "If we go, what message does that send to the rest of the world? That we're afraid? Then my son's death is for nothing."

I squeezed her hands. "Your son's death is a warning, saving others. And you live another day to do the work of Great

Spirit. Please. Go somewhere safe. It's what Great Spirit wants for you."

"But my son's soul is here," she whispered. "I can't go, not yet."

I tried to smile, reassure her. "Hey, I'm a prophet, right? You have to listen to what I say. Please, tell everyone, that's what I want you to do, okay? Get out of here."

She nodded but seemed unconvinced. My stomach tied itself into knots as I wondered . . . would I be able to keep any of these people safe?

As I worked my way through the collection of mourners, my hopes dwindled. While some had taken the attack as a sign to abandon their faith, for others the violence had only strengthened their resolve, to prove their piety in the face of danger. Though I urged people to leave, they seemed to think this was some kind of test, that I was asking them to show their loyalty by putting themselves in harm's way. As I looked out at the vast expanse of tents that remained in place, all those people stubbornly strewn across the beach, I was filled with dread . . . tonight there would be a lot of people in danger.

4

When I returned to the barracks, my friends were waiting for me, faces grim—by now, these new attacks had become public. "What's the plan?" Dawn asked. It was the first time she'd looked to me as a real source of leadership, and my stomach tightened. The truth was, I had no plan. And it sounded like they didn't either.

I thought of all the innocent souls waiting outside, vulnerable, praying to a prophet who couldn't help them. "The general's going to send another patrol out tonight . . ."

"Fat lot of good they did last night," Zack grumbled.

"I think Ciaran and the other sociopaths are blending in with the crowd," I explained. "My mother must have given them some downers."

Layla tentatively suggested, "We have some of those, too, don't we?"

Jude bravely sparked to the idea. "Cops in plainclothes. I'll do it."

Dr. Marko pointed to Jude and Layla. "You're the only ones who can. The drugs that cause Punishment won't work on the rest of us, now that our nanotech's been removed. Non-Outcasts will stick out."

"At least that crap in our brains is useful for something," Jude muttered.

Layla clearly didn't love this plan. "You want me to go into danger again?"

"They're not singling you out . . ." Jude said gently.

Layla was not calmed. "My family has suffered enough . . ."

"I'll go," Zack interrupted.

"You can't," Dawn said, exasperated.

"Yes, I can," he insisted, blush rising in his cheeks. "That crap's still in my head, too."

I was deeply confused. "No, it isn't. I watched you breathe in that gas that removed it."

Zack seemed to shrink, as if trying to disappear. "I didn't actually inhale it. I just pretended."

"Why on earth would you do that?" Dawn asked, echoing the confusion and apprehension of the rest of the room.

Zack looked at me, now beet red. "I'll explain later. Just . . . I can help now."

Irene, usually so quiet, poked her head up to speak. "I'm sorry, don't we have a mole? Does anyone else think this seems a little suspicious?" I had to admit, I shared her concerns.

"If he had a good reason, he should say it," Jude said, gently prodding.

Zack hesitated, then admitted, "I saw what happened to the rest of you, the way your appearances changed, and not always for the better. I didn't want to have that happen to me."

Layla snorted. "Really? You did this because you are vain?" Her laughter lightened the mood a bit—it had been a long time since any of us had laughed.

Zack grew irritated, heading for the door. "I said I'd help. Let me know when we have a plan, and I'll go in with you."

As he stepped out, Irene looked to the rest of us. "I know I'm not a fighter, but I can help, too."

Dawn shook her head. "No way."

Irene seemed offended. "You put yourself in danger all the time . . ."

"No!" Dawn interrupted. I knew she'd already lost her first wife—she wasn't willing to lose another.

As everyone else went silent, watching their confrontation, I said carefully, "I'll go, too."

Dawn turned her ire on me. "Have you all gone crazy? No. You don't have a way to disguise yourself, Grace, and you are too valuable to lose."

I held my voice steady. "I'm the best distraction. If all eyes are on me, no one will be looking for you."

"Absolutely not," Dawn insisted.

"You don't get to tell me no," I said forcefully. "You're the ranking leader of the resistance, but this isn't the resistance anymore. There isn't some grand organization making the rules . . . it's just *us*. Making these decisions together. And I say, I'm going."

Irene tentatively piped in, "What she said."

Dawn stared at me, disbelieving, then turned to her wife. "You better stay alive. Both of you."

I nodded, determined to make sure we did. We didn't have any lives left to spare.

found Zack sequestered in our room, changing clothes. As I entered, I hesitantly gestured to his six-pack, trying to lighten the mood. "Hey, at least it worked, right? No one's going to say you got any less attractive."

Zack put his shirt on, embarrassed. "You're going to make fun of me, too?"

"I will until you give me an explanation," I said. "Since when do you care what you look like?"

"Doesn't everyone care?" he deflected. "Isn't that the world we live in?"

I wasn't going to let him off that easy. "You were a badass CIA agent. Since when are you insecure?"

"Maybe since I stopped being a badass CIA agent and became Prophet Grace's boyfriend," he spat back.

I tried to maintain my composure, a little stung. "I didn't realize that was such a terrible fate."

His eyes filled with sadness, and he suddenly seemed

vulnerable, like a stiff breeze would knock him over. "Do you know how emasculating it is, to be defined only by your famous girlfriend? To lose all sense of yourself, any sense of your own identity?"

Piece by piece, his words filled in the gaps of a puzzle, painted an image. "So what, you want me to be small, so you can feel big?" I stammered. "I thought you were criticizing me because there was something wrong with me. But you just felt bad about yourself, and you needed someone to feel better than?"

"No," he protested. "It's not like that at all. You're wonderful . . . I never meant to make you feel like there was anything wrong with you. I just worry, if I'm not doing anything useful, what am I to you?"

I'd been so caught up in my own insecurities about our relationship, I hadn't even considered Zack might have his own. "You mean you were worried *I'd* leave *you*?" It didn't even seem possible that handsome, confident, brave Zack would worry that he might not measure up.

My shock seemed to reassure him. "You're saying I shouldn't be worried?"

I remembered all the illicit thoughts I'd been having of Jude, the insecurities I still harbored about our relationship. There was a part of me that was still so resentful of Zack, for all the times he'd failed to have my back. But knowing that he had his own fears was a strange kind of comfort. Maybe, if he put aside his, and I put aside mine, we could reshape this relationship into something even stronger. So I shook my head. "You've got nothing to worry about."

He leaned in and kissed me. "I love you." I let all my worries fall away. Let his soothing words and kind eyes sweep me back into our romance. Let myself fall into it like a soft pillow, luxuriate in its comfort.

"I love you, too." Then I added, honestly, "And I'm worried about you, going out into that crowd in disguise."

Zack brushed me off, happy to be back in badass hero mode. "I've taken on Ciaran once, I think I can handle him again."

"Okay," I said, the nervousness building inside of me. Maybe I was playing right into Ciaran's hands, into my mother's hands, by facing down Ciaran myself. But I wasn't willing to sit idly on the sidelines. I was going to find that monster, and I was going to put him back in a cell, where he belonged. Ciaran was a message from my mother, and I was determined to send one back. If she wanted to hurt anyone else, she'd have to go through me first.

inally! Do you know how bored I've been?" Macy asked as we stepped out into the open, flanked by a few dozen soldiers. When she'd gotten wind of our plan, she'd eagerly volunteered to use her status as a beloved guru of Prophet Grace to help with my distraction.

"Don't get too excited. You might get murdered," I muttered back.

"But I probably won't," Macy contended, undeterred. "Look, I already helped spread your lies, not knowing they were lies. I want to do something good for the resistance, you know, on purpose."

"You're doing great," I told her, and she beamed.

"I would have made a really kickass prophet though, right? You're a decent one, so I trust your opinion."

"You would have been—you are—the best," I promised her. "If I could have recruited you as a guru by telling you the truth, I would have wanted you to do everything exactly the same."

Macy smiled, touched—the tension between us finally seemed to be easing.

As we surveyed the scene, I was disappointed to discover that the tent city was just as large as when I'd left it this morning—larger even, perhaps, as new pilgrims seemed to be arriving even now. Last night's attacks had left a buzz in the air; candles burned in vigil and prayer all around the city. Everyone was on edge, waiting, knowing as well as I did that the violence was far from over.

I scanned the crowd, hoping I could spot my friends—Zack, Jude, Layla, and Irene. They'd gone out ahead of me, in disguise, to mingle with the Outcasts. But those disguises were working a little too well; I didn't recognize a single face among the ones staring at me.

"Hello, friends," I called out to the assembled pilgrims. "We'll be here with you tonight, and every night. I'm going to make sure that you stay safe." Macy nodded along, playing her part with solemnity.

I knew if Ciaran was here somewhere, my words would goad him. There was nothing my mother wanted more than to see me break my promises.

"All clear so far." I turned, surprised to see an Outcast woman standing next to me—Layla, in disguise. She barely made eye contact; she was here for the mission and nothing more.

I, however, saw an opportunity to try to repair our friendship. "Thanks," I said tentatively. "And thanks for talking to me again."

She hesitated, then admitted, "You have been putting yourself in danger, too. I know that."

I tried to tread carefully, in case she was softening toward me. "If you want to keep blaming me, I'll understand."

I sensed something inside her harden, just a little. "I don't blame you for my father's death. I blame you for becoming a prophet to begin with."

"I didn't do it on purpose. I didn't want this," I insisted, getting defensive. "I was just trying to get leverage, to free all of you . . ."

Layla pushed back. "You did not think any of it through. If we wanted to create a fake prophet, do you not think we had better options? But now it must be you, and all of our lives depend on you."

"And I screw up a lot," I finished for her.

She shrugged. "You screw up a normal amount. You are just a child."

The more people told me I didn't know what I was doing, the more I wanted to show them that I did. "None of us know what we're doing. You don't, Dawn doesn't. We're all making mistakes. I'm doing the best I can."

"Jude certainly thinks so," she said with a kind of derision that made me unwittingly hopeful. Was she jealous? Was Jude still in love with me? In an instant, a fantasy of him leaving Layla and confessing his love for me flashed through my mind. But I let it go just as quickly. Jude was Layla's, and Zack was mine. Our group had enough rifts already; I didn't need to go adding any more.

I followed Layla's gaze across the expanse in front of us and spotted an Outcast-faced Jude, near the outskirts of the camp, roving through tents. The sight of his face, even in its temporarily mangled form, made my heart beat a little faster. I still loved him, I had to admit that to myself. But more than anything, I wanted him to be happy, and from what I could tell, Layla made him happy. I put on a smile. "Maybe Ciaran and his friends won't come out tonight after all."

Layla smiled back, reassuring. "If they do not, we will come back tomorrow. And the next day."

"Thank you." I felt myself tearing up, looking around at this camp; I was grateful that even if I couldn't protect these people with any kind of supernatural magic, my friends were keeping them safe.

But that relief was broken just as quickly by a scream echoing across the camp—from the place I'd just seen Jude patrolling. Heads turned, attention converging on the sound, trying to see what was happening. Layla and I exchanged a wordless look—perhaps we'd spoken too soon.

I left Macy behind as we ran toward the shouting, fighting against the ever-growing tide of pilgrims running away from it. The soldiers who'd been assigned to protect me sprinted after us, trying to keep pace as I pushed through the crowd.

As we approached the commotion, I discovered a ring of people keeping their distance from an Outcast wielding a bloody knife. The man looked at me, and the twinkle in his eyes told me exactly who it was: Ciaran, in Outcast form. He was filled with bloodlust, brought alive by the excitement of the violence he was committing.

My eyes roved to find his victim: a young girl cowering on the fringes of the circle, clutching her bleeding arm. Though her fear was palpable, her wounds seemed to be superficial. Ciaran hadn't killed anyone yet tonight.

"Everyone, work together to restrain him!" I heard someone shouting. I was relieved to discover the voice belonged to Jude; he was already here, on the scene, helping to wield the crowd against my mother's army.

However, Jude's request was barely needed; clearly, this group was ready to fight back. They drew around Ciaran in a tight circle, closing him in. The soldiers finally caught up with us, raising their rifles, prepared to arrest Ciaran. I breathed a sigh of relief as they moved in—everything seemed to be under control.

But Ciaran still had a devilish smile on his face, one that gave me chills. A smile that didn't subside even as he raised his hands in defeat, let the soldiers approach him . . . Soon enough, I figured out why he was so confident. While the soldiers were focused on Ciaran, another man, disguised as a pilgrim, darted out of the crowd and tased the back of one soldier's neck.

It all happened in a flash. The crowd of pilgrims backed away, startled, opening a path for Ciaran to escape. The soldiers ran after him, as Jude jumped to tackle the Taser-wielding sociopath. As Jude and his opponent struggled, a third assailant shot out of the crowd, brandishing his own Taser.

"Jude, look out!" I cried, but not quickly enough. The two men together subdued Jude, then grabbed him by the arms and began dragging him away.

"No!" I cried out, running after Jude, Layla trailing behind me. I knew I was no physical match for any of these people, but I was desperate to do something, anything. "Stop them!" I cried out to the pilgrims around me. But for the first time in a long time, my words had no impact. I had promised to keep these people safe, and I had failed. They were terrified. I glanced over at Layla, who shared my horror. "Jude!" I cried into the night, feeling helpless.

But not hopeless. As the two men holding Jude pushed their way through the crowd, I sprinted after them doggedly, lungs burning; I'd never run faster in my life, desperate with adrenaline, using my wiry frame to duck through smaller openings in the throng that these soldiers couldn't break through. Surely one of them would catch up soon, would come to Jude's aid.

As the crowd thinned into an open expanse, I lingered on its edges, my whole body vibrating with panic and rage. This is what Ciaran wanted, I was sure of it—to lure me out beyond where I was protected. They must have targeted Jude specifically . . . was there anyone else in our group I'd risk myself for like this? Again, I wanted to fall for my mother's trap. It killed me to let Jude out of my sight. But as I hesitated with indecision, Jude faded away into the night.

It felt like an eternity but must have only been a minute before three soldiers ran up next to me, Layla right behind them, the grief and fury on her face mirroring mine. "They went that way!" I told them, pointing, and they hurried off into the darkness. But already, I knew it would be too late. Jude was gone. And I had no idea how to get him back.

7

As we reconvened in the living room of our apartment, Jude's absence sent a pall over the group. Macy paced anxiously, distraught that her first foray into resistance work had gone so poorly. In the corner, Layla was inconsolable, averting her eyes from me. Right after we'd managed to find some common ground, did she blame me for the loss of another of her loved ones? "We have to find him," she sputtered.

"We will," Dr. Marko promised, trying to soothe the room's fears.

"There *is* one way to save Jude," Dawn said tentatively, looking to Irene.

"How?" I asked, clinging to a tiny bit of hope.

Irene hesitated, then handed me a printout. "An anonymous email address sent me this message. Though it doesn't feel that anonymous to me."

I took the note, and Zack read it over my shoulder: "'This is your last chance to join us.'"

An icy chill went through me. "It's from my mother, isn't it?"

"She still thinks she can convince you to defect?" Zack asked, incredulous.

"She's right," I said quietly. "She has Jude, I have to do what she says." The room filled with angry stares. I grew defensive, insisting, "I can find a way to trick her, to save him, I know I can . . ."

". . . Or that's exactly what she'll expect you to do," Dr. Marko said pointedly.

Zack looked at me with sharp eyes. "We've got this handled, Grace."

I shook my head, refusing to be exiled right now. "It's Jude. I'm not sitting on the sidelines for this one. I've proven I'm not the mole by now, haven't I?"

"Maybe. Maybe not," Zack said stiffly. The others saw the tension rising between us and fell silent, watching.

"You still suspect me?" I asked incredulously. "You."

"I didn't say that," he said gruffly.

"Then what, you're just jealous because it's Jude?" I asked hotly.

The whole room went silent, and Zack's face grew red, his voice firm. "You have two options, Grace. You can stand here and argue with us, which will waste time, time Jude might not have. Or you can let us make a plan to find your friend."

"Without me?" I said, fury rising. "You don't get to decide that." I wasn't willing to accept Zack's word as gospel; I wanted to force my way back into the resistance's inner circle and find a way to help my friend. I looked around the room helplessly but could find no allies—it wasn't just Zack who wanted me out. Even Macy shrugged, no idea how to defend me. Maybe it wouldn't matter, anyway; the truth was I didn't have any bulletproof plans up my sleeve.

"We'll find him, I promise," Zack said, softening, but my anger toward him still felt hard, sharp, biting. These walls he was putting up, keeping me out, were making it grow. I felt like if that anger grew large enough, I'd find a way to claw out of the cage he was putting me in.

"You'd better find him," I snarled, hearing a threat in my voice I hadn't put there on purpose.

Zack heard it as well and nodded solemnly. "Don't worry. You can trust us." I might have trusted the rest of them, but in that moment I didn't trust him. I felt betrayed . . . he was supposed to be the one who had my back. How could this be the same man I'd kissed in the Amazon, the same one I'd adventured with around Redenção? This Zack seemed like a stranger to me.

It felt like my whole world was being swallowed up. Jude, the one person who'd always been on my side, was missing, and there was nothing I could do about it. Zack, my closest ally, was the one shutting me out. I felt deeply powerless. Made worse because on the surface, I had unlimited power. I could control everything and everyone except the people I actually cared about.

As I stepped out of the dining room, Layla followed, pulling me aside. "I want to save him as much as you do," she said softly.

A promise, a thank-you, an apology, wrapped into one simple statement of fact.

I hugged her as tears streamed down both our faces. All anger and competition forgotten, replaced by grief and fear. I'd lost Jude so many times. I didn't know if I could bear to do it for good.

8

After several hours of half-sleep, I awoke in my own bed, alone. After all our fighting recently, I'd wanted so badly to find Zack at my side; his absence unnerved me, as did the buzzing voices coming from the floor below.

I couldn't take it anymore. I had to know what was going on. Tentatively, I crept downstairs, hoping I could overhear something useful. I lurked outside the boardroom, but I couldn't make out anything until Zack exited, expression drawn. From the sliver of the room I could see through the open door, the mood of the rest of the group was just as bleak. When Zack caught sight of me, he went pale. "I didn't realize you were up."

"I couldn't sleep. What's happening?" I asked, worried.

Zack did his best to keep his voice calm. "Grace, I need you to stay out of this."

His bossiness infuriated me. "My friend is missing . . ."

"Is he really just your friend?" Zack snapped.

I was taken by surprise. Zack's accusation seemed to

be coming out of nowhere. "Of course he's just a friend. I mean, we had a little thing, you know that, but that was ages ago . . ."

But Zack didn't seem convinced. "You don't have any feelings for him now?"

I was confused, trying to keep up with what was happening inside his head. "Where is this coming from? Why does this even matter, he's missing . . ."

Zack's voice cracked a little, as he tried not to get too upset. "And you think it's a coincidence that your mother knew to pick him? That he's the one she knew you couldn't handle losing?" Jude and not Zack, that was what he meant. Why he'd chosen now to get his panties in a knot about it, I had no idea.

But I was determined to calm him down. "I don't know why she picked him. Maybe she didn't pick anyone, maybe Ciaran just grabbed the first one of us he found." My words were doing nothing to change the hurt and angry expression on Zack's face. "Look, it doesn't matter, I want to help." Frustrated, I pushed past him. If Zack wasn't taking my side, maybe someone else would.

But as I entered the boardroom, I saw the same suspicious looks from everyone inside. "It's not a good time right now," Layla stammered, and I saw she was comforting a sobbing Irene.

I had a sick feeling in my stomach. "Where's Dawn?" I asked, nervous.

The room went silent, hesitant. "We sent her in as a hostage negotiator," Layla said gravely. "It didn't go well."

I felt lost, adrift. I didn't know what we would do without Dawn. "Didn't . . . is she . . . ?"

"Alive," Dr. Marko said quickly. "As far as we can tell, she's being held captive, with Jude."

"So now we have to find another way to get them out," Zack said, tone still terse. I uncomfortably felt all eyes monitoring me.

I shook my head. "You think Ciaran's going to be a rational negotiator? Or my mother? I could have told you that, if you'd thought to ask me. I know them better than anyone, I should be in here, I should be helping . . ."

"We don't need your help," Layla said firmly. I looked to the others for support, but got none. It was like they were all ganging up on me, for no apparent reason.

"Just trust us, Grace," Zack urged me.

I turned on him, angry. "Why would I trust you, when you don't trust me?"

"Because you're the mole!" Zack shouted.

"Zack . . ." Irene warned, as the whole room tensed.

"I'm not the mole!" I said, deeply offended. But as I looked around the room, my stomach curdled as I realized Zack wasn't the only one who thought so. "You all think I'm sending information back to my mother, don't you?"

Everyone looked at one another. With Dawn gone, there seemed to be confusion over who was in charge, who to take orders from. Finally, Dr. Marko cleared his throat. "Well, you might be."

I was filled with confusion and indignation. Sweet Dr. Marko was the last person I'd expected to lead the charge against me. "I'm innocent," I repeated. "You know me. I swear to you, I'm not betraying our cause, I would never do that."

"I know you wouldn't," Marko said gently. "But Zack's right. You're still the mole."

I looked at the others, trying to make sense of what he was saying. "What are you talking about?"

"Your mother's visit here had a purpose. At first we thought she was trying to recruit you. But eventually we realized, she didn't need to. Esther doesn't need your permission to see what you see, to hear what you hear, to know what you know."

The horror of it engulfed me, as I suddenly realized the truth. "She put something in my head again." I remembered the flash drive she'd given me, to put in the computer. Its purpose hadn't been to show me some stupid Excel documents . . . she'd wanted me to touch it, to infect myself with whatever microscopic technology had covered the surface of the drive. We hadn't needed to worry about a computer virus. We needed to worry about one that would infect my head.

Everyone's nervous glances in my direction suddenly made sense. I hated myself for not seeing it earlier, for not expecting something like this from my mother after everything else she'd done.

"A transmitter," Marko explained. "She knows all your thoughts."

"*All of them*," Zack said pointedly, and the way he said it I realized . . . my friends must have gotten access to them somehow. That was why he'd confronted me like that in the hallway. Everything I'd been feeling for Jude, all my doubts about Zack . . .

My voice cracked. "And so do all of you now."

Layla jumped in. "Please don't ask us too many questions.

Everything you're thinking right now is still being sent back to your mother."

I nodded, as new waves of revulsion crashed over me moment by moment, remembering a million thoughts I never would have wanted Layla to hear, or Zack, or Jude. That was how Ciaran had found us in the crowd . . . my mother had seen through my eyes to pinpoint everyone's locations. That was why he'd taken Jude, because she knew the depth of my feelings for him, that I'd do anything to save him.

I hazarded a glance at Zack, and my heart broke to see his expression. Deep shame, and anger, to know every terrible thing I'd thought about him. Every not so terrible thing I'd thought about another man. I remembered back in the Amazon, how badly I'd wanted to see through his eyes, to know what he thought of me. But maybe I was the lucky one. Zack had gotten a glimpse, and it had nearly broken him.

"Just get Jude back," I told them. "I'll stay out of it."

I fled the boardroom in deep despair. I wondered if my mother could see the humiliation, the burning anger inside of me. The same way she'd seen all my deepest, most embarrassing desires, even watched me have sex. But I knew then, as certain as if I was reading *her* thoughts—she wasn't going to stop unless I stopped her myself. And with no way to make a plan that would surprise her, and friends who couldn't let me help, it seemed like we were doomed to fail.

9

While my friends were working on a plan I wasn't allowed to know about, I wallowed in my frustration. I wanted so badly to help and hated that I couldn't. I was more aware than ever of my idle fantasies about Jude, the wistful, yearning feelings that overtook me when his face crossed my mind . . . knowing all too well that everyone I cared about would see them, too. Would know all the secret desires I harbored about a man who might not survive the night.

I tried to ignore the slamming doors and heated voices downstairs by distracting myself the way I always did: by seeing what people were saying about me online. But after these most recent attacks, praise was hard to find amid the heaps of criticism. I was failing to protect my followers, and faith in me was waning. Even my old friend Eduardo Sousa was expressing skepticism: maybe I was just some kid, full of hot air and broken promises. What hurt most was knowing how right they all were. I closed the laptop, trying to put this despair out of my mind . . . I didn't need my mother to know how worried I was.

I wondered what Esther wanted with my thoughts. If all she wanted to do was invade our city, she could have done it easily. Knowing I couldn't use the nuclear weapons in my possession should have cleared the way for her to send an army to invade ages ago. But she wanted something else . . . she wanted my power. If she killed me outright, she'd make me a martyr. She either had to convince me to join her, or she had to wholly discredit my entire invented religion. So far, she was quite efficiently doing the latter.

I hoped my friends would find some solution, some way to salvage this situation. But as the sun rose, and then neared the horizon again, I could hear just enough sighs and morose tones to infer that whatever they were planning wasn't going well.

Finally, a knock at my door brought a broken-looking Layla. "We need your help."

"How?" I asked feebly. "You convinced me I couldn't."

"The others think you cannot, but . . . we are losing," she said, in a grieving half whisper.

My heart raced. "Is Jude . . ."

"Alive," she reassured me. "But . . . Dr. Marko."

She couldn't say it, so I tried to say it for her. "Something happened."

She nodded. "He tried to sneak in, rescue them, but . . ."

"They took him?"

She shook her head. "Injured him badly. He is in the hospital, critical condition."

The devastation tore through me. My friends were dropping like flies. This was all part of my mother's sick game to get to me. "I'll figure something out," I said with more confidence than I felt.

She nodded. "You will. Because you love him, too." I was filled with a deep shame; she knew every one of my most mortifying thoughts. The ones about her, the ones about her boyfriend. But she still looked at me with friendship, with forgiveness. And with hope, that the love I'd worked so hard to hide would save the man she loved, too.

"I'm sorry," I told her anyway.

She shook her head. "It was not a secret that you still love Jude. At least not to me."

"Oh," I said, embarrassed.

"But you cared for my father. You grieved for him. That I did not know." She teared up as she spoke, and I hugged her.

"No one else dies," I promised her.

We're done playing games, I thought to myself, knowing exactly who would hear my words. *I'm going to make you pay for this.*

10

Where are you going?" Zack asked as I opened the front door.

"I'm going to get Jude and Dawn back," I told him, voice full of a furious determination.

"How?" His voice sounded as skeptical as I felt.

I tried to project some kind of confidence. "I don't know yet. If I did, Esther would know, too."

I could see the hopelessness growing behind his eyes. "If you really think you can stop her, do what you have to," he said, resigned.

I nodded, surprised but relieved that he wasn't trying to boss me around for once. But I knew perfectly well, his despair and futility were probably the only reasons he was willing to entertain my absurd lack of plan. Layla and Irene solemnly joined Zack to watch me leave, faces just a tiny bit optimistic. I was terrified I was about to let everyone down.

As I emerged from the building, onlookers gawked as I

headed out of the city. But I ignored them, focused on retaliation, planning my next move as best I could without actually settling on which words I'd say next. All I knew was, my mother had spent the past year invading my thoughts and stripping away my agency, bit by bit. Whatever shred of power I had left, I was going to use every ounce of it to strike back and make sure my friends came home safe.

When I arrived outside the military base, the soldiers greeted me with wary salutes, surprised by my unexpected presence. "I need to see General Feliciano," I told them. They glanced at one another, their looks filling my stomach with dread. This wasn't going to go well.

It took ten minutes for the general to emerge—an eon, compared to the speed with which she normally greeted me. When she finally appeared, her smile was thin and forced. "Hello, Grace."

The absence of the word *prophet* from her lips unnerved me. "Hey," I said. "Is everything okay?"

"You tell me," she said tersely. "Do you think everything looks okay out there?"

"All part of Great Spirit's plan," I said, trying to spin as best I could.

But she remained cold, and her voice sounded final. "I eagerly await your coming miracle."

"Great Spirit will not disappoint," I promised, though I was sure that promise would be broken.

I'd finally lost the support of our military. And, since my mother was listening to every word of this, my enemies already knew. I was defenseless.

As the general stepped away, I turned to two nearby soldiers, tone clipped. "I'm going outside." Both clearly wanted to advise me against it, but they were still too timid to question the word of a prophet, even a disgraced one. So they dutifully followed me onto the beach to greet the setting sun.

The camp was nothing like I'd last left it. The pilgrims had thinned out—this latest attack had finally confirmed suspicions: it was no longer safe to be a supporter of Grace Luther. The few hundred devotees who remained were hollow-eyed, more desperate-looking than ever. As they heard the gates creak, their bodies turned toward me as though I was a prayer answered. "Can you get me a microphone?" I asked a soldier, and he immediately left to oblige.

A few pilgrims flocked to my feet, keeping a reverent distance. "We are still faithful," one said in a hoarse whisper, proud to be one of the last remaining at my side. "When will we be rewarded?"

I waited until I had the microphone to answer him. "You are my most loyal followers. I thank you." The crowd murmured with delight. Finally, their devotion had been noticed. "And that's why I have one more request for you. First, I want you to turn off all recording devices. All of them." I saw a few people reluctantly lower their phones. Though I knew my mother already knew every word I was speaking, I still didn't want the rest of the world to hear what I was about to say next.

"Out there are monsters, agents of the devil, who are holding two of my friends hostage. I know I've asked you to be patient, to be kind, to be peaceful. But right now, I need to ask you to put all that aside and fight our enemies. They're endangering our cause. These men are unredeemable, and they must be stopped." I gestured to the flyer that the general had distributed around the camp. Anger burned steadily in my heart, fueling me as I nearly shouted into the microphone, "You already have their pictures. Find out where they're hiding and destroy them, by any means necessary. We tried pacifism . . . now we need to try something else. But save the two hostages—they're more vital to our mission than you know."

Bile rose in my throat; I was sickened by my own declaration, and I could tell I wasn't alone; pilgrims and soldiers alike exchanged skeptical looks. This was far different rhetoric than they'd come to expect from me. It was the kind of fire and brimstone I'd made it my brand to preach against. Could this really be the Prophet Grace who'd once inspired them, the one who'd been so different from the other prophets, who was now advocating such darkness?

Some members of the crowd booed and left in disgust. More support dwindling. But a few stayed and nodded. The hunger in their eyes lighting a fire, tapping into an anger already burning within them. Ready to fight, to kill, for someone who would give them an excuse.

I'd created my own little militia, just like the one Prophet Joshua had once wielded, the secret army I'd been a part of. I knew just how powerful that spy network could be. I had to hope that unlike his, mine wouldn't lead to my downfall.

This time, I didn't retreat into some military strong-hold. If my mother had wanted to kill me, she'd had every opportunity, known every step I was taking. I wanted to be out waiting where I knew everyone could find me, so I could hear the moment there was news and direct Jude's rescue mission. My vulnerability felt like a taunt to Esther—and after everything she'd done, I wanted to cause her as much anguish as possible.

As those few gaunt pilgrims eagerly trotted out into the night, competing to be the first to do my bidding, a wave of guilt washed over me, the kind that might have felled me when the nanotech was still in my brain. I was sending these inno-cents directly into harm's way, for my own gain. I was abus-ing their trust, worse than I ever had before, hurting the very people I should have been trying to protect. I knew the mon-strosity of my actions, but the rage that boiled inside of me had completely taken over. I had to strike back at Ciaran and Esther with the only weapon I had left. Even if using that weapon was unforgivable.

The sun began to set behind the hills covered in shanty-towns, but I kept up my confident façade, preaching the word of Great Spirit to the smattering of pilgrims who still lingered at my side, grappling with newfound doubts. "Why is this mission so important to Great Spirit?" they were curious to know. "When is it okay to use violence, and when is it wrong? How will we know, if you aren't around to tell us?"

"I'll be here," I said carefully, worried about condoning any more violence. "That's why we have prophets. If violence hasn't been called for, it's wrong." I saw their nods, their pretending to understand. And though I knew only a small number of people had heard my violent proclamation, I still worried what dark force I might be unleashing, what effects my words might lead to once this mission was complete.

As the reddish sunset light crossed the faces of the soldiers at my side, I saw they were wary. These fighters had been initially converted by my message of peace, by my condemnation of the prophets' hypocritical use of violence. Now I was advocating for those same horrors. Their uneasy looks reminded me of Prophet Joshua's guards, of that moment when his own army had stepped aside and let the crowd slaughter him. Not just the general, but her troops, the most valuable asset I had, were losing faith in me.

"Catch me up, what are we preaching now?" a voice said softly behind me, and I turned to see Macy.

"What are you doing here?" I asked her.

"Thought I'd show the general that there are still people

who believe in you. Though I wish you'd told me we were going Old Testament again." I saw the same doubt and derision on her face as I'd seen growing among the pilgrims.

"You're here to tell me I'm making a mistake, aren't you? That if Dawn were here, she'd say it wasn't worth it to blow everything we have left, just to save two people? Even if one of them is her?"

Macy gave me a grim smile. "I didn't come here to tell you anything, but it sounds like you have some things to tell yourself?"

I found all my fears tumbling out of me. "We were barely keeping our heads above water before. Now I'm destroying the message that made me a prophet in the first place. Dismantling every piece of power I built for myself. Which is exactly what my mother wanted me to do in the first place."

Macy shook her head, overwhelmed. "I have no idea. All these tactical plan things are new to me."

"Same," I said. I remembered what Jude had suggested— that what made me a good prophet was the way I didn't think about tactics, the way I simply tried to improve people's lives. Now here I was doing the opposite, making people's lives worse just to save him. I wondered what he'd think of me . . . if in weaponizing my followers, I'd let Jude down in some fundamental way. And I knew, as I thought about Jude, the love I felt for him must be finding its way back to my mother's server. And also to Zack, if he was still able to see those thoughts.

"You've gotten this far. Just get one step further," she said, encouraging.

"Thanks. You're a pretty good guru."

"I know, right?" she said, grinning.

The soldiers changed shifts, and I realized just how long I'd been standing here, holding court with my followers. My legs were sore, my voice was hoarse from speaking, my stomach rumbled with hunger, and my whole body still quavered with fear and uncertainty. I wondered what I'd unleashed out in those hills, whether my gambit was going to work, or just make everything worse.

Finally, as lamplights began to twinkle across the hills, I saw a figure running toward us. Just a dot of a shadow on the horizon, and then a set of flailing limbs came into view, trying to get my attention. My heart sped up as I recognized the face—one of my pilgrims. Coming with a warning? He shouted in a language I didn't speak, and one of the pilgrims next to me quickly translated into Portuguese: "They found them."

I felt my feet nearly floating off the ground as I left Macy behind and ran out to meet the messenger, my cadre of soldiers following dutifully behind me. "Where are they?" I asked the translator as we came closer.

After a moment of conferring, the translator explained, "In a house not far from here. He says there are many people defending it. Guards in uniform."

So my mother had brought her own army with her. "Take me there."

Everyone looked at me nervously. "Prophet, it's too dangerous," one of the pilgrims said.

I shook my head, determined to follow through on this lead before my mother had a chance to use my own knowledge against me. "Great Spirit tells me this is the only way. I'll be protected. Take me there." Saying the lies almost made me believe them. I began walking toward the hills, nodding to the messenger. "Show me the way." I turned to the soldiers. I was nervous to demand anything right now, but I knew I could use the muscle, if my mother had an army. "If anyone would like to join, you're welcome to."

Out of a dozen soldiers, only one stepped forward—Lieutenant Lopez, whom I recognized from the boat. "I trust you, Prophet," he said, fire in his eyes. Whatever experience he'd had back on the Amazon River must have been something amazing for him to still be following me now.

Reluctantly, the messenger led the way, and the lieutenant and I followed. I nodded goodbye to Macy and steeled myself for my mission. An unarmed fake prophet was heading into battle against the CIA's most highly trained forces. Odds were, we were going to get slaughtered.

12

My mother would be ready for us. If she was still monitoring my thoughts every second, she'd know exactly where I was, exactly where I was headed. My usual move, unexpectedly fake preaching my way out of situations, was unlikely to help me now.

I had to come up with something new, something that used her expectations against her. And I couldn't spend too much time thinking about it either—I had to improvise when I arrived, to make sure she didn't prepare her troops for my plan. If Esther herself was on-site, I thought I might have a chance. At the very least, I hoped she'd spare her own daughter.

We wound through steep, narrow roadways, avoiding motorbikes and averting our eyes from pedestrians. A few Outcasts pointed at me, wondering if it could really be their great prophet, all the way out here. But the rest went about their business, ignoring us. They recognized me . . . they just didn't care. I wondered if my reach had eroded even more than I'd realized.

Even some of the Outcasts of Redenção were indifferent to my presence.

I eyed every passerby with suspicion . . . could that random stranger on the street be a spy for my mother? That other one? I hoped she wouldn't risk a confrontation in the open like this; I assumed she still had a smarter, subtler plan to destroy me.

Finally, our messenger pointed to a concrete building at the top of the hill—more imposing than the other homes on this street. "That's it?" I asked him, and he nodded. I hesitated, half formulating a plan. "Kevlar. Hand me your Kevlar?" The lieutenant reluctantly obliged, and I secured his vest around my chest and pelvis, putting his helmet on my head. Everything but my arms and legs were covered. "Now, go home and get help."

Lopez was confused. "I'm coming in with you," he said bravely.

"No, you're not," I said firmly. "You're going back to Redenção. If I'm not back at the gates in half an hour, come back with whatever army you can muster."

He nodded, nervous, but did as I requested. I waited until he'd begun walking away, then turned back to the doors of the concrete complex. I had an idea of the force my mother would have waiting for me. I hoped I was smart enough to outplay her.

I walked up to the door and knocked. "Come in," I heard a deep voice say. Then I opened the door to a swarm of bullets.

13

My own mother had ordered her firing squad to shoot on sight. I felt numb inside, unwilling to believe that reality.

The concrete entry hall was full of faces I didn't recognize, all in uniform. These must be my mother's CIA forces, the ones she'd told to prepare for my arrival. But I saw no Esther. She must not be on the premises after all. Though a part of me wanted to look her in the eye, confront her about her cruelty, I quickly formulated a plan that would work without her.

I felt the bullets embedding in the Kevlar, biting thuds against my chest. I closed my eyes as the sharp metal pinged against the helmet, rattling my brain. A bullet nicked my arm, and I cried out but tried to keep my focus. I scanned the room, desperate to find cover, but the hall was depressingly bare.

I noticed one man in the corner with his finger on the trigger but not pulling it—afraid he was breaking some kind of a commandment by shooting at a prophet, no doubt. "You," I called out, pointing at him. The bullet fire slowed to a crawl as the agents looked around, confused. "Why aren't you shooting?" I continued, boldly castigating the nonshooter. "Esther told you to kill the prophet on sight, why are you hesitating?"

All the guns lowered now as my invocation of Esther, and seeming foreknowledge of their orders, confused the troops.

"I was shooting," he defended himself.

I shook my head and looked to the others. "Reprimand him. No one questions Esther's orders, ever." They looked around, confused. I continued, "The rest of you, well done. It's no easy feat to pull the trigger on a prophet, and you all passed with flying colors."

My memories of Zack's stories of CIA training gave me a language, a psychology, that I thought might feel familiar to these people. I only hoped that Esther wouldn't be able to act fast enough to contradict and counteract me.

One CIA agent stepped forward, gun still fixed on my heart. "Esther said to take you in by any means necessary."

I let the choking horror of those words pass by me, keeping up my breezy attitude. "And you did. Good job, you've got me." I fixed my eyes on their blank stares. "You really think I could run out of here, if I wanted to? Even if those bullets aren't the kind that kill, they're plenty useful at stopping me."

I knew that would unnerve them, that I knew about their secret, nonlethal bullets. I took off the Kevlar vest and let it drop to the floor, a show of confidence. "Come on, take me in, what are you waiting for?" I asked them, holding my hands in the air in surrender.

My gambit certainly seemed to be successful at confusing them. After a series of puzzled looks were exchanged, one agent hesitantly took my arm and pulled me deeper into the building.

I scoffed as we walked. "Is that it? You don't have handcuffs or anything?" I knew it was a risky play, but I also knew that the safer I pretended I felt, the more they'd trust that I really was safe: that I was in league with Esther, that this was all part of some plan meant to test their loyalty. Just another trick like Esther had employed during their training.

So far, it was working well enough. They led me farther inside the concrete walls, down a hallway I hoped would lead to Jude and Dawn.

Instead, as we turned a corner, that hallway led to Ciaran's devilish grin. He stood in a dank gray room with no windows, in the center of the building, which stank vilely of sweat and sewage. The smell, and the sight of him, made me want to retch. I saw ropes on the walls, which looked like they had once restrained two prisoners . . . but Jude and Dawn were gone.

"Where are they?" I asked, keeping the panic out of my tone. I tried to remain matter-of-fact, militarily stoic.

"Outside. Bathroom break," Ciaran said, and I couldn't tell if he was lying.

"They better be alive. Esther will be pissed if you lost her leverage."

Ciaran smiled, amused. "Pretending you speak for Esther. Cute."

"You know who I am, don't you?" I scoffed.

"Grace Luther. You think I'd forget you? We're old friends," he said with a flirtatious note in his voice. He stepped closer, and I could smell the rankness of his breath. I tried not to cringe.

"I'm also Esther's daughter. You never noticed the resemblance?" He looked at me keenly, and I saw the CIA agents exchanging looks—clearly they *had* noticed it before. Our eyes, the shape of our faces, were almost identical. "Seriously, you think it's a coincidence? We just happened to go on a date the night you got taken in? You think I'm not part of Esther's plan, that we're not working together?" Ciaran seemed struck by that, puzzling through my words.

"To what end?" another agent asked.

"People are getting complacent," I told him, echoing words I remembered hearing a long time ago at Walden Manor. "They see the work of Great Spirit, they see the Revelations, but then they forget. They forget why we have these laws, how lucky we are to have this world. So we remind them. After every religion is established, some number of years later, you get a schism. A Reformation, a holy war that reminds us what we're fighting for. This is all a show, and you're all actors, and Esther didn't bother to tell you. You're pawns in her little game, expendable. But you knew that, you've always known that."

Ciaran scoffed. "And you think you're not a pawn?"

"I'm Esther's only daughter. I'd say that makes me a rook, at least," I said snidely.

"Then why'd she tell us to kill you, if necessary?" he challenged.

My stomach twisted. Could it be true? Had my mother really sent this monster to *kill* me? Could the bullets in those guns have been real after all? I'd put so much faith in my mother's love for me . . . maybe convincing me she really cared had been her biggest con of all.

But a CIA agent stepped in—I could tell from his expression that he still believed my words. "We'll take it from here." I breathed an internal sigh of relief—I'd anticipated my mother perfectly after all.

I'd stayed alive, and safe . . . but she'd gotten exactly what she wanted. Ciaran had done his job—he'd lured me out of my safe, protected haven and right into her hands.

And indeed, moments later, I saw an agent enter and whisper in the ear of my captor—relaying a message from Esther, no doubt. As he listened, his expression hardened, and he quickly told me, "We're keeping you here."

I nodded, still playing my part. I hoped if Esther could read my thoughts, so could Zack. Through my eyes, maybe I could give what remained of the resistance a window into the opposition—a fly-on-the-wall view of the compound, at least.

A few moments later, Dawn and Jude were led inside—both paled when they saw me. I tried to quell the rush of joy I felt to see their faces again. Looking into Jude's eyes filled me with a kind of calm and excitement all at once . . . even though I was the one here to rescue him, I still felt safer in his presence somehow. "Grace . . ." Jude said, but I shook my head. *Not now.*

"Friends of yours?" the agent guarding me asked.

I smiled ruefully. "You could say that. Like I said, we all have our parts to play. Theirs is to be the defeated resistance. Yours is to die valiantly defending the attack that's coming in a few minutes. Mine is to emerge triumphantly and miraculously from the melee, to struggle in vain like the best prophets do, and ultimately take the reins from the old prophets as the voice of the youth. At least, until a couple decades from now, when we do this all over again." I willed the deepest sympathy into my eyes, looking at my captor. "My mother's a genius when it comes to spinning a narrative, but I've never understood her obsession with secrecy. If I were her, I would have clued you all in to the truth, tried to limit casualties. But I guess she has her reasons, and hey, I'm not in charge."

I could see the wheels turning in his head, my words getting to him. In a world where conspiracy theories were real, the plot I was spinning didn't seem so far-fetched to him. And my words seemed downright prophetic a few minutes later, when anxious voices outside started yelling about an army marching up the street with tanks and a whole battalion of soldiers. Lieutenant Lopez had managed to scrape together a decent fighting force after all.

I saw our guards mulling over their options . . . were they really willing to die for Esther's cause, as pawns in some game? One of them nodded to Dawn, Jude, and me. "Take the prisoners outside. Tell them we're willing to make a deal."

A shot of relief and disbelief went through me. I'd miraculously tricked my mother's CIA forces into standing down. We'd won this battle, at least.

I still had no idea how we'd win the war.

14

As the agent shuffled us back through that hallway, I could hear Ciaran's desperate protests. "You're letting them *go*? We were just starting to have fun." A sick part of me wished the lieutenant *would* invade, just so someone would put a bullet through Ciaran's twisted little brain.

But I put him out of my mind as we stepped outside, and my heart swelled to see not only Lieutenant Lopez, but Zack, Layla, and Irene waiting for us as well. Layla rushed to Jude's side, as Irene moved to support a limping Dawn. I approached Zack, who looked slightly different in a way I couldn't put my finger on. He had a tentative smile on his lips. "Good job in there," he said, voice filled with a kind of respect I hadn't heard in a long time.

"Thanks," I said, nervous knowing that he'd not only listened in on every conversation I'd had, but also knew everything I was feeling at this moment. The emotions I'd had seeing Jude again.

"The resistance lives to fight another day," he said, trying to force an optimistic grin, while Lieutenant Lopez whisked us back to the safety of the city as quickly as he could. "I have one other piece of good news. We'd been keeping it from you, because we knew, you know . . ."

"That I was the mole," I finished for him.

"We found out you'd been compromised because we hacked into your mother's computer and found text documents filled with your thoughts." I cringed, imagining it, but Zack continued, "On that same drive, we found the key to repairing the device we stole in Rio. We can get that crap out of your head."

I touched his face, suddenly recognizing the strangeness of it. "You already . . ."

"Took mine out, yeah." His smile sent a wave of relief through me. Though he looked slightly different, perhaps a little less conventionally attractive, he also seemed more at ease— and I strangely found myself more drawn to him than ever. "Ready to rejoin the inner circle? We're going to need your help to figure out what to do next." He then spoke to my eyes like speaking into a microphone, "Because yes, Esther, we aren't giving up yet."

A wave of joy went through me, thinking about being a part of the resistance again. But as I imagined what that might look like, a part of me fell into despair. Even when we'd thought we were winning, my mother had always wrestled us to a stalemate. And what did we have left to fight with? Now that the general had lost faith in me, I was relying on a few scraps of her military . . . that wasn't nearly enough to keep control of Redenção, even if my mother didn't already know exactly what our weaknesses were. I didn't see any way out of this, not with the resources we had left.

Instinctively, I started to pray for answers . . . but I knew I wasn't going to get them from any supernatural source. It had been a long time since I'd felt that connection, that certainty. I thought back to what my mother had said—that good things in life didn't come to those who prayed to the right god, but to those who took action. I finally stopped worrying about what Great Spirit might want, and I thought about what I wanted: a way to end this war. If there was no god to get us out of this, I would have to find a way to do it myself.

And, unencumbered by my hand-wringing over what was right or wrong, I had an idea. "Leave that crap in my brain," I said suddenly, now in the habit of making decisions in the moment. "There's one more thing I need it for."

Zack was stunned. "What would you need it for?"

I looked half at Zack, half at the sky, as though Esther might be watching me from some cloud or satellite somewhere. "We need to call a truce. An end to hostilities."

"A truce? With your mother?" Zack asked, incredulous. "What leverage could we possibly have?"

I smiled, the simplicity of it bowling me over. "We reveal the truth."

Zack's expression was drawn in horror. "But that would be . . ."

"Mass chaos, millions, maybe billions dead, I know. Trust me, I remember all the reasons we haven't done it before. But now, since Esther can read my thoughts, she'll know I'm not bluffing. She won't let all those people die, there's no way."

Zack's measured tone dimmed my excitement. "But if she does . . . Grace, this is the one thing we all agreed we could never do. Not until we find a way to prevent people from feeling that guilt and dying, by removing the bugs from the brains of every single person on the planet. And that could take years . . ."

I shook my head, not sure if I was brilliant or crazy or both. "Not if Esther helps us. If we record a video telling everyone the truth and set it to be released in some way she can't counteract, we leave her with no choice. She has to help us. She has to end this. We win."

Zack's tone was careful. "I know she's your mother . . ."

I cut him off. "My mother's a monster. Believe me, I know that by now. I've given up on convincing her to join our side. But we're going to destroy her life's work, one way or the other. And she won't let that finale be the deaths of millions more people, I know that much."

"You don't know what she's capable of," Zack warned, voice shaking. "Not really."

I thought of the terror inspired in those CIA agents by just the mention of Esther's name, and I wondered if he was right. But I shook my head. "It's our only chance."

"A risky gambit that might kill half the world's population? You don't get to make that choice, for all those people."

I held firm. "Someone has to."

Zack shook his head. "You're starting to sound like her." He meant Esther. Knowing he was right made me queasy.

"It's going to work," I said stubbornly.

Zack hesitated. "I can't condone this. But it's not up to me either."

"Let's put it to a vote," I suggested. "Everyone left in the resistance."

He nodded—not because he wanted to, but because we both knew we had no choice. A handful of us were about to decide the fate of billions of people.

15

We reassembled at the hospital, where Dr. Marko was thankfully awake, but woozy. As a precaution after their brief stint in captivity, Jude and Dawn had been examined, treated, and released, and they joined the cluster around Dr. Marko's bed. This time our group included every single person who knew the truth; Zack had even gathered all the refugees from our Turkish stronghold.

Trying not to be intimidated by the larger crowd, I re-explained my plan and reminded everyone that everything we said and did was being projected back to Esther. As expected, I was met with familiar blank stares, and echoes of all Zack's objections.

"We cannot do this," said a woman I recognized from our transatlantic flight.

"She thinks she can save the world," another stranger grumbled.

"Don't get in the way of Grace and saving the world," Zack quipped.

"It's not that it isn't a good idea," Jude said, coming to my defense. "But it feels risky. Too risky." He looked at me with an apology, sorry he couldn't fully back me.

"That's just it," Irene stepped in. "We know *we* won't die, because *we* know the truth. We're making the decision to risk strangers' lives, and that isn't our call."

Dawn, too, shifted uncomfortably. "For all we know, your mother's tech isn't just reading your thoughts, it's infecting them again. Convincing you to play right into her hands."

Dr. Marko shook his head. "We saw the blueprints on her computer, that's not how it works."

"Unless that's what Esther wanted us to see . . ." Zack said, his old paranoia rising to the surface.

Layla had stayed uncharacteristically quiet as the others leveled their objections. Finally, she spoke up, interrupting. "I think we should do it."

Jude was just as surprised as the rest of us. "You do? Why?"

"They're picking us off one by one," Layla said quietly, and I knew she was thinking of her father. "We are acting like we have some chance of beating them, but we all know they have us backed into a corner. An invasion could come at any minute, and then we are all dead. Yes, Grace's plan is a desperate last resort, you're right, but we are desperate. We lost my father, we almost lost Dawn and Dr. Marko, I almost lost you . . ." she said to Jude, and I could hear her voice cracking as she spoke. "Grace, you and I have never seen eye to eye. I always thought you were naïve, and privileged. And kind of annoying, if I'm honest."

"Thanks," I said, hoping there was a "but" coming.

There was. "But this time I think you are right. I think this is the only way we win."

I looked around the room for support, and I saw Dawn smiling ruefully. "After all the grief you gave me about West Virginia . . ."

I thought of how angry I'd been that she'd put innocent lives at risk and lost them. How naïve I'd been then, like Layla had said. I tried to imagine what me then would have said about me now. I would have thought I was maniacal . . . like the power had gone to my head, drained me of any empathy. And Old Me might have been right. Every cell in my body felt different than it used to—transformed by this year into something harder and wiser, and in some ways crueler. But after fighting this hard, for this long, I couldn't bear the idea that it all had been for nothing. It was the same logic that had led to so many other terrible decisions, made by so many other people . . . but this time, I didn't see any other options.

"I wish I had a better idea. I know you can't tell me any of yours, while my mother can overhear us, but . . . anyone? Anything?"

The others exchanged glances, and Zack said carefully, "Give us a minute, okay?"

I exiled myself outside the hospital room, resisting the temptation to listen in. Deep down, I hoped they'd emerge to tell me I'd been outvoted, that I was off the hook, that someone else had come up with a better plan that wouldn't cross so many moral lines. But when Jude's somber face finally appeared in front of me, I knew no one had. "You won. Barely."

"I don't feel like I won," I told him.

He nodded, understanding. "For what it's worth, I voted in your favor. So did Layla, and Dawn, and Zack."

"Thanks," I said.

"Maybe the world out there doesn't believe in you so much anymore. But your friends do," he reassured me, knowing even before I did, that it was their support I most needed in this moment. Jude always knew what I needed to hear and how to say it in just the right way.

I steeled my courage. "I guess we call my mom now? Make our gambit."

Jude's expression went dark. "Your mother's already here." He showed me a video, streaming live footage from outside Redenção, where my mother was waiting next to a helicopter, its wings slicing through the air ominously. The sight of her face gave me chills. As expected, she'd heard my every word—and she was ready for us.

"Let's record the video," I said. "Let her see just how devastating its effects will be."

I was about to see my mother face-to-face again. I had to pray this time would go better than the last.

16

I left my recorded message in Zack's hands. "We'll set it to upload automatically in a week," he assured me. "Dawn's good with computers, she worked out a fail-safe. No matter what, even if Esther kills us, it'll go live anyway, one week from now. There's no way to stop the release."

"Did you hear that, Mom?" I said to the air above us. "You have to help us. Or you're responsible for killing billions of people." I hoped the trolley problem I'd presented my mother was compelling enough to convince her to acquiesce to our demands. Though I knew she could see the overpowering fear coursing through my veins that maybe she wouldn't. If I'd misread her, if we'd calculated wrong . . . I was about to become the most heinous, genocidal monster the world had ever known.

Zack took my hand, and a little flutter went through me that I was embarrassed my mother would also witness. "Good luck," he said.

"Thanks, I'll need it."

We drove out of the city in near silence, and I could see Zack choosing his words carefully. Finally, he offered, "I'm sorry I wasn't the person I wanted to be. With you, I mean."

"Thanks," I said, surprised by his admission of responsibility. It was strange to see him looking so small and ashamed. When we'd first gotten together, he'd seemed so much older, wiser. Because he had been. That was the problem with falling for someone while still young and naïve—eventually, young and naïve people grow up.

"Considering how little experience you had, and everything . . . I have to admit you did a pretty good job." Though I knew he meant it as a compliment, even now I could hear the condescension in his voice. Some part of him was still sure he could have done it all better. Before, that kind of criticism might have bothered me, but now I simply felt sad for Zack, that he had to live life so hamstrung by his own insecurities. It was clear to me now, he'd never been fully comfortable with me having any kind of power he didn't possess. My strength and wisdom threatened his need to be the strongest and wisest. And if I had to choose between being strong and wise, and dating Zack—I chose my own strength.

In the distance, I could see Esther's helicopter waiting for me. "Do you want me to come with you?" Zack asked. The kindness in his voice melted just a little of the ice that had formed inside my heart.

I shook my head. "I need you here. Making sure that video uploads."

He hugged me tight, like he might be saying goodbye forever. "You can do this," he said, reassuring.

"I hope so."

He teased, "You better—you're Prophet Grace, after all."

"I'm going to miss being called that," I admitted.

"You'll be on one of those 'Where are they now' specials in ten years. 'Remember Prophet Grace?'"

I laughed at the thought. "I hope I'll be on a farm or in the jungle or something. I think I've interacted with enough people in the past few months to last a lifetime."

"You'll be somewhere great. I know that much." I'd forgotten how much warmth I used to feel when he looked at me.

I hugged him again, knowing that if I didn't leave soon, I wouldn't be able to leave at all. The pull of the happy life I'd once imagined I could share with Zack remained strong, even now that I knew all the downsides that came along with it. But that life was gone for good now. So many lives I'd left behind already, in just eighteen short years. "I'll see you soon," I said.

His smile still dazzled, his winks still left me gooey-legged. But something about that goodbye felt final. Like we were saying goodbye to what had been, to us.

Determined and apprehensive, I walked alone toward the dot on the horizon, which would grow into a helicopter, and my mother. It felt familiar—this wasn't the first time I'd met her on the edge of this town. But now the tables were turned: she held all the power, and I was at her mercy.

When I arrived, she tossed me a pair of ear mufflers. "The helicopter gets noisy."

I took them, wary. "No need to talk about why I'm here, I guess? You know what I'm going to ask you?"

Her voice quavered with a kind of resoluteness. "You want

me to turn back the Revelations. To let you tell everyone the truth."

"Yeah, glad you were listening," I said pointedly.

"Well, you're in luck. You're going to get your wish."

It felt like a trick. I treated it like one. "That easy?"

"Easy for your friends, less easy for you." Her gaze, and her words, contained a threat. "Give up your freedom, and the rest of the world will have theirs."

I imagined a dreary life spent in a cold, damp cell. My mother's cell. "Of course," I told her, suppressing my dread. "Whatever it takes."

She nodded, transaction complete. "Get in. Clock's ticking."

"Where are we headed?" I asked, nervously complying.

My mother answered brusquely and uninformatively. "To an airport."

"And then . . . ?"

She smiled, as though taking some joy in taking her daughter on such a journey. "To the seat of the prophets' power. Vatican City."

I buckled my seat belt, trepidation brewing. It was going to be a long trip.

BOOK

SIX

1

As the helicopter took off, flying high above the lush Brazilian landscape, my stomach flip-flopped. My mother had just as easily acquiesced to my demands once before. And the last time, she'd found a way betray me more deeply than I'd thought possible. She hadn't handcuffed me yet, that was a good sign. But the inscrutable look on her face didn't give me any clues about what her true plans might be.

We disembarked at an airport near Salvador, Brazil, and my mother walked us to a private solar plane—one of the many lavish ones owned by the prophets. As we stepped on board, I marveled at the plush leather cushions and the spacious cabin, which was empty save for the two of us. "Do you want anything to drink?" she asked, as the engines revved to life.

I glanced at the pilot, wondering if he was privy to all the same secrets I was. I'd never know—he closed the door behind him, giving us total privacy. "Glass of wine?" I asked, testing her.

She chuckled at the request. "Not till you're twenty-one," she said, brushing by the fact that she and the prophets had outlawed alcohol.

"You're such a responsible mother," I said sarcastically.

"I try," she said, a note of sarcasm in her voice as well.

I wondered what kind of hornet's nest I'd be walking into once we landed in Italy. "Does anyone else know I'm coming?" I asked. "Anyone else you work with?"

"Of course," my mother said.

So they'd be prepared for me. But, I realized, I still didn't know who "they" were. Though I'd spent so much time fighting against this system, I still wasn't totally sure how it worked. "Who's in charge? Of . . . I don't know, the world I guess. Do the prophets answer to anyone?"

She laughed a little. "You mean am I the overlord of all Earth? No, I'm not. There isn't one. To make this system work, every country on the planet had to agree to give up some of their sovereignty. But not all of it. What's left is a democracy of sorts."

"Of sorts," I said ruefully.

"Better than the UN used to be, with just a few rich countries dominating all the decision-making. Or any of the empires before that, where colonized people had no rights at all . . ." she said defensively.

"So because other systems were worse, that makes yours better?"

"I think that's the definition of better, yes," she said, relishing her turn of phrase. A moment later, her face darkened. Perhaps she was remembering why I was here, what we were about to do—dismantle everything she'd built. "Well, we had a good run, at least."

I couldn't bring myself to have any sympathy for her. "And killed a lot of people in the process, yeah, I'd call that a good run."

I'd hoped my words would sting her, but instead, her face softened. "I'm truly sorry about everything that's happened to your friends. To Dr. Smith." Regret burned inside me, realizing that my mother had only been able to assassinate her by reading my thoughts.

"And for invading my mind, you want to apologize for that?" I asked.

"I do," she said, seemingly genuinely. Then she followed with a smirk. "For what it's worth, I'm rooting for Jude." My insides burned, knowing she'd only said that because she could see that deep down, some part of me was rooting for him, too.

As we reached altitude, the exhaustion of the past few days finally hit me. I couldn't remember the last time I'd had a full night's sleep, with all the worrying over my missing friends. Though I wanted to stay alert, keep an eye on my mother, soon I felt my eyelids sliding shut, as my consciousness slipped into the comfort of these luxurious seats.

When I awoke, we were descending into a landscape dotted with aged architecture; we'd made it to Europe. I stretched, rubbing my eyes, and was surprised to see that my mother looked as wide awake and put together as when we'd first boarded. There was a superhuman quality to her, as though she had no concerns for eating or sleeping. She was like a shark—always moving, always on the prowl. And now, her keen eyes watched me closely. "Are you ready?"

Ready to put an end to all this? I'd never been more ready for anything in my life. Adrenaline rushing, I braced for landing . . . and for whatever my mother was planning next.

Alimo arrived to take us from the airstrip to Vatican City, a tiny nation encapsulated by the city of Rome. In its heyday, it had been the seat of the Holy Roman Empire, with popes ruling vast swaths of Europe. Though the city-state's influence had dwindled in the intervening centuries, the Revelations had given the metropolis a new kind of power. Inside these walls lay the collective government of the prophets, a worldwide bureaucracy that coordinated the efforts of people like my mother all around the world. The CIAs and MI6s and ASISs, all working together to ensure their secrets would never be discovered. And now, I was driving through their gates to tear it all down.

"Morning, Tomas," my mother said, nodding to a security guard at the entrance gate.

"Whatever happened to the last pope?" I asked as Esther swiped a card at the gate, opening the doors to the walled-off city. I remembered seeing pictures of a white-haired man outside these buildings when I was little—one whose life had been suspiciously cut short.

She sighed. "We wanted him to join us, obviously. What better prophet to legitimize the cause to millions of Catholics? He hated the idea though. Told us we were committing the greatest sin imaginable, blah blah blah." Apparently his gruesome death in the Revelations had been no accident.

I tried to put my mother's popeicide out of mind as I looked up at the beautiful old buildings. I felt a hint of excitement to be here: the bulk of Vatican City was usually walled off to all outside visitors. Besides employees, only high-ranking clerics, gurus, and prophets were normally allowed access—it was a thrill to enter as a private citizen. Although, I reminded myself, I was still technically a prophet of sorts.

My mother pointed to a tall building—a steel skyscraper built atop a magnificent stone domed structure, almost like it was growing out of it. "That's St. Peter's Tower. That building beneath it is St. Peter's Basilica, but during the Revelations, we had to expand so we'd have more room for joint military operations."

"Exactly what the popes intended," I couldn't help but snark back.

My mother shrugged. "The ancient popes conducted plenty of wars here. Something like five different crusades? Popes were generals just like any kings or dictators, fighting battles to gain and defend their territory. We're just carrying on the tradition."

I rolled my eyes at her sanctimonious justifications. No amount of destruction that had come before could justify the destruction she'd done since. I struggled to keep pace as she marched toward St. Peter's Tower. Something about her demeanor left all the little hairs on my arm on end. She wasn't sad enough, wasn't trying to convince me of anything. Despite her best efforts to pretend otherwise, she was still acting superior, like she held all the cards. Our ploy was supposed to take those cards away from her . . . what was she hiding up her sleeve?

"You know, my video will go live no matter what," I warned her.

"So you said to Zack, I'm aware," she said stoically.

"And my friends know I'm prepared to give my life if that's what it takes."

"We've got time left, I'm not worried." Why *wasn't* she worried? Why was she so sure that removing the nanotech from everyone's heads was going to go off without a hitch? Why was she so complacent about giving up her life's work?

She wasn't planning to. That much was obvious. How she was going to outplay us, I couldn't guess. And I had no choice but to follow her through the gleaming arches of St. Peter's Tower. Whatever plan she'd concocted, at this point I could only be a passenger, watching it go by.

As a kid, on Take Your Child to Work Day, I'd always wished my mother were still alive to take me somewhere more interesting than our worship center. In a sick way, my wish was finally coming true. I followed her into the skyscraper, up a glass elevator. As we rose, I could see all of Vatican City stretching out beneath us: gardens filled with the prophets' acolytes, doing their evil bidding. I hoped I'd be able to finally stop them.

When we arrived at the fiftieth floor, Esther had to swipe a card to get the elevator doors to open, and we emerged on a mezzanine looking out over a bustling command center, dozens of people sitting at computers below us. A wall with hundreds of screens extended two stories high, displaying scenes from all around the world. "What's all this?" I asked her, a little breathless at the scope of these images.

"We keep an eye on things. Make sure world leaders are following the rules, not abusing their power." She nodded to a screen, which showed a war in the Australian bush I hadn't realized was being waged. "Not all of them do. We put a stop to it, and we keep things quiet. Make sure secrets don't slip out." She caught herself. "Until now, at least."

I watched the dronelike key pushers, watching their monitors with dead eyes. "Who are these people?" I asked, wary. "CIA agents? People you've brainwashed or blackmailed to keep your secrets?"

"A job like this, it's too sensitive to trust to just anyone," she said, avoiding my eyes.

"So how do you keep them from spilling the truth?" I asked, curious.

"We have our ways," she deflected obliquely. Looking at those thousand-mile stares, I had a feeling her "ways" might be neurochemical, same as how she kept the rest of us in line. Dr. Marko had suggested the prophets had dozens of different kinds of nanotech, each able to manipulate the brain in a different way. Those "dronelike" workers I was looking at might really just be drones, their personalities and real emotions tamped down in the service of the prophets. Whatever they were victims of, I knew it wasn't pretty.

As I watched the drones type, my worry reached a fever

pitch. All these button pushers, continuing to push their buttons . . . it didn't seem like my mother's brave new world was about to change at all. She wasn't going to acquiesce to our demands; clearly she had something else planned.

"This way," Esther said, pulling me away from the hive of worker bees. We passed a long, dark hallway lined with armed guards who had the same faraway looks as the brainwashed folks at their computers. It seemed Vatican City had a whole new level of security than I'd encountered before—biochemical enforcement of their foot soldiers.

My mother brought me into her corner office that overlooked the city: we could see all of Rome from up here, a beautiful 180-degree view. I glanced at her desk—there were no pictures of me or our family anywhere to be seen. Expected, though my own disappointment at their absence caught me off guard.

My mother moved to a computer, typing furiously. "What are you doing?" I asked nervously.

"I'm accessing your files, the ones that show what's happening in your brain. I want to make sure your friends are still hacked in. They need to see I've ended this, so they can assist the plan on their end. Once the nanotech is out of everyone's heads, we'll have the prophets release their own video, explaining what happened." On her screen, I saw lines of text describing everything I was seeing . . . new paragraphs being written in real time, as I read those very words. Surreal. And terrifying, to see exactly how explicitly my deepest thoughts and feelings were being displayed to everyone I cared about.

Could Esther be telling the truth? Though it seemed unlikely, a tiny bit of hope peeked through. "You can really remove the nanotech from every person in the world, from this office?" I asked, a little skeptical.

"Of course not," she said. "But I can make the phone call that will do it." She watched me carefully. "I can tell without looking at that screen that you're scared. Scared I'm going to let you follow through on this plan, kill all those people."

She was trying to wear me down. I eyed her, a challenge. "You think you could really convince yourself that it's *my* fault everyone died?"

"It *would* be your fault, wouldn't it?" she said, savoring her own argument. "Wouldn't you feel guilty beyond what you could survive? And I don't mean some metal in your head would kill you, I mean you'd want to kill yourself, for what you'd done." She was speaking like someone who could read my mind.

"You're the one with the power to stop it," I reminded her. "You put that technology in people's heads in the first place. You handed your daughter a loaded gun, I just found a way to pull the trigger."

She paused, contemplative, then mused, "You know why I picked guilt as the mechanism to control people? Because it works so well already. Think how ashamed you feel of all the mistakes you've already made. Think of one, any one little transgression, and how it ate you up inside. The cruel things you've said to people. The lives you've taken."

Though I wanted to resist her manipulations, I couldn't help but remember the guard I'd killed in the hospital in New York. Mohammed's death. All the people I'd lied to in the name of my fake prophetship. And she was right, that guilt weighed on me.

Even my smallest high school mistakes still made me ache with shame years later. If I was responsible for the deaths of millions, that guilt would crush me. I'd deserve to be crushed.

I steeled myself. This was why I'd come here, why I'd allowed her to keep reading my thoughts. We were in a staring contest, and I needed her to know I'd never blink, never waver. "You're right. But you know I'm willing to risk that pain, that punishment. That video's going public."

"I know that," my mother said in her usual, icy way. "But by the time anyone hears it, they won't trust a word out of your mouth."

I realized it then, staring at that computer screen. The live feed of my own thoughts. My mother hadn't been trying to convince me of anything. She'd simply prompted me to remember all my darkest moments, my deepest regrets. I'd accidentally armed her with everything she needed to destroy me: my own imperfect past.

"No," I said, tears rolling down my cheek, realizing what was coming next.

Esther's eyes were sad. "I warned you. I warned you what would happen if you kept defying us . . ."

Two large men entered the room, grabbed me and held me down, as my mother reached into her desk drawer and pulled out a syringe. "Mom, what are you doing?" I asked, terrified.

She bristled to hear me use that word—to be identified as my mother in the midst of doing something so cruel. But she kept going, stuck the needle into my vein with a sharp pinch, and a moment later I blacked out.

3

The next thing I remember, I heard voices around me, happily chattering away in what sounded like Italian. My mother hadn't taken me too far, at least. This place smelled of sweat, and I felt strangely disoriented, in a pleasing sort of way. Everything was dark, and even as I opened my eyes, something seemed to be covering my face. My vision was blurred, and it took me a moment to realize I was sprawled facedown on a couch of some kind.

I sat up to realize I was in a booth, at some kind of restaurant, wearing a totally unfamiliar outfit—a sequined, low-cut minidress. Nothing like I'd ever worn in my life. This place was cavernous, lit only by bare overhead bulbs. The Outcast faces I spotted around me suggested I might be somewhere seedy, and the contraband alcohol I spied on nearby tables confirmed it. This was an outlawed establishment—a bar.

As the world spun around me, I realized I was recovering from more than just a sedative . . . they'd put something else inside me as well, I could feel it. I tried to imagine what new tech this might be, until I noticed a red dot on my arm—an injection point, from where my mother had stuck a syringe. Maybe this was nothing more than street drugs, heroin or something like that—plenty embarrassing as a prophet, to be seen wandering in a sedated stupor.

I adjusted my awful, too-revealing dress and got my bearings. I was alone. Was this all part of her plot to discredit me? Who knew what kind of paparazzi might be staged around here, to capture my embarrassment on film. They might not even need to. Random strangers at this bar were snickering, snapping my picture—sending it via texts and social media posts.

I tried to put my thoughts together into a useful shape. A plan. Where were the exits? Was there anyone here who still believed in me, whom I could ask for help? One Outcast girl leaned over, and her camera flashed in my eyes. Disoriented, I reached out and grabbed her hand. "How did I get here?" I mumbled to her.

She recoiled, pulling her hand back—a kind of gesture I hadn't experienced in so long: disgust. My influence had dwindled to nothing. She stifled a giggle. "You don't remember?"

She looked to her friend, standing next to her, and they both cracked up. "I was drugged," I tried to say, but the words were slurred, and in this loud place, no one could hear me. I tried to say it louder, "I was drugged!" Now the whole crowd was laughing at my fumbling speech.

I tried to stand, to get out of there, but my legs were woozy. "Help," I whispered, but no one could hear me over the buzzing crowd. All these people who'd worshipped me only days earlier were now laughing at me. They'd once clamored to touch me, to look into my eyes, to commune with any shred of the sacredness they thought I embodied. Now they kept their distance, mocking me from afar. What had happened, what had my mother done while I was unconscious, to turn everyone against me so quickly?

I found a stranger's phone abandoned on a table nearby and quickly googled my name. In place of the usual worshipful think pieces, now I found takedowns. My mother had found every possible witness on earth who could discredit me. She'd sifted through every one of my worst memories and found a way to display them to the world. Even my old classmates, who'd once sung my praises, were now humming my death march.

I devoured news articles, reading every terrible word being printed about me. "She really wasn't that nice," one former classmate said. It was a girl named Ann, my former partner on a school project back in high school. She'd once heard me talking about her behind my back, and I'd apologized, which I'd thought had been the end of it. But she still resented me, all these years later, especially watching me become a beloved prophet. "I didn't want to burst everyone's bubble, but yeah, she was kind of a self-absorbed mean girl. Really full of herself, sanctimonious. Like someone who'd never really experienced any hardship but felt like she could tell you how to live your life, you know?" Her words stung, because I knew they were true. I felt every bit the failure everyone saw me as.

"Hey! Give me back my phone!" someone said, grabbing it roughly from my hand. My days of being showered with free gifts were over. These Outcasts had loved me for my lies, and now they hated me because of the truth. Everyone's loathing boiled together into a sick sludge, and I felt like I was sinking into it. I needed to find a way out, to contact my friends in the resistance.

I glanced around, certain that my mother would have sent someone to keep an eye on me. I needed to evade whomever she'd assigned to be my tail and find another way out. I spotted a door on the other side of the room that seemed to lead to an exit. Could I make it there, with all these roving eyes on me?

I feigned passing out and dropped beneath the table. It felt almost instinctive to collapse, and once I hit the cool tile floor below, I was strangely comfortable. I didn't even mind the grime; in fact, its grittiness and stickiness on my fingers felt almost pleasant. But I resisted the urge to go back to sleep down here. I ignored the gawking voices, laughing at my fall, and looked around.

I squeezed between the tangle of legs, crawling for the exit. The owners of those legs occasionally cried out, confused, but I pressed on, determined, finally finding an empty booth in a corner to hide beneath.

"Where'd she go?" I heard someone say in English. I'd managed to evade notice; I was safe for now at least, hiding in this tiny little crawlspace beneath these tables. Maybe I could wait here until the bar emptied out, confuse my tail into thinking I'd escaped. Sober up, at least.

But just as I felt my head clearing, to my dismay, a strange face ducked beneath the table. A dark-haired man in his twenties, smiling wickedly. "No, you can't wait here until the bar empties out," he said.

It was such a perfect echo of my plans, it took me a moment to process exactly what he'd said. How had he known what I was thinking? And then I remembered—my mother's nanotech was still in my brain. My enemies had a perfect representation of all my thoughts, which meant this man must be an enemy. There was no escape; I couldn't plot one even if I tried.

I stayed put. As long as I was under this booth, they couldn't kill me. No one could make me look like a fool. Or at least, no more a fool than I'd already made of myself, and I was doing plenty of that on my own. "Come on," he said, low enough so that only I could hear. "You did a good job. You're done for the night. Let's go back."

Woozy, I wanted to acquiesce. But I braced myself against the sides of the booth. If he wanted to take me out of here, he'd have to drag me. "What's going on?" I heard a stranger ask.

The agent answered the stranger, playing a part. "The prophet chick? I don't know, she just came up and started trying to make out with me earlier. I was worried about her. Then she ran in here, I think to have another drink. She was talking about some guy she broke up with, Zack."

"Her boyfriend?" someone said, delighted to hear such juicy gossip about a disgraced prophet.

"Turns out, he never believed in her. He always thought she was just some silly kid—he knew she was full of crap before the rest of us did." Hearing the truth mixed into his fabrication hurt worse somehow. He could have made up a lie, and I wouldn't have cared . . . having everyone know the truest, worst things about me filled me with a new kind of shame I'd never experienced before.

Instinctively, I moved for the exit. I knew escape was un-likely, but at least I was going to try. I popped up among a few confused patrons and noticed my dress had ridden up to my waist, exposing my underwear. Embarrassed, I pulled it down and elbowed my way through the crowd, making a beeline for the door on the opposite side of the room. I had a significant lead on my tail, and for a moment, it seemed like I was getting away.

But suddenly a figure stepped in front to block me. Another guard? As I looked up, a wave of shock washed over me—the man blocking my path was my father.

4

I hadn't seen my father since I'd left him in the stadium in South Africa, and he looked older now, sadder, tired. How had he found me here? I hoped that he knew me well enough to see through my mother's ruse, that he'd know I was being set up. Could he be here to rescue me? But the look on his face proved that couldn't be further from the truth. "Dad, how did you . . ."

"I saw you on the news," he said tersely. "I've been seeing you, all over Europe."

"What are you talking about?" I asked, confused.

"The car you stole in Paris? The drunken cursing fit in Barcelona? It wasn't hard to find you tonight, the paparazzi outside were a dead giveaway." The breadth of my supposed crimes startled me. Had my mother staged all that with a double?

"It's not real . . ." I begged him, but he wouldn't listen.

"I don't want to hear it!" he roared. "Another lie, you can't stop lying, can you? You've committed blasphemy and worse, and you don't even show any remorse!"

Tears rolled down my cheeks—he might have been talking about falsified transgressions, but I knew all the real crimes I'd committed. Ones far worse than he could imagine. Again, it was the truth in his words, not the falsehoods, that pierced to my core.

I glanced behind me to see that my tail was grinning ear to ear, as patrons filmed every word of our fight on their cellphone cameras. Being berated by my own father at an Outcast dive bar? This was playing perfectly into my mother's narrative. At the very least, I knew I had a moment of reprieve, here with my father. "Dad, I need your help," I begged him, eyes still wet with tears.

He shook his head futilely. "How can I help you? With what you've become?" His voice cracked as he said, "My little girl . . ."

"Dad . . ."

But he wouldn't let me finish, too busy drowning himself in nostalgia. "It feels like just yesterday that I was taking you to ballet, watching you help your mother in the garden."

My mother, I could tell him about my mother. "Mom, she's not . . ."

But again, he interrupted me. "Do you remember, after she died, how we tried to keep her garden going?"

I did, and it was one of my more bitter memories, especially now that I knew she hadn't died at all. After my mother's supposed death, seeing her flowers withering in the backyard had been a constant reminder of her absence. Even though I had no skills, no experience, nine-year-old me had set about trying to make them grow again. "Yeah," I said. "I remember."

"And the hydrangeas, you kept replanting, and replanting,

but they kept dying. And you were just inconsolable, like if you could make those hydrangeas grow, you could bring your mother back. I kept telling you, plant them a little deeper. Dig deeper. We tried so hard, we almost dug up the whole back-yard. But we were never going to make those hydrangeas grow. And I realized, sometimes we have to accept defeat. I've accepted defeat, now. I thought I could bring you back into the fold, help you purge your sinful ways, but . . ."

I grabbed him by the arms, interrupting his frustrating ram-blings about flowers. "Dad. I need your help. Please. You don't understand; Mom is alive . . ."

My father pulled away before I could finish. "I can't hear another one of your crazy stories. I'm sorry."

"Dad! Listen to me." I remembered how I was dressed, how I must appear to him, and shame overtook me. He was never going to listen.

My father finally looked up and noticed all the cameras film-ing us. "I can't be here," he stuttered, backing away from me. Of course, even in a moment like this, he had to think of his reputa-tion. I followed him out the door of the bar, only to be greeted by flashbulbs; a mob of paparazzi, as promised. Startled, I took a step back, and in that moment my father disappeared into the crowd. Reporters were bearing down on me, laughing at my tearstained face.

I ducked back inside, trying to compose myself. Though my dad had been dismissive before, it had never been like this. He'd just given up on me when I needed it most. I knew he thought this was tough love, letting me hit rock bottom, but it didn't feel like love at all. I'd been on this side of his concern, his judgment, his pity . . . but never his disdain. I was wrecked. Both my parents had abandoned me in the span of just a few days. I'd lost touch with my friends, alienated my allies, and ruined my reputation. I had nothing left and nowhere to turn.

Except back to my tail, the smirking CIA agent. He walked up to meet me, flanked by two more men in matching black suits. I was surrounded by enemies. "Let's get you home," my tail said, wrapping his arm around me like a friend.

I pushed him away; I wasn't going to let this man touch me.

My captor was undeterred. "You've got two options. You walk out with me now, we ride in the back seat of that limo. Or you stay here, and leave in the trunk." *Play nice or die*, his message came in loud and clear.

Seeing no way out, I reluctantly walked alongside him, keeping as much distance as I could, heading toward a back door. I looked for an escape route—was there anywhere else I could turn? Could the paparazzi help me maybe?

"Don't even try it," my guard whispered to me, and I remembered that he seemed to have a real-time feed of my thoughts in his ear. "You're right, I do," he said, in answer to the question I hadn't asked out loud. "So do what I tell you to, okay?"

I nodded, feeling sick. I hated being penned in like this . . . the claustrophobia of all these people mocking me, watching me march to my death . . . it made my stomach swirl with nausea. Or . . . maybe that was just actual nausea. I stooped, gasping for breath, and then hurled my guts out onto the shiny loafers of a waitress carrying a tray of drinks.

"Prophet Grace just barfed on my shoes!" she cried out, like it was the most hilarious thing in the world.

"Maybe they're a holy relic now," a bartender joked.

As they walked off laughing, I continued retching bile. When I finally stabilized, the agent put an arm around me, helping me up, as I cringed. "Let's get you somewhere you can sleep this off," he said, loud enough for everyone around me to hear.

I wiped my mouth with my arm and adjusted my dress again, trying to regain some semblance of dignity. But there was nothing I could do to quiet the jeers of the crowd or the sarcastic chants of, "Pro-phet Grace! Pro-phet Grace!" It was even worse than my mother had predicted—I wasn't a footnote, I was a laughingstock.

I couldn't wait to be forgotten.

As we exited the building, I put my head down, trying to ignore the flashbulbs, knowing there was nothing I could do to avoid further humiliation. A limo approached, furthering my mother's claims that I was living the self-absorbed high life, out of touch. But I didn't hesitate as I got inside. My enemies had won, and now I just wanted to be alone, to stop giving people more ammunition to shame me with.

The guard closed the door behind us, and the limo drove off. I turned to him. "Where are you taking me?"

He smiled, seemingly friendly. "You're going to get a good night's sleep. Long time coming." Though the words were comforting, there was something menacing about them. If I wasn't going to a prison cell, I had a feeling there was only one other place Esther's colleagues would tolerate keeping me—and it was also six feet underground.

As we drove, I examined my captor—I wondered if they'd picked him because of how much he looked like Zack. From the public's perspective, he was the perfect choice to play my fake "rebound guy." I wondered how much like Zack he really was. Beneath his gruff exterior, could there be a good person, capable of empathy and independent thought? I tested him, "You know what Esther's really like, right? What the truth is?"

"I know everything you know," he reminded me. So yes, he knew the truth.

"Then why are you doing this? Working for them?" I asked.

This stranger looked at me with venom. "To make sure people like you don't destroy what we've built."

I missed the days when my words were magic, when they got me whatever I wanted. It had given me this bluffing confidence that I could talk my way out of anything, anywhere. I felt so powerless now that those same words got me nothing. And I felt hollow, knowing that without my silver tongue, I was defenseless, helpless, hopeless . . . soon to be lifeless.

We settled into silence as I watched the lights of Rome whizz by outside. How much I would have loved to explore this city as a normal teenager: to visit the Coliseum, to down absurd quantities of pasta and gelato. I'd been blessed to get to see so many things in my travels with the resistance, but my heart still ached thinking of everything I wouldn't get to do. Of a whole lifetime, which had disappeared the moment I stepped on that plane with my mother. This car ride had a kind of finality to it; I was en route to my final destination, and there was nothing I could do but accept it, say my final prayers.

So I did. I wasn't sure whether to say them to Great Spirit . . . after prophesizing so many false things in His name,

I felt uncomfortable asking for anything else. So I didn't. In my head, I just prayed, *Great Spirit, God, Allah, whatever you want me to call you . . . If I'm on my way out of this world, please take care of it.* Like my father and those stupid hydrangeas, I finally accepted there was nothing I could do and put my faith in a higher power I wasn't even sure was listening, if only to ease my troubled mind. Everyone else's fate was out of my hands now, so I tried to put it in the best care I could find.

I'd spent so much time worrying about what this deity might want from me, how to please it . . . but in the end, the god I had left wasn't a taskmaster or an overlord, but a gift. A gift of peace, in the midst of a time of turmoil. And maybe that was all that faith in a god, real or imagined, was ever supposed to be.

Our limo pulled up outside a ritzy hotel, and I warily followed my guard inside. I glanced at the patrons filling the lobby's lavish chairs and wondered which of them worked for the prophets. Which of them were here to take me down if I tried to run. "Not telling you." The guard smirked, and I cringed, hating him more and more with each forced step I took. Where else could this night end except with my demise, in some deeply humiliating fashion? The final straw, to cement my disgrace.

But still, I followed him into the elevator, to the top floor: the penthouse. The luxury accommodations of Redenção had nothing on the ritziest parts of Rome, with all the wealth and glamour that came from living at the feet of the prophets. Every bit of furnishing looked priceless and fragile. As we entered our suite, my guard plopped himself on the king-size bed and gestured to the two glasses of champagne that had been left on the bedside table. "Drink?"

I shook my head, still feeling a little woozy from whatever they'd pumped in me earlier. And I certainly wasn't going to voluntarily eat or drink anything this man had to offer, for fear of whatever he might have drugged it with.

I shrank into a corner, as far as I could get from my captor. "I'm not going to hurt you," he promised, but I didn't believe him. "Go to the bathroom, I know you need to."

I blushed, realizing he knew everything—every sensation I was feeling, every urge, every fear. I tentatively opened the door, expecting it to contain something fatal, but it was just a normal, opulent bathroom. I locked the door behind me, afraid to touch anything. Had they planted some transdermal drug on the toilet seat? The sink handles?

I pulled off a roll of toilet paper and began to obsessively clean everything, embarrassed to realize that my every action was being monitored by multiple people. Finally, I sat down to use the toilet, and think. There had to be some way out of here, besides in a body bag.

As I exited the bathroom, my guard turned on loud music. "What's that for?" I asked, nervous.

He shrugged. "Privacy."

The room felt hot, and my heart beat wildly. I tried to find a way to stall. "Can you give me a minute?" I asked, pointing to the balcony.

He shrugged. Sure."

As I stepped into the chilly night outside, I realized why he'd been so blasé—at fifty stories up, there was nowhere for me to go. He would have loved it if I'd tried to escape, jumped to my death . . . it'd make his job much easier. Maybe that was his plan all along, to stage exactly that scene. I stared out at the city lights. Was this it? My final moments?

And then something caught my eye on the corner of the balcony. *Hydrangeas.* Poetic. Or . . . perhaps something else. I saw a thin piece of wire, running from the pot, along the edge of the roof. My heart stopped for a second as I moved over to it. Could it be some kind of explosive? Had they planned for me to go out a different way, in a terrorist attack of some sort?

But no . . . this wasn't my mother's doing. *It was my father's.* My breath caught in my throat, remembering my father's instructions: "Dig deeper."

So I dug, frantic, disbelieving. And indeed, as my fingernails tore through the loose dirt, they ran into something hard. I yanked out this mystery object and brushed off the soil: it was a harness, attached to that wire I'd seen.

I could hear my tail running toward the balcony, his footsteps urgent; he'd heard every one of my thoughts and figured out what was happening. I hurriedly wrapped the straps of the harness around my chest, locking myself in. And just as I closed the final carabiner, as the guard was moments away from tackling me, something thrust me skyward.

The force of the tug knocked the wind out of me, and I screamed—I was suddenly hanging in midair, as if from nothing. The guard reached to grab me, but I was already above him, flying inexplicably up, up into the sky, whipping through the icy night breeze.

My hotel balcony was just a dot now as my high heels fell off, one by one, tiny little projectiles headed to the earth far below. I gripped onto the harness, terrified that it would come loose. But for once I didn't care that I was flashing my underwear to the whole world. I was free!

But free how, and where? I glanced up; the wire extended above me to something that looked almost like a missile. Whatever was propelling me upward must have been planted on the roof, disguised somehow. Set off at the perfect moment to send me into the sky.

I could barely catch my breath as I flew up and up, over the Tiber. Amid the terror that was beating my heart wildly, there was a little bit of joy at the absurdity of what was happening. Though my bare skin shook fiercely against the cold winds, adrenaline kept me vigilant: I was flying up above Rome, toward the Italian countryside. It was impossibly, terrifyingly magical.

And then, almost imperceptibly at first, I felt myself starting to slow down. The rocket, whatever it was, was losing acceleration. For a moment, it felt like I was hovering in midair. Until . . . my stomach lurched, and I began to fall.

And fall fast.

My mind raced in terror as I desperately examined the harness. I must have missed some instruction that showed me how to release the parachute. Had there been a note buried in the flowerpot that I'd failed to find? I saw no tab to pull, nothing that signaled how to stop my sudden acceleration toward the earth. I'd never been skydiving, but I had a feeling it was more fun when it didn't end in death.

I spread my limbs and leaned forward, hoping that I could slow myself a little at least by increasing the wind resistance. But I kept falling, faster and faster. Panic surged through me like a storm, engulfing everything.

It was over. My life was over. I closed my eyes, bracing for the worst . . .

And then I felt myself being jerked upward again, and sideways this time. It hurt like heck, knocking the breath out of me and rattling my brain in its cage. What on earth was happening? When I managed to orient myself and get my bearings, I looked up to see that a small plane had caught onto the wire and was now towing me, high above the city of Rome. My friends had staged the strangest, most impossible rescue.

I breathed half a sigh of relief. The other half would have to wait until I was safely in that plane.

I saw a familiar face lean out of the plane, pulling up on the wire attached to my harness: Jude. He shouted something to me, which I assumed was, "Are you okay down there?" I didn't respond; I knew he wouldn't be able to hear me, and I definitely didn't feel okay. He reeled me in slowly. It felt like ages until I was finally gripping on to his hand, then on to the side of the plane. I could hear him now, loud and clear. "I've got you, just hold on."

One final jolt of terror, as I let him pull me up and in, and then Dawn shut the side of the plane door. Collapsed on the floor of the plane, I gulped in air, letting the fear spill out of me. I was, somehow, alive.

"Don't move," Dr. Marko said, and I realized he was here, too, walking into my peripheral vision. I was still disoriented from flying through the air and the residual doping, so I barely noticed as he placed a gas mask over my face. I recognized the sound of the whirring machine immediately: he was removing my nanotech, the new nanotech that recorded all my thoughts. Finally, my brain's connection to my mother's computer was being severed.

After a moment, he removed the gas mask, and I looked around. Jude, Dr. Marko, and Dawn were all clustered around me. "Are you okay?" Jude asked, concerned, and I nodded.

"Your thoughts are off the grid again," Dr. Marko reassured

me. "Speaking of . . ." Marko looked to the pilot, an Outcast with a cheery disposition. A nod from the cockpit, and suddenly the plane tilted, changing course, evading my mother.

I breathed a sigh of relief—I was starting to like these sighs of relief. "How did you guys find me?"

"Your mother let us stay hacked into her system, so we could see all your thoughts." Dawn explained, as she covered me with a blanket—I was still shivering from the cold air outside. "I think she expected us to fold, to see that our plan had failed and find a way to pull the plug on the video."

"But instead we used it to track your location," Jude said proudly. "The hard part was figuring out how to rescue you without letting you and your mother know what was happening."

"My dad," I said, remembering who had given me the key clue. "How did you find him? And, you know, convince him I wasn't the devil . . ."

Dawn smiled. "We didn't. He found *us* in Redenção after you disappeared. He knew the pictures he was seeing on the news weren't you. Even if you'd gone crazy, he was sure you were still a good person underneath, that you wouldn't be doing things that hurt people, no matter what. So we removed his nanotech, told him the truth, and he joined up with us."

I could barely believe it. "My dad. He's on our side?"

"Waiting to meet us outside Vatican City."

"Vatican City?" I asked, confused. "Shouldn't we be getting the heck away from there?"

Dawn shook her head. "The video is still set to go live in four days. Which means our plan has to go forward, and we need your help."

Every inch of my body was still searing with pain from my trip into the sky, and my head ached from all the substances that had been in it recently. The last thing I wanted to do was put myself in the middle of another high-stress, life-or-death mission. But I could tell by their faces, this wasn't something that could wait.

"What do you need me to do?" I asked.

Dawn took a deep breath. "We need you to be your mother."

Before I could ask for more details, Dawn handed me a parachute pack. "Put this on."

I stared at her, incredulous. "You want me to go skydiving again? No way. I didn't love it the first time." Every cell in my body rebelled at the idea of leaving this plane.

"Sorry, but the prophets will be tracking the airfields near here. If we want to get out alive, this is our only option." I glanced over at the Outcast pilot, horrified. If this plane was going down, was he going down with it?

Dr. Marko followed my gaze and said softly, "He agreed to this going in. We needed someone willing to accept whatever consequences arose, and . . . he's still willing to do anything for you. One of the few left." I felt ill at the thought of yet another human being sacrificing their life for me, dying for a lie.

I'd done enough lying. "I'm not willing to let him do that."

Dawn stepped in this time, trying to reassure me, "He'll take the plane as far as he can and then jump himself. Hopefully the prophets won't find him. But if they do, maybe it'll be before they find us. Give us a bit of a head start."

Her words, careful as they were, still twisted my stomach with guilt. But as I looked down at the rolling green hills below us, I realized Dawn was right—if we wanted to have any chance at finishing our mission, this was our only way out. "Okay," I relented, taking the harness from Dawn. What was one more life on a conscience that already bore the burden of so many lost lives?

"You've come this far," Jude said, reassuring. "We'll get you to safety."

Thankfully I wouldn't be alone in the air this time—Jude strapped himself into the two-person harness with me and showed me how to work the parachute, which thankfully existed this time. "Don't worry, I'll be the one to pull it," he promised. My heart fluttered a little to be this close to him. And I was relieved that finally, my thoughts and feelings were mine alone.

My heart fluttered much more wildly as we stepped to the edge of the plane, looking down at the ground so far below us. "Ready?" Jude asked me.

"You've done this before, right?" I asked him.

"At least once more than you," he joked, trying to be reassuring. I'd been so grateful to have two feet perched on something solid again; everything inside of me resisted going back to free fall. But I knew I had two choices—jumping now, or jumping when our plane was under fire from the prophets.

I tried to exterminate my fears. "Ready," I said, taking a deep breath.

I wasn't sure if I could will my feet forward, but then I heard Jude's steady, "One, two, three," and suddenly we were jumping.

I closed my eyes as we hurtled toward the earth, my stomach flip-flopping, the wind whipping my hair everywhere. My body ached—I just wanted it to be over, to be safely back on the warm ground again. But then, Jude pulled the parachute, yanking us out of free fall, and suddenly the wind slowed.

I opened my eyes to see the Tuscan landscape below us. On the edge of the horizon, the first few rays of sunrise were beginning to peek through, and I watched as the pink light slowly crept up the edges of the sky below us. "It's beautiful," I said. Jude squeezed my hand, and for a moment I forgot how cold I was, forgot how scared I was, how much my body was hurting. For a moment, up here, I was safe, with someone I loved. I had no idea when or how that might happen again, so I decided to enjoy this brief moment of peace. In truth, there was nowhere else in the world I would have wanted to be.

We slowly floated down to a field crisscrossed with dark lines, a vineyard, I discovered as we grew closer. "Brace yourself," Jude told me, but I still wasn't ready for the force of the earth moving up to meet us—a heavy smack against the soles of my bare feet. I clung to Jude, trying to keep from losing my balance, and he steadied us. As our motion stilled, I took a deep breath. "I guess we're alive," he said with a grin.

My heart was still pounding, but I felt a sense of deep relief. "That was easier than last time," I muttered, removing my harness and readjusting my sequined dress.

"You've had a busy day," he joked, gathering up our parachute.

I scanned the horizon and saw an unfamiliar car driving toward us with its lights off. An instinctive shot of dread whipped through me. Had the prophets found us already? I prodded Jude's arm, alerting him, and we ducked behind the grapevines—not much cover, but better than nothing, in case it was an enemy.

The car stopped near us, engine still running, and I heard a car door slam. I looked at Jude—should we run? But then I saw the familiar figure walking toward us—it was Zack. Our getaway vehicle. Energized, I stood up straighter, limping toward the car with aching limbs that felt like they'd aged decades in a matter of hours.

Jude put an arm around me to help me move, as Zack ran to meet us, putting an arm around my other side. "Have they spotted us?" Jude asked Zack.

Zack's face remained expressionless. "Hard to tell. We seem to be in the clear, but we've been outplayed before."

As we approached the car, I saw a second figure in the driver's seat—my father. I broke away from Jude and Zack, ignoring the pain, limp-running toward the car. "Dad!" He opened the door and hopped out to hug me. As he wrapped his arms around me, I started crying. I hadn't realized how badly I'd been missing my father's love and approval.

"Grace. I'm so glad you're okay . . ."

"Thank you for believing me," I said, choking up.

"Took me long enough," he said, and in that moment all my anger at him was erased. I had my father back, finally.

"We need to move," Jude said as politely as he could. We loaded ourselves into the car, as my dad took the wheel again, hurtling off down this winding rural road.

"Where are Dawn and Dr. Marko?" I asked.

"Macy spotted them in the air not far from here," Jude said. "She's on her way to pick them up now. We're reconvening at a castle nearby."

"A castle?" Just when I thought this day couldn't get any weirder.

"Well, in a manner of speaking," Jude said.

When we arrived, I discovered it was indeed a castle only in a manner of speaking. The roof had long ago collapsed, and it was covered by a tarp to keep out the rain, which was only sort of working; the floor was sticky with mud. "I feel like a princess," I joked as we entered.

"Sorry this isn't up to the luxury of your private jets," my father ribbed me back.

Thinking of that jet reminded me: "Dad, did they tell you who took me on it?"

My dad's face grew dark. "I still don't quite believe it. I wouldn't have, but they showed me a picture they took of her in captivity in Redenção."

"I wanted to tell you so badly," I told him. "Back in Johannesburg."

My father admitted, "I wouldn't have believed you. I was so angry at you, for making fools of everyone, pretending to be a prophet. I couldn't face the fact that I was the fool."

"No more a fool than the rest of us," I reassured him.

My father nodded. "I decided the only way to stop being one

was to admit that I was one." Before he could say anything else, we heard another car drive up—it was Macy, with Dawn and Dr. Marko in tow.

"We did it!" Macy crowed excitedly.

As they entered, Dr. Marko's hair was wild and askew, and he seemed overwhelmed. "I never want to do that again," he said.

"Try doing it without a parachute," I said bitterly.

Dawn, however, was already back to business. "Are we all here? Let's get started." Our little castle went silent, as Dawn unfurled blueprints of St. Peter's Tower. "We need to get in here."

"How?" I asked, skeptical. "That place is crazy secure. Guards on every level."

"That's why we need your mother's help to get in. That is, you, posing as your mother."

I considered it. "I don't know if I can pull it off. Even under a burqa, won't they be able to tell I'm someone else?"

"Maybe they won't look too closely," Jude suggested.

"I'll try," I said unconvincingly.

"What are we searching for once Grace gets inside?" my father asked.

Dr. Marko chimed in, "Well, one of the things Grace wasn't privy to, when she was the mole and we were keeping information from her, is I've spent the past few weeks developing a virus that will rewrite the code of the nanotech in our heads. The problem is, I don't have the source code for the bugs themselves. I need that to implement the virus."

"How do we know the source code is at St. Peter's Tower?" I asked.

"Your mother let us see through your eyes when you were inside," Zack explained. "And in the process, we figured out where we can access the source code, on an advanced nanofabricator. We need you to use it to create Dr. Marko's virus, then smuggle it back out." I remembered the heavily guarded hallway my mother had whisked me past—I had a hunch that was the location my friends were referring to.

I considered . . . could my mother have given us that lead as bait? "And what if they're ready for us?"

Dr. Marko stared at me soberly. "Then you'll have to move quickly. The moment you rewrite the code, you'll have only a short window to get outside."

This was it, our last chance, and it rested entirely on me. I hoped that this time I wouldn't let everyone down.

7

We drove back into Rome in the middle of rush hour, camouflaging ourselves among the thousands of other commuting cars. The closer we got to Vatican City, the more my stomach filled with dread. I ducked down in the back seat, worried the prophets might be searching for anyone who matched the description of the disgraced missing prophet. Or for any of us, really. My father turned on the car radio, and we listened for news reports of my startling escape. Surely a teenage girl shooting into the sky would make headlines? But somehow my mother had kept a lid on mainstream Italian media sources at least. I guessed those drones in her office had something to do with that.

My father parked the car a half mile from the gates of Vatican City. "You'll need to go by foot from here," Zack told me.

"Where is Esther right now?" I wondered. This plan wouldn't work if I crossed paths with her.

I could hear the fear in Jude's voice. "We aren't sure. Maybe in Vatican City somewhere. Maybe in Timbuktu."

"So luck, we're betting on luck here," I said darkly.

Zack handed me a small comms device, which I placed inside my ear. "So we can communicate while you're in the field."

I looked at these three men, who all meant so much to me, and felt them giving me strength. "Get back safe," my father told me. Worry was etched deep into his voice; this was his first resistance mission after all. And his first time watching his daughter walk into mortal danger.

"I'll get back with what we need," I promised him.

I left Zack and my father behind as Jude walked with me toward an alley, handing me a burqa. "Layla's parting gift. She sewed it herself."

I'd been wondering where Layla was but hadn't found an appropriate moment to ask. "Why didn't she come with you?"

Jude hesitated, and I saw the answer on his face. "She wanted to stay behind with her family. She felt like we had enough help here. And . . . well, because of the fallout, after what she saw in your mother's files, that you were thinking . . ."

"I'm sorry," I sputtered. "I didn't mean . . ."

"No," he admitted. "It wasn't just you. She didn't leave because of you, I mean. She left because of me."

My breath caught in my throat. "Oh."

He seemed almost bashful, nervously gauging my expression as he spoke. "She knew how I felt about you. I think she always knew, hoped it would fade. *I* hoped it would fade. But after all this time . . . Ten years from now, twenty years from now . . . I guess some part of me will always love you."

I couldn't quite believe those words had just escaped his mouth. I wanted to grab him, hug him. "I love you, too," I whispered.

He took my hand, face pained. "Right now, all that matters is you get back to us, safe."

"I'll do my best," I promised him. A part of me wished I didn't know what he'd just told me, that I didn't have a reason to want to survive this mission. Because the truth was, there was a decent chance that the fate of the world rested on me making a sacrifice that would keep me from Jude forever.

With an encouraging brush of my arm, he was off, retreating back to the car, and I ached, watching him go. But I knew, nothing I felt for him mattered unless our plan succeeded. I steadied myself, slipping the burqa over my head. It matched my mother's exactly—Layla had done a great job replicating it. I felt a pang of guilt and gratitude for my friend, whom I'd unwittingly hurt, wondering if I'd ever see her again.

As I walked toward the Vatican, the thick black fabric blocked the sun's rays. After being so cold flying through the air, it was a welcome change to overheat. I pushed through the throngs of tourists to the entrance of Vatican City. Gripping my fake key card with sweaty fingers, I approached the gate, nodding to the guard with an imitation of my mother's melodic, authoritative tone. "Morning, Tomas." I wondered if he remembered me walking through this door with my mother only days earlier. If he did, he didn't recognize me—my performance was fooling him so far.

I did my best to mimic my mother's crisp, efficient gait as I moved to the door and swiped my key card, which obviously didn't work. Pretended to be startled when the knob didn't turn. Glanced back at Tomas, letting him look into my eyes; I knew I had my mother's eyes, and filling them with her cold annoyance completed the picture. Without looking at me too closely, Tomas nervously pressed a button. I heard the door unlatch. "Morning, Esther."

He couldn't see my victorious smile beneath the burqa as I stepped inside. So far, as long as I acted like I belonged, I looked enough like I did to pass through without being hassled. Thankfully, the most important people in the prophets' organization weren't subject to the same levels of scrutiny as mere mortals.

But as I stepped inside the gates, my insides twisted up as I saw her: Esther, across the square, walking toward me. The moment I'd most feared was happening already. Our plan was about to fail.

8

She's here," I whispered into my comms.

"Already?" Zack asked, distressed. None of us had expected to encounter Esther so soon.

My voice shook as I confirmed, "Walking across the square toward me."

"Hang by the doors, we'll need you to let in backup."

"Copy," I said, hoping that loitering near the entrance wouldn't attract too much attention. Would Esther spot me as easily as I'd spotted her? In our all-black attire, we stuck out like sore thumbs.

"Now," I heard Zack's voice say a few moments later, and I opened the door I'd just walked through to see my father heading toward the entrance, eyed suspiciously by the guard.

"Peter!" I said brightly, thinking of the first fake name that popped into my brain. I wished I'd thought of one that wasn't also the name of the building we were about to break into.

"Esther!" he said, and we shook hands like old colleagues as

I held the door open for him. The guard's suspicions seemed assuaged, and I let my father inside the gates.

"Go get her," I whispered, hanging back behind a nearby building, watching from out of Esther's sight.

My father was still a few yards away when Esther spotted him and stopped in her tracks. "Valerie!" he called out, anger in his voice. She immediately turned tail, walking in the opposite direction, as he stalked her across the square. "Valerie, I know that's you!"

As much as I wanted to watch my parents' long overdue confrontation, I knew my father's presence here would raise suspicions all on its own. My father's job was to distract Esther, play on her emotions. To keep her from turning him in, and from thinking about why he might be here, besides to witness the aliveness of the wife who'd faked her death.

My job was to get into St. Peter's Tower. There would be no guard to social engineer at its entrance, and my key card wouldn't get me to where I needed to go. Panic bloomed inside me. What if I couldn't do this? But as I waited for the elevators, I noticed the respectful looks of other employees standing next to me. They bought my disguise completely. Why wouldn't they? Who'd expect an impostor beneath her uniform, especially one whose eyes looked like hers?

I remembered to act important as I strode onto the elevator, taking a spot in the back. "Which floor?" someone asked, and I gestured to the top, giving a slow little wave like the one I always remembered my mother making. Without even saying the number, I'd gotten a drone to swipe me onto the top floor.

When I emerged onto the mezzanine, I moved quickly. Ignoring the mass of drones at their monitors below, I swung by my mother's office, grabbing a set of keys from her desk drawer.

Then I headed straight for the heavily guarded hallway I'd noted the first time I was here, moving toward the room where Dr. Marko had said I'd be able to clone the tech. My disguise as Esther allowed me to move unfettered past the rows and rows of doors that lined the hall. According to their intel, I was looking for a green one.

But when I approached that door, I found an armed guard waiting, eyeing me suspiciously. My breath caught in my throat; this man wasn't simply going to step aside. The tech controlling his brain would force him to follow instructions to a letter. "What are you doing here?"

I steadied myself. "Can you give me a moment?" I asked politely, trying to give my voice the same melodic, officious timbre my mother's possessed, as I jingled the keys in my hand so he'd know I was allowed to be here.

His eyes narrowed. "Do you have global approvals?"

"Did you see what happened last night?" I snapped back at him. For a moment, it was as though my mother was speaking through me, as I told him, voice cracking, "My daughter was shot into the sky last night. Someone kidnapped her, out of our clutches. We have a rogue prophet out there somewhere, and we don't have time to sit around and get Denmark to approve fixing the problem. I gave them a chance to deal with this the way they wanted to, and now look where we are. I'm going to fix this myself, and you are going to let me. Now, move."

The guard cowered, overwhelmed. "I can't . . ."

"Go, make the call, tell everyone what I'm doing. I'll live

with the consequences. What I won't live with is my daughter hiding out in some hole somewhere, sending messages that undermine the fabric of the world we live in. That will get millions, maybe billions of innocent people killed. Not again."

I could see the anger rising in him, but he didn't lift his gun. He strode off past me in a huff, presumably to make that call. I inhaled deeply, shaking from the effort, and fumbled until I found the key that fit this lock. I entered, relocking the door behind me, adrenaline rushing as I tried to avert pure panic.

I'd solved one problem but created another. I now had very limited time in this room to follow Dr. Marko's instructions. And then, I knew there was only one way I could transport the nanotech out of here: in my own body.

9

This machine was the most complex thing I'd ever seen—a thousand times more powerful than the device we'd stolen in Rio. It was an advanced 3-D nanofabricator, which could combine atoms into molecules at a higher rate than any other machine on the planet. Its precision and dexterity could produce just about any substance, and soon, it would spit out the one Dr. Marko had concocted. My fingers fumbled as I typed in the series of letters and numbers that he'd made me memorize: the formula he'd concocted that, when combined with the source code in this machine, would create a virus that could rewrite the nanotech in our brains.

I braced myself, overcome with doubt and trepidation. I'd had so many different pieces of machinery inside my head over the years—changing my body, changing my thoughts, reading them and broadcasting them. Did I really want to put something else in there? Especially some new experimental bug that had never been tried on a human being before? Dr. Marko thought this would work on paper, sure, but no one had ever tested out the real thing. I'd agreed to be not just the carrier pigeon, but the guinea pig.

But that was it: I'd already agreed to it. As the printer finished its job, I regarded its contents with wariness. The vial that emerged contained a dense, sticky fluid. Dr. Marko had explained that just one drop contained enough of the nanotech to infect me in a few minutes—its replication rate was a thousand times faster than any previous form of the bugs. I opened the vial and dipped my finger into the liquid—it was still warm. I exhaled, knowing I didn't have much time, and then inhaled the liquid off my finger.

It felt strange as it made its way through my nostrils, into my sinuses. It would be in my bloodstream soon, reproducing by feeding off the sugars in my blood, then invading my lungs. I sat and waited, tried to see if I could feel the tech moving through me, but its presence was just as invisible as every previous generation of the technology.

The first time I'd been infected, I'd thought it was a gift from a god, as I sat in my father's worship center waiting for Great Spirit to judge me. Had I been good or bad? Though I'd recalled a thousand little sins, they were the sins of a child. Nothing compared to all my new adult sins.

I wondered how I might fare now, with this new invasive weapon inside of me. Would my guilt kill me? I'd taken uppers before I left, just in case, but I still worried—what if they didn't work the way we expected with this new tech? What if my crimes as a false prophet were enough to take me out for good?

But as the nanotech took hold, my appearance never changed. Instead, I felt the tickle in the back of my throat that Dr. Marko had said would signal that the tech was working as expected. "My throat feels scratchy," I said into my comms.

I heard Dr. Marko's voice echoing back to me. "Good. Now get out of there." Hoping I hadn't missed some other vital step, I dropped the rest of the vial into an incinerator in the corner of the room, then reached beneath my burqa into my pocket for the small electromagnetic pulse device I'd brought with me—a weapon that delivered a small but powerful burst that would destroy all electronics in the immediate vicinity. We could leave behind no evidence of what we'd just built. I set off the weapon; the lights above my head flickered off, and the screen on the monitor went dark. The most powerful machine in the world for creating new nanotech was now destroyed. Permanently. "The virus is deployed, and the EMP destroyed the nanofabricator," I said quietly into comms.

"Good," Dawn said. "Esther's gotten away from your father, and she's headed for the building. You're running out of time."

I peeked out into the hall, where the lights had gone dark, too. By now, the guards were onto me. As I attempted to make my escape, heading into the hallway, two of them quickly cornered me, pulling off my veil, revealing my face. "The real Esther wants to know what you're up to," one sneered.

The tickle in my throat moved up to my nose, and I sneezed—right in his face. "Sorry," I said, unable to hide my victorious smile. "Got a little cold."

While one of the guards held on to me, the other stepped

inside the machine room to see what I'd been doing in there. When he emerged, a few moments later, he was livid. "What did you do to that machine?"

"Oh, is something wrong?" I asked, taunting him a little. "It looked fine when I left."

He nodded to his comrade, cold. "Lock her in a cell. See if she'll talk in a few days." But the guard who was holding on to me didn't move; he was rubbing his throat, eyebrows furrowed. The other guard glared at him. "What's going on?"

But the guard holding me didn't respond, just stared into space, as though trying to get his bearings. "Give me a minute."

The first guard rolled his eyes and grabbed my arm. "Fine, I'll take her."

But as he walked me toward the elevator, his gait slowed, as he moved to touch his own throat. He looked at me quizzically, as though seeing me for the first time. *Our plan was working.*

There was a reason I had to be the one to carry out the tech—it wasn't just a computer virus. It was a literal virus, transmitted from person to person. But this one, once caught, disabled any nanotech in a person's brain. And it spread the way any other virus did—by replicating in its victims' lungs, over-producing mucus, and causing them to sneeze. My every breath carried the disease of truth. We weren't just stealing a piece of tech—we were striking a deathblow into the heart of Vatican City along with it. My mother thought that by brainwashing her security force, she'd keep herself safer; in actuality, she'd given me one simple way to disable all of them at once.

As the guard wheezed into the crowd of office drones, some of whom were already grabbing at their throats, sniffling, I walked past him. No one stopped me—the tech in their heads no longer demanded they blindly obey the prophets.

I stepped into the elevator, and the doors closed in front of me. Now alone, I tossed off the burqa, and instead covered my head with a large hat I'd kept in my pocket. I made sure to cover every shred of my hair—my wild mane would be the most obvious giveaway.

When the elevator doors opened, I saw a phalanx of armed guards waiting to meet me. I smiled at them, trying to exit, but they pushed me back in. "Prophet Grace?" So much for the hat as a disguise.

I reluctantly stepped back, as they all piled in with me. And then I sneezed. "Bless you," one of them said.

"Thanks," I said.

By the time our elevator reached the bottom floor, and the elevator doors opened up to a dank stone basement that looked like a prison, I saw hands moving to throats. In the small space of that elevator, the tech had dispersed quickly, filling all the available air. The guards seemed confused about what to do with me, what to do with themselves. I reached over to hit the button for lobby, and the elevator quickly rocketed back to the main level.

Back on the ground floor, I pushed past the confused guards and out onto the main square of Vatican City, where I broke into a run. My lungs were filled with mucus, the results of my sudden onset cold, and every part of my body still ached from my various trips through the sky. But I saw freedom now—it was so close. Just on the other side of that gate.

But as I was about to open the door, escape back into the

expanse of Rome, an arm grabbed me. Esther, with no nano-tech for the virus to destroy. My mother, furious. "What the hell did you do?" Her voice was brittle, hollow. A woman who had lost everything.

"What's done is done," I told her with a kind of finality, and I twisted from her grip, running out of the gates, past a confused Tomas, and onto the streets of Rome. I ran and ran, pushing past pedestrians, and hopped onto a crowded bus. The digital letters on its front broadcast its final destination: *Aeroporto*. As I looked around at the other passengers, noses already starting to run, I felt a smile come across my face. There was nothing that could stop us now.

When we arrived at the airport, sneezing passengers spilled out ahead of me into the terminal. I saw Jude waiting on the curb and walked to meet him. "Your mom is coming," he warned me. "You have to do this fast."

I nodded, pulling off my hat, as Jude pointed his phone at me, starting to roll. For a second I wondered how I looked, thought to reach for some makeup to be on-camera . . . before I remembered that it didn't matter, that nothing mattered besides what I had to say. "The second Revelation is coming," I said into the lens. "It's already on its way to you. You'll see for your-selves, soon enough. And in four days, I'll tell you everything."

Jude ended the recording and hit a few strokes on his phone. "It's out there." The video was in the wind, and so was the virus that would destroy everyone's nanotech. It was spreading like wildfire, and there was nothing the prophets could do to stop it.

I hugged Jude with relief. "Where do you want to go now?" he asked.

I knew what he meant. We'd always talked about where we'd want to go when we got our real lives back. Nova Scotia, Tokyo. "Tutelo. I want to go home."

"Me, too." I knew he hadn't seen his parents in years. Soon he'd be able to.

Or maybe not. In the distance, we saw a convoy of military vehicles, sirens blaring.

"Run," I said, but there was nowhere to go. My mother had surrounded us from every angle. We weren't going anywhere but prison.

10

As Jude and I sat in the back of a military vehicle, for the first time in a long time, I wasn't afraid. Esther could do what she wanted with us—in a matter of days, that virus would spread around the world, and we could finally tell people the truth, without risking their lives. It was over, and there was nothing she could do about it.

Jude stared at me with a mixture of awe and apprehension. "You really think your mom's out of tricks up her sleeve?"

"I don't know," I said, fear rising inside of me. My mother had surprised us so many times before.

"Whatever's ahead, we'll face it together," he promised me. His smile was so genuine, so kind as always. I wondered, with a shot of embarrassment: How many details did he know about my fantasies of him?

"I'm not sure if you read . . ." I began.

"Your thoughts?" he interrupted.

"Yeah," I said, relieved not to have to finish that sentence.

"No way in hell," he promised.

"Really?" I asked, surprised by his definitive tone.

He shook his head. "Layla tried to tell me a couple things, but I told her to stop. That was messed up, what your mom did. I get that they had to keep reading, you know, to save you. But I didn't want to be involved."

Despite everything he'd been through, he was still the sweet young man I'd fallen in love with. More than that, because tragedy had carved him into someone more resilient. "Thanks," I said. "You're a good person."

"So are you. And I don't have to read what's inside your head to know that," he joked.

"I don't know if I'm so good anymore," I muttered.

"You're less perfect, that's true," he admitted. "But to be good I think you have to stop being perfect."

"You sure about that?" I asked, skeptical.

"You're braver. And you accept people on their terms, instead of trying to enforce your own. You're kinder, even if it doesn't feel like it." His words knocked down a wall inside of me I hadn't even realized I'd built. The idea that there might still be good in me, despite everything I'd done, filled me with hope. That whatever I'd sacrificed to get us here, it hadn't been my soul.

For so long, I'd been holding my feelings for Jude in a box deep inside my heart, and now that Layla was gone, I felt them pouring out. "If we get out of here," I began, and instead of letting me finish, he squeezed my hand. Looked into my eyes.

"Yeah," he answered. "If we get out of here."

It was at once the realization of a long-held dream, and a

wish that would remain unfulfilled. My hopes were dwindling that we would find a way out of my mother's clutches.

The van stopped, and two agents opened the back doors and grabbed me, pulling me out of the van, away from Jude. I reached for him, to hold his hand one last time, but our fingers just barely missed each other. "Grace!" he called out, but then I was out of the van, as the agents hauled me into an imposing stone building: a women's prison.

After a brief intake exam, a guard led me onto the dank and crowded main floor, and the room tittered with excitement—a hundred heads turned to watch my every move. I could hear the victorious murmurs of those who hated me, the ones who thought I deserved my place here. More quietly, too, I heard the reverent whispers of those few devotees who might still believe in me.

But I didn't care about any of it. In a few days, it would all be over. The people who loved me would hate me for lying, and the ones who hated me might have a little more sympathy now that I was finally telling the truth. I barely ate; every spare moment I had, I huddled around the TV in the common room, making sure it was tuned to the news and fighting off anyone who wanted to change the channel.

On the fourth day, a few hours before I knew my announcement would be going live, the other prisoners overpowered me, putting on some soccer game. I still hovered, anxious, looking for any opportunity to change it back, as my fellow prisoners cheered with hoarse voices—they, too, of course, had fallen victim to the virus I'd carried in here with me.

"Prophet Grace, I still believe in you," one sniffling young woman whispered to me as I fumed in the corner.

"You won't soon," I told her.

But as soccer transitioned to car racing, a news broadcast interrupted it all. "Breaking news. The strange virus that's raced around the world, causing mild coldlike symptoms, might finally have an explanation. A scientist claims it's part of ending a decades-long conspiracy, and a video from the disgraced Prophet Grace, recorded last week, seems to back up that theory." The whole room went silent, looking at me, as the television played my speech, the one that had been set to automatically upload.

My face was from only a week ago, but it seemed so innocent. I felt like I was watching a stranger, who intoned with gravity, "My friends, I have an apology to make. What I'm about to tell you won't be easy for me to say, or easy for you to hear. But it has to be said, and heard. You've put your trust in me, and I abused that trust. Because I knew something you didn't. That this world we live in, it's a lie. Punishments and Forgiveness aren't the work of Great Spirit, but of mere mortals. The prophets around the world have worked together to conceal that fact. My own prophetship was meant to challenge their power, to give me the chance to do what I'm doing now—to reveal the truth to you. While I wish I could have done it sooner, I'm just grateful I could do it at all. Know that Great Spirit will not Punish you for doubting Him, for questioning His power, His existence. You're all safe now, I promise. I hope we can all find a way to move forward together, peacefully, without leaning on the crutch of an imaginary religion to save us."

I drank in every word, the broadcast warming my cold soul.

We'd finally done it—we'd gotten the truth out there. When the video finished, an interviewer turned to Dr. Marko, who'd found his way to media outlets to explain the science behind what had happened to all of us—nanotechnology, serotonin receptors, everything I'd learned last year. The other inmates lingered around me in a strange kind of silence, watching with apprehension and confusion.

It was only a matter of time now. They'd arrest Esther, and the rest of the prophets, and I'd be exonerated. I took a deep breath, and I waited.

11

B ut as the days passed, I started to worry. Why was I still in here? Weren't my friends passionately working on my case? Days turned into weeks, and the agony of not knowing gnawed at me. Why wasn't anyone coming to see me? I felt like I was back in Redenção—isolated, with no idea what the resistance was planning. Once again, unsure if my friends had even survived.

My eyes stayed glued to the TV, desperate for any clues about what was happening in the outside world. I saw my mother and the other prophets being led away in handcuffs, as the talking heads decried the depth of their crimes. It took nearly a week before I saw any mention of my friends: the first footage of Dawn at a bail hearing. The news described her as "an accomplice of Prophet Grace," a phrase that both made me laugh and made my stomach turn.

Dawn played into the narrative, defending me at every turn.

"Grace did everything she could to bring peace to this world," she told the news cameras, as she valiantly argued her innocence. It was surreal, to see her describing me as someone she admired. And I was moved, realizing it wasn't just an act . . . my mentor actually believed in me that much. As the case played out, the public seemed swayed to Dawn's side.

They did not, however, seem convinced of *my* innocence. Pundits tore apart my speeches, looking for every possible ulterior motive. Why had I *really* done all this? I was Esther's daughter, after all . . . I couldn't be as blameless as I claimed. I tried to hold on to hope. The truth was the only thing that could set me free.

The continued wary looks from my fellow prisoners slowly drained that hope. If they weren't swayed to my side, how would I ever convince strangers? The news continued its unrelenting, damning coverage of my actions, blaming me not only for the world my mother had created, but also the one that had followed.

And that world, I was horrified to discover, was nothing like the one I'd expected to create. Without Punishments to keep people in line, crime was higher than ever before. All those years, being restrained from behaving badly, had taken away people's self-discipline. Now they were resentful at being deceived, and they were lashing out—at property, at their neighbors, at themselves.

Where once walls had come down, they were being built again. Where once there had been peace, armies were readying for war. Where once people had shared their wealth without a second thought, now they began to hoard. Famines sprung up. Violence against the "other," whomever the other happened to be today.

As I witnessed calamity after calamity through my tiny little screen, I was reminded of my mother's spreadsheets, of the lives she'd claimed to have saved. Though I would never agree with her methods, I finally saw the rationale behind what she'd been trying to do. This globe we lived on was big and violent and out of control, and trying to find a way to rein that in, on a larger scale . . . The monstrous society she'd created had been genius, in its own sick way. I'd always understood my mother's impulse to fight for a better world, but this was the first time I truly understood the brutality she'd been struggling against all along.

More than anything, I wanted to go back out there and try again. Say something to apologize for the violent world I'd brought back. Say something that might ease that violence. My words had once inspired people; I was certain they must still have some small value, to someone. But within these prison walls, I was helpless. Voiceless.

I was starting to lose hope; maybe I would be here forever. Until finally, a guard appeared at my cell door with a message. I had a visitor. She led me to meet an unfamiliar woman in a suit: my lawyer. "You're being extradited," she told me.

"Where? Why?" I asked.

"To America. Because that's where you're from. You're going to be tried there, with the rest of the American prophets and gurus."

"No, I'm not working with them," I protested. "I was working *against* them."

She shrugged. "That's for an American court to decide."

The reality finally sunk in. I wasn't being hailed as a hero, and I never would be. I was being put on trial.

12

That's how I found myself in Arlington Federal Prison, surrounded by a horde of newly minted criminals who'd taken advantage of their newfound freedoms to commit all kinds of unspeakable crimes. Jude visited me on my first day. "What's happening?" I asked him. "Where have you guys been?"

"We've been dealing with legal issues of our own," he admitted. "Dawn finally got cleared, which is a good sign for the rest of us."

"I'm so confused," I said. "They know everything now. Why doesn't anyone believe me?"

"They do," he said carefully. "The prosecutors aren't trying you for anything you didn't do."

My hopes dripped into a puddle at my feet. The truth wasn't going to set me free. Everyone knew the truth, and they hated me anyway. All those crimes I'd been worried Great Spirit would Punish me for . . . that wasn't the Punishment I was going to get. I was going to stand trial, by a jury of my peers, and they'd decide whether I'd acted righteously.

I knew then, long before the opening arguments, the testimony, the deliberation, exactly what verdict that jury was going to give. I'd watched hours upon hours of those television pundits, and it was clear. People weren't mad at me for my crimes as prophet. They were mad about being deceived. And they were mad that I'd had the gall to stop deceiving them, to thrust them back into a world of war and crime and hatred. That not only had I made them fools, I'd told them they were foolish.

Two months later, a jury of my peers would find me guilty and sentence me to fifteen years in prison.

13

I know it's been a while since you heard from me. It's been longer since you wanted to. Why did I emerge after all this time, to tell you my story? Why bother, when the verdict on Grace Luther was handed down so long ago?

It turns out, I *was* looking for your forgiveness, your understanding. I wanted you to see *why* I made the choices I made. Why I hurt you, when I was only trying to help. Fifteen years is a long time to sit and think about what you've done, about the mistakes you've made. I've thought of a hundred things I could have done differently, ways I could have been better. Everything is easier in hindsight. Everyone is wiser once they've made their mistakes.

There's plenty I regret, but I don't regret telling you the truth. I've thought a lot about what my mother said—about how much simpler the world she created was. The one where gods were real, and morality was law, and goodness was rewarded. Where the hard decisions were taken out of most people's hands. Where living your life every day was a little easier. As much as some people hate me for it, I don't regret taking that away from you.

I don't regret giving you a world where you're free to make mistakes—the same kinds of mistakes I made. To be human, to be complicated. Free to doubt, free to sin and blaspheme, free to worship whatever the heck you want to. And yes, perhaps the prophets' world felt safer; but it wasn't true safety, because none of it was true. The world I gave you might be sad and uncertain, but at least it's real. And I don't regret giving you something real.

What I regret is not finding a way to be out there with you now. Helping to rebuild. I've hated watching from inside a cell, not being able to change things. Especially as someone who managed to change so much, so young. But a long time ago, I declared my willingness to give up my freedom, in order to grant freedom to the rest of the world. I think as trades go, that one was worth it.

These past fifteen years, though things have slowly been getting better, they haven't moved as quickly as I'd hoped. I thought we would remember the good we'd once found in ourselves, back when we were forced to be good. I thought we'd remember the cruelty of judging one another based on appearances. I thought we'd find ways to love people who were different from us. I thought we would learn from our mistakes, remember how to work together. I thought we'd all agreed that imposing our beliefs on others was how we'd gotten into this mess. I thought we'd had our fill of false prophets, hypocritical leaders. I thought we'd all learned empathy, and forgiveness.

I've looked long and hard at my faults. But now, I'm asking you to look at yours. That's my one last request: I'm asking you to do what I never could and find a way to be wise but also good, merciful but strong. Take it from someone who's learned the hard way: that's the only way we're going to rebuild this world. And it pains me, every day, that I can't be the one to lead that charge.

I need one of you to lead. I need one of you to be brave, to be the voice I tried to be and failed. I wanted to save the world, and despite everything I accomplished, I fell short. But this story doesn't have to be over yet. I might be in here, but the rest of you still have the power to change things. Make this right.

Make this world as peaceful as my mother hoped it would be. As just as Zack did. Fun, for Macy. Kind, for Layla. Meaningful, for my father. Loving, for Jude.

I know it's a hard ask. If no one else has been able to do it, why should I expect you to do anything? I tried my hardest, succeeded beyond my wildest expectations, and yet there is still so much pain and injustice in our world. We're free, yes, but as my mother said, free to make mistakes.

My prayer to you is the same one I once gave to Great Spirit. Please take care of this world, since I can't anymore.

I've finally found my religion, and it's you. Your compassion, your drive, your kindness. I believe in your power to make the world better. I no longer believe in Great Spirit, but I believe in you.

EPILOGUE

The gates of the prison creaked open, and I stepped out into the sunlight. Fifteen years, it had been a long time. Everything looked different than I remembered. The buildings in the distance a little bigger. The sky a little darker. The birds a little quieter. I breathed in, and the smell was familiar. Smoke and pollen—springtime.

I'd expected cameras, but the warden had kept the press at bay. Their absence was lonely, in a way. I thought this moment deserved a little more fanfare, wanted someone else to mark with me how meaningful it felt. But the air outside hung silent, save for the rumble of the nearby highway.

I thought of my friends, how their lives had gone on without me. Dawn and Irene, still married, with a couple kids . . . they must be in middle school by now. The last time Dawn had visited me in prison, she'd remarked how simple and easy things felt. Too easy. "After all those years fighting, grieving, how can

I just accept this? While you're in here, when there are people who didn't make it?"

"You earned it," I'd told her. If anyone deserved happiness, I knew it was our fearless leader, who'd sacrificed so much for so many others.

Zack, too, I'd heard, had moved on. Embraced his fame as a hero of the resistance, an inside man who took down the prophets. I resented that the public looked at him so fondly, when they still hated me, but I was happy he'd found his place. Also married, with a baby on the way.

Layla, they told me, had ended up in Paris. Macy was in Philadelphia. Dr. Marko with his family in Berlin. All living normal lives, rarely talking about their histories with the resistance. Life always goes on, with or without you. And for fifteen years, the world had continued without me. It ached a bit; there was a part of me that wanted everything to stop in my absence. More than that though, I wanted the people I loved to enjoy the freedom we'd worked so hard to achieve.

But still, I was alone. Or I thought was, until I heard a familiar, deep voice. "Grace!" I turned to see a face I recognized. One that had visited me every week, for all these years. Grin hidden by a thin layer of scruff, eyes still bright and shining. His company had kept me sane all these years, and yet, he'd been so far away, through that glass. As he walked toward me, I felt that same old feeling resurging inside. Like no matter how long we stayed apart, something inside of us would always be connected. He was a different person, once again, and yet the same Jude I'd always loved. The same one I always would love.

"You came," I said, and as I hugged him, relief washed over me. I'd never felt freer than in that moment.

"Always," he said. And I forgot all the years we'd lost, those Nova Scotia summers we might have shared. All I saw was the man standing in front of me, miraculously, taking my hand. Together, we'd survived a thousand deaths, a thousand rebirths, and now, we had a whole future to explore. A new, unfamiliar world, where I'd lost everything. But still, something good, somehow, remained.

"So where are we going?" I asked, opening the passenger door of his car.

"No idea," he said. And as the engine roared to life, we drove ahead.

ACKNOWLEDGMENTS

First off, to Eva: I've known Eva since she was nine years old, but even then she was wise beyond her years. We used to tell each other stories back and forth, and her creativity blew me away. I told her we should start writing down some of her ideas, and since my typing skills were faster at the time, I became her stenographer. Before we knew it, over the course of several sessions, she had more than forty pages of content. "You're writing a novel," I told her, and she seemed surprised, but undeterred. We kept going.

I'll admit—it was her bravery, facing down that blank page, that inspired me to write my own novel. Books were something I'd wanted to tackle for years, but writing one had always seemed too hard. Watching this young girl breathlessly crafting an epic fantasy, I thought—if she can do this, I, the professional writer, should certainly be able to. Thanks to Eva, I faced my fears. Though technically I was supposed to be her mentor, I always tell people that the mentorship really went in the other direction. It's been a privilege to watch her grow up into such a fearless, inspiring young woman, and I know she'll excel at whatever she chooses to pursue in her future.

Many, many thank-yous to all my friends and family who read and gave feedback on this book, especially in the midst of the difficult period in which I was writing it: Ann Acacia Kim, Laura Herb, Sarah Hawley, Derek Leben. And last but not least, my amazing mother, Becky Ridgeway, for reading this manuscript at its roughest and convincing me I had what it took to finish. I'm so lucky to have had you as my cheerleader for all these years, and I'm going to miss you so much. Thank you all for your ideas and encouragement and general fabulousness.

I'm forever indebted to both my incredible editor, Tessa Woodward, and my wonderful agent, Peter Steinberg, for being so understanding throughout this editorial process. Tessa, thank you for your deft and incisive notes, which helped me solve so many issues I'd been banging my head against the wall over. Peter, your kindness and support over the past year went above and beyond, and I am so grateful.

Thank you as well to Elle Keck, Laurie McGee, Christina Joell, and everyone else at Harper Voyager for all of your help bringing this book out into the world! And of course, those who helped get this world off the ground: Claire Abramowitz, Randy Kiyan, Ari Levinson, Priyanka Krishnan, Rebecca Lucash, and David Pomerico.

Dad, thanks for buying up most of the stock of my last two books! And as always, my family, my friends, my colleagues, my teachers and mentors, and everyone else who has read and promoted this series: thank you from the bottom of my heart for all of your support!

ABOUT THE AUTHOR

Sarah Tarkoff is the author of *Sinless* and *Fearless*, the first two novels in the Eye of the Beholder trilogy, and wrote for the CW series *Arrow*. Her other television writing credits include ABC's *Mistresses* and Lifetime's *Witches of East End*. She graduated from the University of Southern California with a degree in screenwriting and currently lives in Los Angeles.

Sarah Tarkoff's
Eye of the Beholder Series

SINLESS

With shades of Scott Westerfeld's *Uglies* and Ally Condie's *Matched*, this cinematic dystopian novel—the first in the thrilling *Eye of the Beholder* series—is set in a near future society in which "right" and "wrong" are manifested by beauty and ugliness.

Despite all her efforts to live a normal teenage life, Grace Luther is faced with a series of decisions that will risk the lives of everyone she loves—and, ultimately, her own.

FEARLESS

A young woman will imperil her future and her world to expose the global shadow network that uses its power to play God and control humanity.

In a dangerous world filled with lies and betrayals, Grace can't trust anyone. And the choices she makes will either save her friends, the resistance, and the hope of attaining free will—or secure the Prophets' power and ultimate control.

RUTHLESS

Grace risks everything to expose a conspiracy controlling her world in this heart-pounding finale to the *Eye of the Beholder* series, a thrilling saga set in a near-future dystopian society.

As the government's reign of terror intensifies, rebel after rebel is targeted and killed. Yet there is one last hope. With the future at stake, Grace must overcome her fears to expose and destroy the government's false prophets forever. Though she has many doubts, there's one thing she's certain of: she will lead the rebellion to victory . . . or die trying.